Famous Monster Tales

Famous Monste

D. VAN NOSTRAND COMPANY, INC.

Princeton, New Jersey   Toronto   London   Melbourne

Collected by Basil Davenport

Foreword by Clifton Fadiman

Tales

ACKNOWLEDGMENTS

Acknowledgment is made to the following for permission to use material owned by them. Every reasonable effort has been made to clear the use of the stories in this volume with the copyright owners. If notified of any omissions the publisher will gladly make the proper corrections in future editions.

"Smoke Ghost" by Fritz Leiber first appeared in *Unknown Worlds.* Copyright 1941 by Street and Smith Publications, Inc.

"The Phantom Farmhouse" by Seabury Quinn is reprinted by permission of the author. Copyright 1923 by Popular Fiction Publishing Co. Copyright 1946 by Health Knowledge, Inc. by special arrangement with the author. Copyright 1965 by Health Knowledge, Inc. by special arrangement with the author.

"The Thing on Outer Shoal" by P. Schuyler Miller appeared in *The Other Side of the Moon,* copyright 1949 by August Derleth.

"The Outsider" by H. P. Lovecraft is reprinted by permission of the author.

"Second Night Out" by Frank Belknap Long is reprinted by permission of the author.

"It" by Theodore Sturgeon appeared in *Unknown* magazine in 1940, copyright by Street and Smith Publications, Inc., and in *Who Knocks,* edited by August Derleth, copyright 1946 by August Derleth. Reprinted by permission of the author.

"The Dancing Partner" by Jerome K. Jerome is from *Novel Notes* published by J. M. Dent & Sons Ltd., London. Reprinted by permission.

"Skeleton" by Ray Bradbury is reprinted by permission of the author.

"The Thing in the Pond" by Paul Ernst appeared in *Astounding Stories,* copyright 1934 and 1961 by Street and Smith Publications, Inc. Used by permission.

"Negotium Perambulans" by Edward Frederic Benson appeared in *Invisible and Invisible* by E. F. Benson, copyright 1923 by George H. Doran Company.

"The Fifty-first Dragon" by Heywood Broun is copyright 1921 and 1941 by Heywood Hale Broun. Reprinted by permission of Heywood Hale Broun and Constance M. Broun.

CONTENTS

FOREWORD

THESE MONSTROUS TALES WERE SELECTED AND ARE PREFACED BY the late Basil Davenport. His untimely death precluded the writing of the general introduction for which my comments must serve as an inadequate substitute. For many years he was my colleague on the Board of Judges of the Book-of-the-Month Club. I valued him not only as a professional critic of high competancy but as a friend and as a Johnsonian personality of an order rarely to be found in our time. Basil Davenport's scholarship ranged over many fields. Especially was he a notable authority on the minor literature of the odd: ghost and murder stories, thrillers and detective tales, fantasy and science-fiction. In this specialized area his anthologies are treasured by amateurs of the grotesque and arabesque. The collection of *frissonades* now in the reader's trembling hands provides additional evidence of his exacting and severe taste for the pleasingly uneasy-making.

These pages rustle with the stealthy movements of strictly orthodox, old-fashioned monsters: werewolves and horrors spawned by the great deep; quasi-humans and robots, vampires and fearsome survivors from the dark abysm of the remote past, abortions from the scientist's laboratory. Such creatures present a wholesome, indeed a cheerful contrast to the psychological deformities of contemporary sick humor, the pretentious sadisms of the latest modern Gothic tale, the revolting hokum of television. The stories in which they lurk and gibber do not claim to be prophecy or obscure existentialist fables or devastating black satire. With the classical monster tale you know precisely where you are: in the hands of a canny projector of the uncanny, a businesslike narrator who has no purpose ulterior to that of making your flesh creep for an idle half-hour. Such a tale does not cheat you by poking fun at itself: even the sly "Fifty-first Dragon" and the folk-humorous "Thing on Outer Shoal" are not parodic in tone. The self-conscious "camp" note—whether high, low, or medium camp—does not intrude. These appealing monsters make only a single claim on us. They beg to be taken— just for a moment—seriously. And, as Mr. Harry Golden would say, they're entitled.

Long and noble is the genealogy of the monster story. One supposes it all started with paleolithic man who, living among real monsters, quite properly, in the interests of a good fireside tale, exaggerated his adventures. Monsters meet us at the very dawn of written literature. Ancient Assyro-Babylonian tablets tell of the slaying by the hero Marduk of the dread dragon of chaos, Tiamat. Hercules and his monsters we know well. *Beowulf* has two splendid monsters—Grendel and Grendel's mother, all the more dreadful for being nameless. Nor has our machine century mocked the monster story into obsolescence. Indeed, hyper-technology, itself the most monstrous of monsters, has given the genre a shot of adrenalin. Science-fiction supplies us with more and better monsters, terrene and extra-terrene, than ever before. We may be living in a golden age of monsterizing.

What lies back of the lure such tales have exerted over count-less centuries? Some might be of the opinion that today the fan-tasticated horror serves as a kind of escape hatch, the grisliest of stories being but moonlight, roses, and violin music compared with the realities of Belsen and Treblinka, Hiroshima and Viet-nam and the even greater horrors the future promises us. But, while fictional monsters may be used for consolatory or escapist purposes, most of us are drawn to them because a good harmless scare seems to satisfy something in our quirky human natures. The French philosopher Fontenelle located tragic drama's appeal in the circumstance that the audience, knowing the harrowing events portrayed to be but imaginary, is comforted by a sense of safety. Perhaps an effect of this sort operates in the case of monster fiction.

Yet a good monster story on occasion seems to offer more than the pleasures of gooseflesh followed by relief. Does it not call out to something buried deep in our unconscious selves? Perhaps, as has been speculated, the memory of the race lies coiled in us still. Perhaps that memory reaches back to our dawn-time when our brute ancestors confronted an unpredictable world, alive with a thousand nameless fears.

The existence of racial memory, however, defies demonstration. Much more apparent is the fact that we want to believe the unbelievable. Irrationality answers to something permanently implanted in our natures; and the ghost story, the monster story is as satisfactorily irrational as anyone could desire.

Finally, there remains that last faint eerie doubt, the low-muttered question, Who knows? "Who knows," asks Mr. Davenport, "what there is in the sea that we have never heard of?" And again: "Who knows what exactly are the conditions which once brought forth life?"

Who indeed? Do we really know what is beneath our feet, above our heads, or even by our very side, nonexistent only because we are blinded and deafened and anesthetized by our pitiful five senses? Today the chess-playing robot is a commonplace. Tomorrow some strange organism will spring to life in a test tube. The astronaut of the future may well encounter beings far more fantastic than any who live out their brief paper lives within these pages. The monster story makes no claim to be based on fact. Nonetheless, we cannot but be uneasily aware that as yet the facts are not all in. Who knows? . . .

Here, for the pleasure of your shudder, is a fine clutch of horrors, a witches' cauldron of grue, a circle of poisonous mushrooms suddenly sprouting in the garden of fantastic fiction.

—CLIFTON FADIMAN

In John Buchan's novel The Dancing Floor, *the hero has a recurring dream, which began in his childhood and comes on the same night every year. He dreams that he is in a pleasant room.*

"In one corner was a door which led to the outer world, and through this door he knew that he might on no account pass. Another door faced him, and he knew that he had only to turn the handle for it to open. But he did not want to, for he understood quite clearly what was beyond. There was a second room just like the first one; he knew nothing about it except that opposite the entrance another door led out of it. Beyond was a third chamber, and so on interminably. There seemed to the boy to be no end to this fantastic suite. Yes, but there *was* an end. Somewhere far away in one of the rooms was a terror waiting on him, or, as he feared, coming towards him."

Later "He knew clearly—though how he knew he could not tell—that each year the something came a room nearer, and was even now but twelve rooms off."
—*There is another story—I believe by E. F. Benson, but I have not been able to trace it—of a boy at school who slept in an old-fashioned dormitory with many beds. He dreamed that the boy who slept nearest the door was made away with by a monstrous creature: "It was not a man, nor a dog, nor an ape, nor a bear, but it had resemblances to all these." And every night it came one bed nearer his own.*

Among the ghost stories of Montague Rhodes James (who wrote more first-rate stories in that genre than any one who ever lived) there is one called "The Mezzotint," about a print showing a handsome old house with a lawn around it, and a figure just showing at the edge of the picture. Every time the owner looks at it, the cloaked figure is nearer the house. In another of his stories, "Mr. Humphreys and His Inheritance," Mr. Humphreys inherits a country house in a park containing a topological maze, which has a monument in the center of it. A gardener, guiding him through the maze, puts down his hat for a mark, and when they get back he says, "I made sure I left that down over against a bramble-bush, and you can see for yourself there ain't no bram-

*ble-bush, not in this walk at all." Later in the story Mr. Hum-
phreys, looking out of the window, notices "a small Irish yew,
thin and black, which stood like an outpost of the shrubbery
through which the maze was approached." Later still, as he is
showing off the place to a lady, he says, "That bush-thing under
the library window: you would have that away, wouldn't you?"
These episodes are separated by several pages, and a careless
reader might miss the fact that they all belong together: that
Something is coming nearer and nearer the house.*

That is the worst sort of spook.

SMOKE GHOST
Fritz Leiber

MISS MILLICK WONDERED JUST WHAT HAD HAPPENED TO MR. WRAN.
He kept making the strangest remarks when she took dictation.
Just this morning he had quickly turned around and asked,
"Have you ever seen a ghost, Miss Millick?" And she had tittered
nervously and replied, "When I was a girl there was a thing in
white that used to come out of the closet in the attic bedroom
when I slept there, and moan. Of course it was just my imagination. I was frightened of lots of things." And he had said, "I
don't mean that kind of ghost. I mean a ghost from the world
today, with the soot of the factories on its face and the pounding
of machinery in its soul. The kind that would haunt coal yards
and slip around at night through deserted office buildings like
this one. A real ghost. Not something out of books." And she
hadn't known what to say.

He'd never been like this before. Of course he might be joking, but it didn't sound that way. Vaguely Miss Millick wondered
whether he mightn't be seeking some sort of sympathy from her.
Of course Mr. Wran was married and had a little child, but that
didn't prevent her from having daydreams. The daydreams were
not very exciting, still they helped fill up her mind. But now he
was asking her another of those unprecedented questions.

"Have you ever thought what a ghost of our times would look

like, Miss Millick? Just picture it. A smoky composite face with the hungry anxiety of the unemployed, the neurotic restlessness of the person without purpose, the jerky tension of the high-pressure metropolitan worker, the uneasy resentment of the striker, the callous opportunism of the scab, the aggressive whine of the panhandler, the inhibited terror of the bombed civilian, and a thousand other twisted emotional patterns. Each one overlying and yet blending with the other, like a pile of semitransparent masks?"

Miss Millick gave a little self-conscious shiver and said, "That would be terrible. What an awful thing to think of."

She peered furtively across the desk. Was he going crazy? She remembered having heard that there had been something impressively abnormal about Mr. Wran's childhood, but she couldn't recall what it was. If only she could do something—laugh at his mood or ask him what was really wrong. She shifted the extra pencils in her left hand and mechanically traced over some of the shorthand curlicues in her notebook.

"Yet, that's just what such a ghost or vitalized projection would look like, Miss Millick," he continued, smiling in a tight way. "It would grow out of the real world. It would reflect all the tangled, sordid, vicious things. All the loose ends. And it would be very grimy. I don't think it would seem white or wispy or favor graveyards. It wouldn't moan. But it would mutter unintelligibly, and twitch at your sleeve. Like a sick, surly ape. What would such a thing want from a person, Miss Millick? Sacrifice? Worship? Or just fear? What could you do to stop it from troubling you?"

Miss Millick giggled nervously. There was an expression beyond her powers of definition in Mr. Wran's ordinary, flat-cheeked, thirtyish face, silhouetted against the dusty window. He turned away and stared out into the gray downtown atmosphere that rolled in from the railroad yards and the mills. When he spoke again his voice sounded far away.

"Of course, being immaterial, it couldn't hurt you physically —at first. You'd have to be peculiarly sensitive even to see it, or be aware of it at all. But it would begin to influence your actions. Make you do this. Stop you from doing that. Although only a projection, it would gradually get its hooks into the world of things as they are. Might even get control of suitably vacuous minds. Then it could hurt whomever it wanted."

Miss Millick squirmed and read back her shorthand, like books said you should do when there was a pause. She became aware of the failing light and wished Mr. Wran would ask her to turn on the overhead. She felt scratchy, as if soot were sifting down onto her skin.

"It's a rotten world, Miss Millick," said Mr. Wran, talking at the window. "Fit for another morbid growth of superstition. It's time the ghosts, or whatever you call them, took over and began a rule of fear. They'd be no worse than men."

"But"—Miss Millick's diaphragm jerked, making her titter inanely—"of course there aren't any such things as ghosts."

Mr. Wran turned around.

"Of course there aren't, Miss Millick," he said in a loud, patronizing voice, as if she had been doing the talking rather than he. "Science and common sense and psychiatry all go to prove it."

She hung her head and might even have blushed if she hadn't felt so all at sea. Her leg muscles twitched, making her stand up, although she hadn't intended to. She aimlessly rubbed her hand back and forth along the edge of the desk.

"Why, Mr. Wran, look what I got off your desk," she said, showing him a heavy smudge. There was a note of clumsily playful reproof in her voice. "No wonder the copy I bring you always gets so black. Somebody ought to talk to those scrubwomen. They're skimping on your room."

She wished he would make some normal joking reply. But instead he drew back and his face hardened.

"Well, to get back to that business of the second class mailing privileges," he rapped out harshly, and began to dictate.

When she was gone he jumped up, dabbed his finger experimentally at the smudged part of the desk frowned worriedly at the almost inky smears. He jerked open a drawer, snatched out a rag, hastily swabbed off the desk, crumpled the rag into a ball and tossed it back. There were three or four other rags in the drawer, each impregnated with soot.

Then he strode over to the window and peered out anxiously through the gathering dusk, his eyes searching the panorama of roofs, fixing on each chimney and water tank.

"It's a neurosis. Must be compulsions. Hallucinations," he muttered to himself in a tired, distraught voice that would have made Miss Millick gasp. "It's that damned mental abnormality cropping up in a new form. Can't be any other explanation. But it's so damned real. Even the soot. Good thing I'm seeing the psychiatrist. I don't think I could force myself to get on the elevated tonight—" His voice trailed off, he rubbed his eyes, and his memory automatically started to grind.

It had all begun on the elevated. There was a particular little sea of roofs he had grown into the habit of glancing at just as the packed car carrying him homeward lurched around a turn. A dingy, melancholy little world of tarpaper, tarred gravel, and smoky brick. Rusty tin chimneys with odd conical hats suggested abandoned listening posts. There was a washed-out advertisement of some ancient patent medicine on the nearest wall. Superficially it was like ten thousand other drab city roofs. But he always saw it around dusk, either in the smoky half-light, or tinged with red by the flat rays of a dirty sunset, or covered by ghostly wind-blown white sheets of rain-splash, or patched with blackish snow; and it seemed unusually bleak and suggestive, almost beautifully ugly, though in no sense picturesque; dreary, but meaningful. Unconsciously it came to symbolize for Catesby Wran certain disagreeable aspects of the frustrated, frightened century in which he lived, the jangled century of hate and heavy industry and total wars. The quick, daily glance into the half darkness became an integral part of his life. Oddly, he never saw it in the morning, for it was then his habit to sit on the other side of the car, his head buried in the paper.

One evening toward winter he noticed what seemed to be a shapeless black sack lying on the third roof from the tracks. He did not think about it. It merely registered as an addition to the well-known scene and his memory stored away the impression for further reference. Next evening, however, he decided he had been mistaken in one detail. The object was a roof nearer than he had thought. Its color and texture, and the grimy stains around it, suggested that it was filled with coal dust, which was hardly reasonable. Then, too, the following evening it seemed to have been blown against a rusty ventilator by the wind— which could hardly have happened if it were at all heavy. Perhaps it was filled with leaves. Catesby was surprised to find himself anticipating his next daily glance with a minor note of apprehension. There was something unwholesome in the posture of the thing that stuck in his mind—a bulge in the sacking that suggested a misshapen head peering around the ventilator. And his apprehension was justified, for that evening the thing was on the nearest roof, though on the farther side, looking as if it had just flopped down over the low brick parapet.

Next evening the sack was gone. Catesby was annoyed at the momentary feeling of relief that went through him, because the whole matter seemed too unimportant to warrant feelings of any sort. What difference did it make if his imagination had played tricks on him, and he'd fancied that the object was crawling and hitching itself slowly closer across the roofs? That was the way any normal imagination worked. He deliberately chose to disregard the fact that there were reasons for thinking his imagination was by no means a normal one. As he walked home from the elevated, however, he found himself wondering whether the sack was really gone. He seemed to recall a vague, smudgy trail leading across the gravel to the nearer side of the roof, which was marked by a parapet. For an instant an unpleasant picture formed in his mind—that of an inky humped creature crouched behind the parapet, waiting. Then he dismissed the whole subject.

The next time he felt the familiar grating lurch of the car, he caught himself trying not to look out. That angered him. He turned his head quickly. When he turned it back, his compact face was definitely pale. There had only been time for a fleeting rearward glance at the escaping roof. Had he actually seen in silhouette the upper part of a head of some sort peering over the parapet? Nonsense, he told himself. And even if he had seen something, there were a thousand explanations which did not involve the supernatural or even true hallucination. Tomorrow he would take a good look and clear up the whole matter. If necessary, he would visit the roof personally, though he hardly knew where to find it and disliked in any case the idea of pampering a silly fear.

He did not relish the walk home from the elevated that evening, and visions of the thing disturbed his dreams and were in and out of his mind all next day at the office. It was then that he first began to relieve his nerves by making jokingly serious remarks about the supernatural to Miss Millick, who seemed properly mystified. It was on the same day, too, that he became aware of a growing antipathy to grime and soot. Everything he touched seemed gritty, and he found himself mopping and wiping at his desk like an old lady with a morbid fear of germs. He reasoned that there was no real change in his office, and that he'd just now become sensitive to the dirt that had always been there, but there was no denying an increasing nervousness. Long before the car reached the curve, he was straining his eyes through the murky twilight, determined to take in every detail.

Afterward he realized that he must have given a muffled cry of some sort, for the man beside him looked at him curiously, and the woman ahead gave him an unfavorable stare. Conscious of his own pallor and uncontrollable trembling, he stared back at them hungrily, trying to regain the feeling of security he had completely lost. They were the usual reassuringly wooden-faced people everyone rides home with on the elevated. But suppose he had pointed out to one of them what he had seen—that sodden, distorted face of sacking and coal dust, that boneless paw which waved back and forth, unmistakably in his direction, as if reminding him of a future appointment— He involuntarily shut his eyes tight. His thoughts were racing ahead to tomorrow evening. He pictured this same windowed oblong of light and packed humanity surging around the curve—then an opaque monstrous form leaping out from the roof in a parabolic swoop —an unmentionable face pressed close against the window, smearing it with wet coal dust—huge paws fumbling sloppily at the glass—

Somehow he managed to turn off his wife's anxious inquiries. Next morning he reached a decision and made an appointment for that evening with a psychiatrist a friend had told him about. It cost him a considerable effort, for Catesby had a well-grounded distaste for anything dealing with psychological abnormality. Visiting a psychiatrist meant raking up an episode in his past which he had never fully described even to his wife. Once he had made the decision, however, he felt considerably relieved. The psychiatrist, he told himself, would clear everything up. He could almost fancy him saying, "Merely a bad case of nerves. However, you must consult the oculist whose name I'm writing down for you, and you must take two of these pills in water every four hours," and so on. It was almost comforting, and made the coming revelation he would have to make seem less painful.

But as the smoky dusk rolled in, his nervousness returned and he let his joking mystification of Miss Millick run away with him until he realized that he wasn't frightening anyone but himself.

He would have to keep his imagination under better control, he told himself, as he continued to peer out restlessly at the massive, murky shapes of the downtown office buildings. Why, he had spent the whole afternoon building up a kind of neomedieval cosmology of superstition. It wouldn't do. He realized then that he had been standing at the window much longer than he'd thought, for the glass panel in the door was dark and there was no noise coming from the outer office. Miss Millick and the rest must have gone home.

It was then he made the discovery that there would have been no special reason for dreading the swing around the curve that night. It was, as it happened, a horrible discovery. For, on the shadowed roof across the street and four stories below, he saw the thing huddle and roll across the gravel and, after one upward look of recognition, merge into the blackness beneath the water tank.

As he hurriedly collected his things and made for the elevator, fighting the panicky impulse to run, he began to think of hallucination and mild psychosis as very desirable conditions. For better or for worse, he pinned all his hopes on the psychiatrist.

"So you find yourself growing nervous and . . . er . . . jumpy, as you put it," said Dr. Trevethick, smiling with dignified geniality. "Do you notice any more definite physical symptoms? Pain? Headache? Indigestion?"

Catesby shook his head and wet his lips. "I'm especially nervous while riding in the elevated," he murmured swiftly.

"I see. We'll discuss that more fully. But I'd like you first to tell me about something you mentioned earlier. You said there was something about your childhood that might predispose you to nervous ailments. As you know, the early years are critical ones in the development of an individual's behavior pattern."

Catesby studied the yellow reflections of frosted globes in the dark surface of the desk. The palm of his left hand aimlessly rubbed the thick nap of the armchair. After a while he raised his head and looked straight into the doctor's small brown eyes.

"From perhaps my third to my ninth year," he began, choosing the words with care, "I was what you might call a sensory prodigy."

The doctor's expression did not change. "Yes?" he inquired politely.

"What I mean is that I was supposed to be able to see through walls, read letters through envelopes and books through their covers, fence and play Ping-pong blindfolded, find things that were buried, read thoughts." The words tumbled out.

"And could you?" The doctor's expression was toneless.

"I don't know. I don't suppose so," answered Catesby, long-lost emotions flooding back into his voice. "It's all confused now. I thought I could, but then they were always encouraging me. My mother . . . was . . . well . . . interested in psychic phenomena. I was . . . exhibited. I seem to remember seeing things other people couldn't. As if most opaque objects were transparent. But I was very young. I didn't have any scientific criteria for judgment."

He was reliving it now. The darkened rooms. The earnest assemblages of gawking, prying adults. Himself sitting alone on a little platform, lost in a straighbacked wooden chair. The black silk handkerchief over his eyes. His mother's coaxing, insistent questions. The whispers. The gasps. His own hate of the whole business, mixed with hunger for the adulation of adults. Then the scientists from the university, the experiments, the big test. The reality of those memories engulfed him and momentarily made him forget the reason why he was disclosing them to a stranger.

"Do I understand that your mother tried to make use of you as a medium for communicating with the . . . er . . . other world?"

Catesby nodded eagerly.

"She tried to, but she couldn't. When it came to getting in touch with the dead, I was a complete failure. All I could do— or thought I could do—was see real, existing, three-dimensional objects beyond the vision of normal people. Objects anyone could have seen except for distance, obstruction, or darkness. It was always a disappointment to mother."

He could hear her sweetish patient voice saying, "Try again, dear, just this once. Katie was your aunt. She loved you. Try to hear what she's saying." And he had answered, "I can see a woman in a blue dress standing on the other side of Dick's house." And she had replied, "Yes, I know, dear. But that's not

Katie. Katie's a spirit. Try again. Just this once, dear." The doctor's voice gently jarred him back into the softly gleaming office.

"You mentioned scientific criteria for judgment, Mr. Wran. As far as you know, did anyone ever try to apply them to you?"

Catesby's nod was emphatic.

"They did. When I was eight, two young psychologists from the university got interested in me. I guess they did it for a joke at first, and I remember being very determined to show them I amounted to something. Even now I seem to recall how the note of polite superiority and amused sarcasm drained out of their voices. I suppose they decided at first that it was very clever trickery, but somehow they persuaded mother to let them try me out under controlled conditions. There were lots of tests that seemed very businesslike after mother's slipshod little exhibitions. They found I was clairvoyant—or so they thought. I got worked up and on edge. They were going to demonstrate my super-normal sensory powers to the university psychology faculty. For the first time I began to worry about whether I'd come through. Perhaps they kept me going at too hard a pace, I don't know. At any rate, when the test came, I couldn't do a thing. Everything became opaque. I got desperate and made things up out of my imagination. I lied. In the end I failed utterly, and I believe the two young psychologists got into a lot of hot water as a result."

He could hear the brusque, bearded man saying, "You've been taken in by a child, Flaxman, a mere child. I'm greatly disturbed. You've put yourself on the same plane as common charlatans. Gentlemen, I ask you to banish from your minds this whole sorry episode. It must never be referred to." He winced at the recollection of his feeling of guilt. But at the same time he was beginning to feel exhilarated and almost light-hearted. Unburdening his long-repressed memories had altered his whole viewpoint. The episodes on the elevated began to take on what seemed their proper proportions as merely the bizarre workings of overwrought nerves and an overly suggestible mind. The doctor, he anticipated confidently, would disentangle the obscure subconscious causes, whatever they might be. And the whole business would be finished off quickly, just as his childhood experience—which was beginning to seem a little ridiculous now—had been finished off.

"From that day on," he continued, "I never exhibited a trace of my supposed powers. My mother was frantic and tried to sue the university. I had something like a nervous breakdown. Then the divorce was granted, and my father got custody of me. He did his best to make me forget it. We went on long outdoor vacations and did a lot of athletics, associated with normal, matter-of-fact people. I went to business college eventually. I'm in advertising now. But," Catesby paused, "now that I'm having nervous symptoms, I've wondered if there mightn't be a connection. It's not a question of whether I really was clairvoyant or not. Very likely my mother taught me a lot of unconscious deceptions, good enough to fool even young psychology instructors. But don't you think it may have some important bearing on my present condition?"

For several moments the doctor regarded him with a slightly embarrassing professional frown. Then he said quietly, "And is there some . . . er more specific connection between your experiences then and now? Do you by any chance find that you are once again beginning to . . . er . . . see things?"

Catesby swallowed. He had felt an increasing eagerness to unburden himself of his fears, but it was not easy to make a beginning, and the doctor's shrewd question rattled him. He forced himself to concentrate. The thing he thought he had seen on the roof loomed up before his inner eye with unexpected vividness. Yet it did not frighten him. He groped for words.

Then he saw that the doctor was not looking at him but over his shoulder. Color was draining out of the doctor's face and his eyes did not seem so small. Then the doctor sprang to his feet, walked past Catesby, threw open the window and peered into the darkness.

As Catesby rose, the doctor slammed down the window and said in a voice whose smoothness was marred by a slight, persistent gasping, "I hope I haven't alarmed you. I saw the face of . . . er . . . a Negro prowler on the fire escape. I must have frightened him, for he seems to have gotten out of sight in a hurry. Don't give it another thought. Doctors are frequently bothered by *voyeurs* . . . er . . . Peeping Toms."

"A Negro?" asked Catesby, moistening his lips.

The doctor laughed nervously. "I imagine so, though my first odd impression was that it was a white man in blackface. You see, the color didn't seem to have any brown in it. It was dead-black."

Catesby moved toward the window. There were smudges on the glass. "It's quite all right, Mr. Wran." The doctor's voice had acquired a sharp note of impatience, as if he were trying hard to reassume his professional authority. "Let's continue our conversation. I was asking if you were"—he made a face—"seeing things."

Catesby's whirling thoughts slowed down and locked into place. "No, I'm not seeing anything that other people don't see, too. And I think I'd better go now. I've been keeping you too long." He disregarded the doctor's halfhearted gesture of denial. "I'll phone you about the physical examination. In a way you've already taken a big load off my mind." He smiled woodenly. "Good night, Dr. Trevethick."

Catesby Wran's mental state was a peculiar one. His eyes searched every angular shadow, he glanced sideways down each chasmlike alley and barren basement passageway, and kept stealing looks at the irregular line of the roofs, yet he was hardly conscious of where he was going. He pushed away the thoughts that came into his mind, and kept moving. He became aware of a slight sense of security as he turned into a lighted street where there were people and high buildings and blinking signs. After a while he found himself in the dim lobby of the structure that housed his office. Then he realized why he couldn't go home—

because he might cause his wife and baby to see it, just as the doctor had seen it.

"Hello, Mr. Wran," said the night elevator man, a burly figure in blue overalls, sliding open the grillework door to the old-fashioned cage. "I didn't know you were working nights now."

Catesby stepped in automatically. "Sudden rush of orders," he murmured inanely. "Some stuff that has to be gotten out."

The cage creaked to a stop at the top floor. "Be working very late, Mr. Wran?"

He nodded vaguely, watched the car slide out of sight, found his keys, swiftly crossed the outer office, and entered his own. His hand went out to the light switch, but then the thought occurred to him that the two lighted windows, standing out against the dark bulk of the building, would indicate his where-abouts and serve as a goal toward which something could crawl and climb. He moved his chair so that the back was against the wall and sat down in the semidarkness. He did not remove his overcoat.

For a long time he sat there motionless, listening to his own breathing and the faraway sounds from the streets below: the thin metallic surge of the crosstown streetcar, the farther one of the elevated, faint lonely cries and honkings, indistinct rum-blings. Words he had spoken to Miss Millick in nervous jest came back to him with the bitter taste of truth. He found him-self unable to reason critically or connectedly, but by their own volition thoughts rose up into his mind and gyrated slowly and rearranged themselves, with the inevitable movement of planets.

Gradually his mental picture of the world was transformed. No longer a world of material atoms and empty space, but a world in which the bodiless existed and moved according to its own obscure laws or unpredictable impulses. The new picture illumined with dreadful clarity certain general facts which had always bewildered and troubled him and from which he had tried to hide: the inevitability of hate and war, the diabolically timed machines which wrecked the best of human intentions, the walls of willful misunderstanding that divided one man from another, the eternal vitality of cruelty and ignorance and greed. They seemed appropriate now, necessary parts of the picture. And superstition only a kind of wisdom.

Then his thoughts returned to himself, and the question he had asked Miss Millick came back, "What would such a thing want from a person? Sacrifices? Worship? Or just fear. What could you do to stop it from troubling you?" It had become a practical question.

With an explosive jangle, the phone began to ring. "Cate, I've been trying everywhere to get you," said his wife. "I never thought you'd be at the office. What are you doing? I've been worried."

He said something about work.

"You'll be home right away?" came the faint anxious question. "I'm a little frightened. Ronny just had a scare. It woke him up. He kept pointing to the window saying, 'Black man, black man.' Of course it's something he dreamed. But I'm frightened. You will be home? What's that, dear? Can't you hear me?"

"I will. Right away," he said. Then he was out of the office, buzzing the night bell and peering down the shaft.

He saw it peering up the shaft at him from the deep shadows three floors below, the sacking face pressed against the iron grillework. It started up the stair at a shockingly swift, shambling gait, vanishing temporarily from sight as it swung into the second corridor below.

Catesby clawed at the door to the office, realized he had not locked it, pushed it in, slammed and locked it behind him, retreated to the other side of the room, cowered between the filing cases and the wall. His teeth were clicking. He heard the groan of the rising cage. A silhouette darkened the frosted glass of the door, blotting out part of the grotesque reverse of the company name. After a little the door opened.

The big-globed overhead light flared on and, standing just inside the door, her hand on the switch, he saw Miss Millick.

"Why, Mr. Wran," she stammered vacuously, "I didn't know

you were here. I'd just come in to do some extra typing after the movie. I didn't . . . but the lights weren't on. What were you—"

He stared at her. He wanted to shout in relief, grab hold of her, talk rapidly. He realized he was grinning hysterically.

"Why, Mr. Wran, what's happened to you?" she asked embarrassedly, ending with a stupid titter. "Are you feeling sick? Isn't there something I can do for you?"

He shook his head jerkily, and managed to say, "No, I'm just leaving. I was doing some extra work myself."

"But you *look* sick," she insisted, and walked over toward him. He inconsequentially realized she must have stepped in mud, for her high-heeled shoes left neat black prints.

"Yes, I'm sure you must be sick. You're so terribly pale." She sounded like an enthusiastic, incompetent nurse. Her face brightened with a sudden inspiration. "I've got something in my bag that'll fix you up right away," she said. "It's for indigestion."

She fumbled at her stuffed oblong purse. He noticed that she was absent-mindedly holding it shut with one hand while she tried to open it with the other. Then, under his very eyes, he saw her bend back the thick prongs of metal locking the purse as if they were tinfoil, or as if her fingers had become a pair of steel pliers.

Instantly his memory recited the words he had spoken to Miss Millick that afternoon. "It couldn't hurt you physically—at first . . . gradually get its hooks into the world . . . might even get control of suitably vacuous minds. Then it could hurt whomever it wanted." A sickish, cold feeling came to a focus inside him. He began to edge toward the door.

But Miss Millick hurried ahead of him.

"You don't have to wait, Fred," she called. "Mr. Wran's decided to stay a while longer."

The door to the cage shut with a mechanical rattle. The cage creaked. Then she turned around in the door.

"Why, Mr. Wran," she gurgled reproachfully, "I just couldn't think of letting you go home now. I'm sure you're terribly unwell. Why, you might collapse in the street. You've just got to stay here until you feel different."

The creaking died away. He stood in the center of the office motionless. His eyes traced the course of Miss Millick's footprints to where she stood blocking the door. A sound that was almost a scream was wrenched out of him.

"Why, Mr. Wran," she said, "you're acting as if you were crazy. You must lie down for a little while. Here, I'll help you off with your coat."

The nauseously idiotic and rasping note was the same; only it had been intensified. As she came toward him he turned and ran through the storeroom, clattered a key desperately at the lock of the second door to the corridor.

"Why, Mr. Wran," he heard her call, "are you having some kind of fit? You must let me help you."

The door came open and he plunged out into the corridor and up the stairs immediately ahead. It was only when he reached the top that he realized the heavy steel door in front of him led to the roof. He jerked up the catch.

"Why, Mr. Wran, you mustn't run away. I'm coming after you."

Then he was out on the gritty gravel of the roof, the night sky was clouded, and murky, with a faint pinkish glow from the neon signs. From the distant mills rose a ghostly spurt of flame. He ran to the edge. The street lights glared dizzily upward. Two men walking along were round blobs of hat and shoulders. He swung around.

The thing was in the doorway. The voice was no longer solicitous but moronically playful, each sentence ending in a titter.

"Why, Mr. Wran, why have you come up here? We're all alone. Just think, I might push you off."

The thing came slowly toward him. He moved backward until his heels touched the low parapet. Without knowing why or what he was going to do, he dropped to his knees. The face he dared not look at came nearer, a focus for the worst in the world, a gathering point for poisons from everywhere. Then the lucidity of terror took possession of his mind, and words formed on his lips.

"I will obey you. You are my god," he said. "You have supreme power over man and his animals and his machines. You rule this city and all others. I recognize that."

Again the titter, closer. "Why, Mr. Wran, you never talked like this before. Do you mean it?"

"The world is yours to do with as you will, save or tear to pieces." He answered fawningly, as the words automatically fitted themselves together into vaguely liturgical patterns. "I recognize that. I will praise, I will sacrifice. In smoke and soot and flame I will worship you forever."

The voice did not answer. He looked up. There was only Miss Millick, deathly pale and swaying drunkenly. Her eyes were closed. He caught her as she wobbled toward him. His knees gave way under the added weight and they sank down together on the edge of the roof.

After a while she began to twitch. Small noises came from her throat, and her eyelids edged open.

"Come on, we'll go downstairs," he murmured jerkily, trying to draw her up. "You're feeling bad."

"I'm terribly dizzy," she whispered. "I must have fainted. I didn't eat enough. And then I'm so nervous lately, about the war and everything, I guess. Why, we're on the roof! Did you bring me up here to get some air? Or did I come up without knowing it? I'm awfully foolish. I used to walk in my sleep, my mother said."

As he helped her down the stairs, she turned and looked at him. "Why, Mr. Wran," she said, faintly, "you've got a big black smudge on your forehead. Here, let me get it off for you." Weakly she rubbed at it with her handkerchief. She started to sway again and he steadied her.

"No, I'll be all right," she said. "Only I feel cold. What

happened, Mr. Wran? Did I have some sort of fainting spell?"
He told her it was something like that.

Later, riding home in an empty elevated car, he wondered
how long he would be safe from the thing. It was a purely
practical problem. He had no way of knowing, but instinct told
him he had satisfied the brute for some time. Would it want
more when it came again? Time enough to answer that question
when it arose. It might be hard, he realized, to keep out of an
insane asylum. With Helen and Ronny to protect, as well as
himself, he would have to be careful and tight lipped. He began
to speculate as to how many other men and women had seen the
thing or things like it.

The elevated slowed and lurched in a familiar fashion. He
looked at the roofs again, near the curve. They seemed very
ordinary, as if what made them impressive had gone away for
a while.

I am not saying this story is about werewolves—maybe it isn't— but werewolves are mentioned quite early in it, and that is excuse enough for talking about them here. The word were *is an old English word for* man, *coming from the same root as the Latin* vir; *the French* garou *is an adaptation of it, like Guillaume for William. The belief in were-animals is almost as widespread as that in ghosts or in magic itself. The belief is always attached to the largest and most dangerous animal known to a people; there are were-bears in Scandinavia, were-tigers in India, were-leopards in Africa. And in New England? Read on and find out.*

THE PHANTOM FARMHOUSE

Seabury Quinn

I HAD BEEN AT THE NEW BRIARCLIFF SANITARIUM NEARLY THREE weeks before I actually saw the house.

Every morning, as I lay abed after the nurse had taken my temperature, I wondered what was beyond the copse of fir and spruce at the turn of the road. The picture seemed incomplete without chimneys rising among the evergreens. I thought about it so much I finally convinced myself there really was a house in the wood. A house where people lived and worked and were happy.

All during the long, trying days when I was learning to navigate a wheelchair, I used to picture the house and the people who lived in it. There would be a father, I was sure; a stout, good-natured father, somewhat bald, who sat on the porch and smoked a cob pipe in the evening. And there was a mother, too; a waistless, plaid-skirted mother with hair smoothly parted over her forehead, who sat beside the father as he rocked and smoked, and who had a brown work-basket in her lap. She spread the stocking feet over her outstretched fingers and her vigilant needle spied out and closed every hole with a cunning no mechanical loom could rival.

Then there was a daughter. I was a little hazy in my conception of her; but I knew she was tall and slender as a hazel wand, and that her eyes were blue and wide and sympathetic.

Picturing the house and its people became a favorite pastime with me during the time I was acquiring the art of walking all over again. By the time I was able to trust my legs on the road I felt I knew my way to my vision-friends' home as well as I knew the by-ways of my own parish; though I had as yet not set foot outside the sanitarium.

Oddly enough, I chose the evening for my first long stroll. It was unusually warm for September in Maine, and some of the sturdier of the convalescents had been playing tennis during the afternoon. After dinner they sat on the veranda, comparing notes on their respective cases of influenza, or matching experiences in appendicitis operations.

After building the house bit by bit from my imagination, as a child pieces together a picture puzzle, I should have been bitterly disappointed if the woods had proved empty; yet when I reached the turn of the road and found my dream house a reality, I was almost afraid. Bit for bit and part for part, it was as I had visualized it.

A long, rambling, comfortable-looking farmhouse it was, with a wide porch screened by vines, and a whitewashed picket fence about the little clearing before it. There was a tumbledown gate in the fence, one of the kind that is held shut with a weighted chain. Looking closely, I saw the weight was a disused ploughshare. Leading from gate to porch was a path of flat stones, laid unevenly in the short grass, and bordered with a double row of clam shells. A lamp burned in the front room, sending out cheerful golden rays to meet the silver moonlight.

A strange, eerie sensation came over me as I stood there. Somehow, I felt I had seen that house before; many, many times before; yet I had never been in that part of Maine till I came to Briarcliff, nor had anyone ever described the place to me. Indeed, except for my idle dreams, I had had no intimation that there was a house in those pines at all.

"Who lives in the house at the turn of the road?" I asked the fat man who roomed next to me.

He looked at me as blankly as if I had addressed him in Choctaw, then countered, "What road?"

"Why, the south road," I explained. "I mean the house in the pines—just beyond the curve, you know."

If such a thing had not been obviously absurd, I should have thought he looked frightened at my answer. Certainly his already prominent eyes started a bit further from his face.

"Nobody lives there," he assured me. "Nobody's lived there for years. There isn't any house there."

I became angry. What right had this fellow to make my civil question the occasion for an ill-timed jest? "As you please," I replied. "Perhaps there isn't any house there for *you;* but I saw one there last night."

"My God!" he ejaculated, and hurried away as if I'd just told him I was infected with smallpox.

Later in the day I overheard a snatch of conversation between him and one of his acquaintances in the lounge.

"I tell you it's so," he was saying with great earnestness. "I thought it was a lot of poppycock, myself; but that clergyman saw it last night. I'm going to pack my traps and get back to the city, and not waste any time about it, either."

"Rats!" his companion scoffed. "He must have been stringing you."

Turning to light a cigar, he caught sight of me. "Say, Mr. Weatherby," he called, "you didn't mean to tell my friend here that you really saw a house down by those pines last night, did you?"

"I certainly did," I answered, "and I tell you, too. There's nothing unusual about it, is there?"

"Is there?" he repeated. "*Is* there? Say, what'd it look like?"

I described it to him as well as I could, and his eyes grew as wide as those of a child hearing the story of Bluebeard.

"Well, I'll be a Chinaman's uncle!" he declared as I finished. "I sure will!"

"See here," I demanded. "What's all the mystery about that farmhouse? Why shouldn't I see it? It's there to be seen, isn't it?"

He gulped once or twice, as if there were something hot in his mouth, before he answered:

"Look here, Mr. Weatherby, I'm telling you this for your own good. You'd better stay in nights; and you'd better stay away from those pines in particular."

Nonplussed at this unsolicited advice, I was about to ask an explanation, when I detected the after-tang of whisky on his breath. I understood, then. I was being made the butt of a drunken joke by a pair of racecourse followers.

"I'm very much obliged, I'm sure," I replied with dignity, "but if you don't mind, I'll choose my own comings and goings."

"Oh, go as far as you like"—he waved his arms wide in token of my complete free-agency—"go as far as you like. I'm going to New York."

And he did. The pair of them left the sanitarium that afternoon.

A slight recurrence of my illness held me housebound for several days after my conversation with the two sportively inclined gentlemen, and the next time I ventured out at night the moon had waxed to the full, pouring a flood of light upon the earth that rivaled midday. The minutest objects were as readily distinguished as they would have been before sunset; in fact, I remember comparing the evening to a silver-plated noon.

As I trudged along the road to the pine copse I was busy formulating plans for intruding into the family circle at the farmhouse; devising all manner of pious frauds by which to scrape acquaintance.

"Shall I feign having lost my way, and inquire direction to the sanitarium; or shall I ask if some mythical acquaintance, a John Squires, for instance, lives there?" I asked myself as I neared the turn of the road.

Fortunately for my conscience, all these subterfuges were unnecessary, for as I neared the whitewashed fence, a girl left the porch and walked quickly to the gate, where she stood gazing pensively along the moonlit road. It was almost as if she were coming to meet me, I thought, as I slackened my pace and assumed an air of deliberate casualness.

Almost abreast of her, I lessened my pace still more, and looked directly at her. Then I knew why my conception of the girl who lived in that house had been misty and indistinct. For the same reason the venerable John had faltered in his description of the New Jerusalem until his vision in the Isle of Patmos.

From the smoothly parted hair above her wide, forget-me-not-eyes to the hem of her white cotton frock, she was as slender and lovely as a Rossetti saint; as wonderful to the eye as a mediaeval poet's vision of his lost love in paradise. Her forehead, evenly framed in the beaten bronze of her hair, was wide and high, and startlingly white, and her brows were delicately penciled as if laid on by an artist with a camel's-hair brush. The eyes themselves were sweet and clear as forest pools mirroring the September sky, and lifted a little at the corners, like an Oriental's giving her face a quaint, exotic look in the midst of these Maine woods.

So slender was her figure that the swell of her bosom was barely perceptible under the light stuff of her dress, and, as she stood immobile in the nimbus of moon rays, the undulation of the line from her shoulders to ankles was what painters call a "curve of motion."

One hand rested lightly on the gate, a hand as finely cut as a bit of Italian sculpture, and scarcely less white than the limed wood supporting it. I noticed idly that the forefinger was somewhat longer than its fellows, and that the nails were almond shaped and very pink—almost red—as if they had been rouged and brightly polished.

No man can take stock of a woman thus, even in a cursory, fleeting glimpse, without her being aware of the inspection, and in the minute my eyes drank up her beauty, our glances crossed and held.

The look she gave back was as calm and unperturbed as

though I had been non-existent; one might have thought I was
an invisible wraith of the night; yet the faint suspicion of a
flush quickening in her throat and cheeks told me she was
neither unaware nor unappreciative of my scrutiny.

Mechanically, I raised my cap, and, wholly without conscious
volition, I heard my own voice asking:

"May I trouble you for a drink from your well? I'm from the
sanitarium—only a few days out of bed, in fact—and I fear I've
overdone myself in my walk."

A smile flitted across her rather wide lips, quick and sympathetic as a mother's response to her child's request, as she
swung the gate open for me.

"Surely—" she answered, and her voice had all the sweetness
of the south wind soughing through her native pines—"surely
you may drink at our well, and rest yourself, too—if you wish."

She preceded me up the path, quickening her pace as she
neared the house, and running nimbly up the steps to the porch.
From where I stood beside the old-fashioned well, fitted with
windlass and bucket, I could hear the sound of whispering
voices in earnest conversation. Hers I recognized, lowered
though it was, by the flutelike purling of its tones; the other
two were deeper, and, it seemed to me, hoarse and throaty.
Somehow, odd as it seemed, there was a queer, canine note in
them, dimly reminding me of the muttering of not too friendly
dogs—such fractious growls I had heard while doing missionary
duty in Alaska, when the savage, half-wolf malemutes were not
fed promptly at the relay stations.

Her voice rose a trifle higher, as if in argument, and I fancied
I heard her whisper, "This one is mine, I tell you; mine. I'll
brook no interference. Go to your own hunting."

An instant later there was a reluctant assenting growl from
the shadow of the vines curtaining the porch, and a light laugh
from the girl as she descended the steps, swinging a bright tin
cup in her hand. For a second she looked at me, as she sent the
bucket plunging into the stone-curbed well; then she announced,
in explanation:

"We're great hunters here, you know. The season is just in, and Dad and I have the worst quarrels about whose game is whose."

She laughed in recollection of their argument, and I laughed with her. I had been quite a Nimrod as a boy, myself, and well I remembered the heated controversies as to whose charge of shot was responsible for some luckless bunny's demise.

The well was very deep, and my breath was coming fast by the time I had helped her wind the bucket-rope upon the windlass; but the water was cold as only spring-fed well water can be. As she poured it from the bucket it shone almost like foam in the moonlight, and seemed to whisper with a half-human voice, instead of gurgling as other water does when poured.

I had drunk water in nearly every quarter of the globe; but never such water as that. Cold as the breath from a glacier: limpid as visualized air, it was yet so light and tasteless in substance that only the chill in my throat and the sight of the liquid in the cup told me that I was doing more than going through the motions of drinking.

"And now, will you rest?" she invited, as I finished my third draught. "We've an extra chair on the porch for you."

Behind the screen of vines I found her father and mother seated in the rays of the big kitchen lamp. They were just as I had expected to find them; plain, homely, sincere country folk, courteous in their reception and anxious to make a sick stranger welcome. Both were stout, with the comfortable stoutness of middle age and good health; but both had surprisingly slender hands. I noticed, too, that the same characteristic of an over-long forefinger was apparent in their hands as in their daughter's, and that both their nails were trimmed to points and stained almost a brilliant red.

"My father, Mr. Squires," the girl introduced, "and my mother, Mrs. Squires."

I could not repress a start. There people bore the very name I had casually thought to use when inquiring for some imaginary person. My lucky stars had surely guided me away from that attempt to scrape an acquaintance. What a figure I should have cut if I had actually asked for Mr. Squires!

Though I was not aware of it, my curious glance must have stayed longer on their reddened nails than I had intended, for Mrs. Squires looked deprecatingly at her hands. "We've all been turning, putting up fox grapes"—she included her husband and daughter with a comprehensive gesture. "And the stain just won't wash out; has to wear off, you know."

I spent, perhaps, two hours with my new-found friends, talking of everything from the best methods of potato culture to the surest way of landing a nine-pound bass. All three joined in the conversation and took a lively interest in the topics under discussion. After the vapid talk of the guests at the sanitarium, I found the simple, interested discourse of these country people as stimulating as wine, and when I left them it was with a hearty promise to renew my call at an early date.

"Better wait until after dark," Mr. Squires warned. "We'd be glad to see you any time; but we're so busy these fall days, we haven't much time for company."

I took the broad hint in the same friendly spirit it was given.

It must have grown chillier than I realized while I sat there, for my new friends' hands were clay-cold when I took them in mine at parting.

Homeward bound, a whimsical thought struck me so suddenly I laughed aloud. There was something suggestive of the dog tribe about the Squires family, though I could not for the life of me say what it was. Even Mildred, the daughter, beautiful as she was, with her light eyes, her rather prominent nose and her somewhat wide mouth, reminded me in some vague way of a lovely silver collie I had owned as a boy.

I struck a tassel of dried leaves from a cluster of weeds with my walking stick as I smiled at the fanciful conceit. The legend of the werewolf—those horrible monsters, formed as men, but capable of assuming bestial shape at will, and killing and eating their fellows, was as old as mankind's fear of the dark, but no mythology I had ever read contained a reference to dog-people. Strange fancies strike us in the moonlight, sometimes.

September ripened to October, and the moon, which had been as round and bright as an exchange-worn coin when I first visited the Squires house, waned as thin as a shaving from a silversmith's lathe.

I became a regular caller at the house in the pines. Indeed, I grew to look forward to my nightly visits with those homely folk as a welcome relief from the tedious gay companionship of the over-sophisticated people at the sanitarium.

My habit of slipping away shortly after dinner was the cause of considerable comment and no little speculation on the part of my fellow convalescents, some of whom set it down to the eccentricity which, to their minds, was the inevitable con-comitant of a minister's vocation, while others were frankly curious. Snatches of conversation I overheard now and then led me to believe that the objective of my strolls was the subject of wagering, and the guarded questions put to me in an effort to solve the mystery became more and more annoying.

I had no intention of taking any of them to the farmhouse with me. The Squires were my friends. Their cheerful talk and unassuming manners were as delightful a contrast to the atmosphere of the sanitarium as a breath of mountain balsam after the fetid air of a hothouse; but to the city-centered crowd at Briarcliff they would have been only the objects of less than half scornful patronage, the source of pitying amusement.

It was Miss Leahy who pushed the impudent curiosity further than any of the rest, however. One evening, as I was setting out, she met me at the gate and announced her intention of going with me.

"You must have found something *dreadfully* attractive to take you off every evening this way, Mr. Weatherby," she hazarded as she pursed her rather pretty, rouged lips at me and caught step with my walk. "We girls really *can't* let some little country lass take you away from us, you know. We simply can't."

I made no reply. It was scarcely possible to tell a pretty girl, even such a vain little flirt as Sara Leahy, to go home and mind her business. Yet that was just what I wanted to do. But I would not take her with me; to that I made up my mind. I would stop at the turn of the road, just out of sight of the farmhouse, and cut across the fields. If she wanted to accompany me on a cross-counry hike in high-heeled slippers, she was welcome to do so.

Besides, she would tell the others that my wanderings were nothing more mysterious than nocturnal explorations of the nearby woods; which bit of misinformation would satisfy the busybodies at Briarcliff and relieve me of the espionage to which I was subjected, as well.

I smiled grimly to myself as I pictured her climbing over fences and ditches in her flimsy party frock and bearded pumps, and lengthened my stride toward the woods at the road's turn.

We marched to the limits of the field bordering the Squires' grove in silence, I thinking of the mild revenge I should soon wreak upon the pretty little busybody at my side, Miss Leahy too intent on holding the pace I set to waste breath in conversation.

As we neared the woods she halted, an expression of worry, almost fear, coming over her face.

"I don't believe I'll go any farther," she announced.

"No?" I replied, a trifle sarcastically. "And is your curiosity so easily satisfied?"

"It's not that." She turned half round, as if to retrace her steps. "I'm afraid of those woods."

"Indeed?" I queried. "And what is there to be afraid of? Bears, Indians, or wildcats. I've been through them several times without seeing anything terrifying." Now she had come this far, I was anxious to take her through the fields and underbrush.

"No-o," Miss Leahy answered, a nervous quaver in her voice, "I'm not afraid of anything like that; but—oh, I don't know what you call it. Pierre told me all about it the other day. Some kind of dreadful thing—loop—loop—something or other. It's a French word, and I can't remember it."

I was puzzled. Pierre Geronte was the ancient French-Canadian gardener at the sanitarium, and, like all doddering old men, would talk for hours to anyone who would listen. Also, like all *habitants,* he was full of wild folklore his ancestors brought overseas with them generations ago.

"What did Pierre tell you?" I asked.

"Why, he said that years ago some terrible people lived in these woods. They had the only house for miles 'round; and travelers stopped there for the night, sometimes. But no stranger was ever seen to leave that place, once he went in. One night the farmers gathered about the house and burned it, with the family that lived there. When the embers had cooled down they made a search, and found nearly a dozen bodies buried in the cellar. That was why no one ever came away from that dreadful place.

"They took the murdered men to the cemetery and buried them; but they dumped the charred bodies of the murderers into graves in the barnyard, without even saying a prayer over them. And Pierre says—Oh, Look! *Look!*"

She broke off her recital of the old fellow's story, and pointed a trembling hand across the field to the edge of the woods. A second more and she shrank against me, clutching at my coat with fear-stiffened fingers and crying with excitement and terror.

I looked in the direction she indicated, myself a little startled by the abject fear that had taken such sudden hold on her.

Something white and ungainly was running diagonally across the field from us, skirting the margin of the woods and making for the meadow that adjoined the sanitarium pasture. A second glance told me it was a sheep; probably one of the flock kept to supply our table with fresh meat.

I was laughing at the strength of the superstition that could make the girl see a figure of horror in an innocent mutton that had strayed away from its fellows and was scared out of its silly wits, when something else attracted my attention.

Loping along in the trail of the fleeing sheep, somewhat to the rear and a little to each side, were two other animals. At first glance they appeared to be a pair of large collies; but as I looked more intently I saw that these animals were like nothing I had ever seen before. They were much larger than any collie— nearly as high as St. Bernards—yet shaped in a general way like Alaskan sledge-dogs—huskies.

The farther one was considerably the larger of the two, and ran with a slight limp, as if one of its hind paws had been injured. As nearly as I could tell in the indifferent light, they were a rusty brown color, very thick-haired and unkempt in appearance. But the strangest thing about them was the fact that both were tailless, which gave them a terrifyingly grotesque look.

As they ran, a third form, similar to the other two in shape, but smaller, slender as a greyhound, with much lighter hued fur, broke from the thicket of short brush edging the wood and took up the chase, emitting a series of short, sharp yelps.

"Sheep-killers," I murmured, half to myself. "Odd. I've never seen dogs like that before."

"They're not dogs," wailed Miss Leahy against my coat. "They're not dogs. Oh, Mr. Weatherby, let's go away. Please, please take me home."

She was rapidly becoming hysterical, and I had a difficult time with her on the trip back. She clung whimpering to me, and I had almost to carry her most of the way. By the time we reached the sanitarium, she was crying bitterly, shivering, as if with a chill, and went in without stopping to thank me for my assistance.

I turned and made for the Squires farm with all possible speed, hoping to get there before the family had gone to bed. But when I arrived the house was in darkness, and my knock at the door received no answer.

As I retraced my steps to the sanitarium I heard faintly, from the fields beyond the woods, the shrill, eerie cry of the sheep-killing dogs.

A torrent of rain held us marooned the next day. Miss Leahy was confined to her room, with a nurse in constant attendance and the house doctor making hourly calls. She was on the verge of a nervous collapse, he told me, crying with a persistence that bordered on hysteria, and responding to treatment very slowly.

An impromptu dance was organized in the great hall and half a dozen bridge tables set up in the library; but as I was skilled in neither of these rainy day diversions, I put on a waterproof and patrolled the veranda for exercise.

On my third or fourth trip around the house I ran into old Geronte shuffling across the porch, wagging his head and muttering portentously to himself.

"See here, Pierre," I accosted him, "what sort of nonsense have you been telling Miss Leahy about those pine woods down the south road?"

The old fellow regarded me unwinkingly with his beady eyes, wrinkling his age-yellowed forehead for all the world like an elderly baboon inspecting a new sort of edible. *"M'sieur* goes out alone much at nights, *n'est-ce-pas?"* he asked, at length.

"Yes, Monsieur goes out alone much at night," I echoed, "but what Monsieur particularly desires to know is what sort of tales have you been telling Mademoiselle Leahy. *Comprenez vous?"*

The network of wrinkles about his lips multiplied as he smiled enigmatically, regarding me askance from the corners of his eyes.

"M'sieur is *Anglaise,"* he replied. "He would not understand —or believe."

"Never mind what I'd believe," I retorted. "What is this story about murder and robbery being committed in those woods? Who were the murderers, and where did they live? *Hein?"*

For a few seconds he looked fixedly at me, chewing the cud of senility between his toothless gums, then, glancing carefully about, as if he feared being overheard, he tiptoed up to me and whispered:

"M'sieur mus' stay indoors these nights. W'en the moon, she shine, yes; w'en she not show her face, no. There are evil things abroad at the dark of the moon, *M'sieur.* Even las' night they keel t'ree of my bes' sheep. Remembair, *M'sieur,* the *loup-garou,* he is out when the moon hide her light."

And with that he turned and left me; nor could I get another word from him save his cryptic warning, "Remembair, *M'sieur;* the *loup-garou.* Remembair."

In spite of my annoyance, I could not get rid of the unpleasant sensation the old man's words left with me. The *loup-garou*— were-wolf—he had said, and to prove his goblin-wolf's presence, he had cited the death of his three sheep.

As I paced the rain-washed porch I thought of the scene I had witnessed the night before, when the sheep-killers were at their work.

"Well," I reflected, "I've seen, the *loup-garou* on his native heath at last. From causes as slight as this, no doubt, the horrible legend of the werewolf had sprung. Time was when all France quaked at the sound of the *loup-garou's* hunting call and the bravest knights in Christendom trembled in their castles and crossed themselves fearfully because some renegade shepherd dog quested his prey in the night. On such a foundation are the legends of a people built."

Whistling a snatch from *Pinafore* and looking skyward in search of a patch of blue in the clouds, I felt a tug at my rain-coat sleeve, such as a neglected terrier might give. It was Geronte again.

"M'sieur," he began in the same mysterious whisper, "the *loup-garou* is a verity, certainly. I, myself, have nevair seen him" —he paused to bless himself—"but my cousin, Baptiste, was once pursued by him. Yes.

"It was near the shrine of the good Sainte Anne that Baptiste lived. One night he was sent to fetch the curé for a dying woman. They rode fast through the trees, the curé and my cousin Baptiste, for it was at the dark of the moon, and the evil forest folk were abroad. And as they galloped, there came a *loup-garou* from the woods, with eyes as bright as hell-fire. It followed hard, this tailless hound from the devil's kennel; but they reached the house before it, and the curé put his book, with the Holy Cross on its cover, at the doorstep. The *loup-garou* wailed under the windows like a child in pain until the sun rose; then it slunk back to the forest.

"When my cousin Baptiste and the curé came out, they found

its hand marks in the soft earth around the door. Very like your hand, or mine, they were, *M'sieur*, save that the first finger was longer than the others."

"And did they find the *loup-garou?*" I asked, something of the old man's earnestness communicated to me.

"Yes, *M'sieur*; but of course," he replied gravely. "T'ree weeks before a stranger, drowned in the river, had been buried without the office of the Church. W'en they opened his grave they found his finger nails as red as blood, and sharp. Then they knew. The good curé read the burial office over him, and the poor soul that had been snatched away in sin slept peacefully at last."

He looked quizzically at me, as if speculating whether to tell me more; then, apparently fearing I would laugh at his outburst of confidence, started away toward the kitchen.

"Well, what else, Pierre?" I asked, feeling he had more to say.

"*Non, non, non,*" he replied. "There is nothing more, *M'sieur*. I did but want *M'sieur* should know my own cousin, Baptiste Geronte, had seen the *loup-garou* with his very eyes."

"Hearsay evidence," I commented, as I went in to dinner.

During the rainy week that followed I chafed at my confinement like a privileged convict suddenly deprived of his liberties, and looked as wistfully down the south road as any prisoned gipsy ever gazed upon the open trail.

The quiet home circle at the farmhouse, the unforced conversation of the old folks, Mildred's sweet companionship, all beckoned me with an almost irresistible force. For in this period of enforced separation I discovered what I had dimly suspected for some time. I loved Mildred Squires. And, loving her, I longed to tell her of it.

No lad intent on visiting his first sweetheart ever urged his feet more eagerly than I when, the curtains of rain at last drawn up, I hastened toward the house at the turn of the road.

As I hoped, yet hardly dared expect, Mildred was standing at the gate to meet me as I rounded the curve, and I yearned toward her like a hummingbird seeking its nest.

She must have read my heart in my eyes, for her greeting

smile was as tender as a mother's as she bends above her babe.

"At last you have come, my friend," she said, putting out both hands in welcome. "I am very glad."

We walked silently up the path, her fingers still resting in mine, her face averted. At the steps she paused, a little embarrassment in her voice as she explained, "Father and mother are out; they have gone to a—meeting. But you will stay?"

"Surely," I acquiesced. And to myself I admitted my gratitude for this chance of Mildred's unalloyed company.

We talked but little that night. Mildred was strangely distrait, and, much as I longed to, I could not force a confession of my love from my lips. Once, in the midst of a long pause between our words, the cry of the sheep-killers came faintly to us, echoed across the fields and woods, and as the weird, shrill sound fell on our ears, she threw back her head, with something of the gesture of a hunting dog scenting its quarry.

Toward midnight she turned to me, a panic of fear having apparently laid hold of her.

"You must go!" she exclaimed, rising and laying her hand on my shoulder.

"But your father and mother have not returned," I objected. "Won't you let me stay until they get back?"

"Oh, no, no," she answered, her agitation increasing. "You must go at once—please." She increased her pressure on my shoulder, almost as if to shove me from the porch.

Taken aback by her sudden desire to be rid of me, I was picking up my hat, when she uttered a stifled little scream and ran quickly to the edge of the porch, interposing herself between me and the yard. At the same moment I heard a muffled sound from the direction of the front gate, a sound like a growling and snarling of savage dogs.

I leaped forward, my first thought being that the sheep-killers I had seen the other night had strayed to the Squires place. Crazed with blood, I knew, they would be almost as dangerous to men as to sheep, and every nerve in my sickness-weakened body cried out to protect Mildred.

To my blank amazement, as I looked from the porch I beheld Mr. and Mrs. Squires walking sedately up the path, talking composedly together. There was no sign of the dogs or any other animals about.

As the elderly couple neared the porch I noticed that Mr. Squires walked with a pronounced limp, and that both their eyes shone very brightly in the moonlight, as though they were suffused with tears.

They greeted me pleasantly enough; but Mildred's anxiety seemed increased, rather than diminished, by their presence, and I took my leave after a brief exchange of civilities.

On my way back I looked intently in the woods bordering the road for some sign of the house of which Pierre had told Miss Leahy; but everywhere the pines grew as thickly as though neither axe nor fire had ever disturbed them.

"Geronte is in his second childhood," I reflected, "and like an elder child, he loves to terrify his juniors with fearsome witch-tales."

Yet an uncomfortable feeling was with me till I saw the gleam of the sanitarium's lights across the fields; and as I walked toward them it seemed to me that more than once I heard the baying of the sheep-killers in the woods behind me.

A buzz of conversation, like the sibilant arguments of a cloud of swarming bees, greeted me as I descended the stairs to breakfast next morning.

It appeared that Ned, one of the pair of great mastiffs attached to the sanitarium, had been found dead before his kennel, his throat and brisket torn open and several gaping wounds in his flanks. Boris, his fellow, had been discovered whimpering and trembling in the extreme corner of the dog house, the embodiment of canine terror.

Speculation as to the animal responsible for the outrage was rife, and, as usual, it ran the gamut of possible and impossible surmises. Every sort of beast from a grizzly bear to a lion escaped from the circus was in turn indicted for the crime, only to have a complete alibi straightway established.

The only one having no suggestion to offer was old Geronte, who stood sphinx-like in the outskirts of the crowd, smiling sardonically to himself and wagging his head sagely. As he caught sight of me he nodded sapiently, as if to include me in the joint tenancy to some weighty secret.

Presently he worked his way through the chattering group and whispered, "*M'sieur*, he was here last night—and with him was the other tailless one. Come and see."

Plucking me by the sleeve, he led me to the rear of the kennels, and, stooping, pointed to something in the moist earth. "You see?" he asked, as if a printed volume lay for my reading in the mud.

"I see that someone has been on his hands and knees here," I answered, inspecting the hand prints he indicated.

"*Something*," he corrected, as if reasoning with an obstinate child. "Does not *M'sieur* behol' that the first finger is the longest?"

"Which proves nothing," I defended. "There are many hands like that."

"Oh—yes?" he replied with that queer upward accent of his. "And where has *M'sieur* seen hands like that before?"

"Oh, many times," I assured him somewhat vaguely, for there was a catch at the back of my throat as I spoke. Try as I would, I could recall only three pairs of hands with that peculiarity.

His little black eyes rested steadily on me in an unwinking stare, and the corners of his mouth curved upward in a malicious grin. It seemed, almost, as if he found a grim pleasure in thus driving me into a corner.

"See here, Pierre," I began testily, equally annoyed at myself and him, "you know as well as I that the *loup-garou* is an old woman's tale. Someone was looking here for tracks, and left his own while doing it. If we look among the patients here we shall undoubtedly find a pair of hands to match these prints."

"God forbid!" he exclaimed, crossing himself. "That would be an evil day for us, *M'sieur*. Here, Bor-ees," he snapped his fingers to the surviving mastiff, "come and eat."

The huge beast came wallowing over to him with the ungainly gait of all heavily-muscled animals, stopping on his way to make a nasal investigation of my knees. Scarcely had his nose come into contact with my trousers when he leaped back, every hair in his mane and along his spine stiffly erect, every tooth in his great mouth bared in a savage snarl. But instead of the mastiff's fighting growl, he emitted only a low, frightened whine, as though he were facing some animal of greater power than himself, and knew his own weakness.

"Good heavens!" I cried, thoroughly terrified at the friendly brute's sudden hostility.

"Yes, *M'sieur*," Geronte cut in quickly, putting his hand on the dog's collar and leading him a few paces away. "It is well you should call upon the heavenly ones; for surely you have the odor of hell upon your clothes."

"What do you mean?" I demanded angrily. "How dare you—?"

He raised a thin hand deprecatingly. "*M'sieur* knows that he knows," he replied evenly; "and what I also know."

And leading Boris by the collar, he shuffled to the house.

Mildred was waiting for me at the gate that evening, and again her father and mother were absent at one of their meetings.

We walked silently up the path and seated ourselves on the porch steps where the waning moon cast oblique rays through the pine branches.

I think Mildred felt the tension I was drawn to, for she talked trivialities with an almost feverish earnestness, stringing her sentences together, and changing her subjects as a Navajo rug weaver twists and breaks her threads.

At last I found an opening in the abattis of her small talk.

"Mildred," I said, very simply, for great emotions tear the ornaments from our speech, "I love you, and I want you for my wife. Will you marry me, Mildred?" I laid my hand on hers. It was cold as lifeless flesh, and seemed to shrink beneath my touch.

"Surely, dear, you must have read the love in my eyes," I urged, as she averted her face in silence. "Almost from the night I first saw you. I've loved you! I—"

"O-o-h, don't!" Her interruption was a strangled moan, as if wrung from her by my words.

I leaned nearer her. "Don't you love me, Mildred?" I asked. As yet she had not denied it.

For a moment she trembled, as if a sudden chill had come on her, then, leaning to me, she clasped my shoulders in her arms, hiding her face against my jacket.

"John, John, you don't know what you say," she whispered disjointedly, as though a sob had torn the words before they left her lips. Her breath was on my cheek, moist and cold as air from a vault.

I could feel the litheness of her through the thin stuff of her gown, and her body was as devoid of warmth as a dead thing.

"You're cold," I told her, putting my arms shieldingly about her. "The night has chilled you."

A convulsive sob was her only answer.

"Mildred," I began again, putting my hand beneath her chin and lifting her face to mine, "tell me, dear, what is the matter?" I lowered my lips to hers.

With a cry that was half scream, half weeping, she thrust me suddenly from her, pressing her hands against my breast and lowering her head until her face was hidden between her outstretched arms. I, too, started back, for in the instant our lips were about to meet, hers had writhed back from her teeth, like a dog's when he is about to spring, and a low, harsh noise, almost a growl, had risen in her throat.

"For God's sake," she whispered hoarsely, agony in every note of her shaking voice, "never do that again! Oh, my dear, dear love, you don't know how near to a horror worse than death you were."

"A—horror—worse—than—death?" I echoed dully, pressing her cold little hands in mine. "What do you mean, Mildred?"

"Loose my hands," she commanded with a quaint reversion

to the speech of our ancestors, "and hear me. I do love you. I love you better than life. Better than death. I love you so I have overcome something stronger than the walls of the grave for your sake, but John, my very love, this is our last night together. We can never meet again. You must go, now, and not come back until tomorrow morning."

"Tomorrow morning?" I repeated blankly. What wild talk was this?

Heedless of my interruption, she hurried on. "Tomorrow morning, just before the sun rises over those trees, you must be here, and have your prayer book with you."

I listened speechless, wondering which of us was mad.

"By that corncrib there"—she waved a directing hand—"you will find three mounds. Stand beside them and read the office for the burial of the dead. Come quickly, and pause for nothing; heed no sound from behind you. And for your own safety, come no sooner than to allow yourself the barest time to read your office."

Finally, I rose to go. "You will do what I ask?" she implored.

"Certainly not," I answered firmly.

"John, John, have pity!" she cried, flinging herself to the earth before me and clasping my knees. "You say you love me. I only ask this one favor of you; only this. Please, for my sake, for the peace of the dead and the safety of the living, promise you will do this thing for me."

Shaken by her abject supplication, I promised, though I felt myself a figure in some grotesque nightmare as I did it.

"Oh, my love, my precious love," she wept, rising and taking both my hands. "At last I shall have peace, and you shall bring it to me. No," she forbade as I made to take her in my arms at parting. "The most I can give you, dear, is this." She held her icy hands against my lips. "It seems so little, dear; but oh! it is so much."

Like a drunkard in his cups I staggered along the south road, my thoughts gone wild with the strangeness of the play I had just acted.

Across the clearing came the howls of the sheep-killers, a sound I had grown used to of late. But tonight there was a deeper, fiercer *timbre* in their bay; a note that boded ill for man as well as beast. Louder and louder it swelled; it was rising from the field itself, now, drawing nearer and nearer the road.

I turned and looked. The great beasts I had seen pursuing the luckless sheep the other night were galloping toward me. A cold finger seemed traced down my spine; the scalp crept and tingled beneath my cap. There was no other object of their quest in sight. I was their elected prey.

My first thought was to turn and run; but a second's reasoning told me this was worse than useless. Weakened with long illness, with an uphill road to the nearest shelter, I should soon be run down.

No friendly tree offered asylum; my only hope was to stand and fight. Grasping my stick, I spread my feet, bracing myself against their charge.

And as I waited their onslaught, there came from the shadow of the pines the shriller, sharper cry of the third beast. Like the crest of a flying, wind-lashed wave, the slighter, silver-furred brute came speeding across the meadow, its ears laid back, its slender paws spurning the sod daintily. Almost, it seemed as if the pale shadow of a cloud were racing toward me.

The thing dashed slantwise across the field, its flight converging on the line of the other two's attack. Midway between me and them it paused; hairs bristling, limbs bent for a spring.

My eyes went wide with incredulity. It was standing in my defense.

All the savageness of the larger beasts' hunting cry was echoed in the smaller creature's bay, and with it a defiance that needed no interpretation.

The attackers paused in their rush; halted, and looked speculatively at my ally. They took a few tentative steps in my direction; and a fierce whine, almost an articulate curse, went up from the silver-haired beast. Slowly the tawny pair circled and trotted back to the woods.

I hurried toward the sanitarium, grasping my stick firmly in readiness for another attack.

But no further cries came from the woods, and once, as I glanced back, I saw the light-haired beast trotting slowly in my wake, looking from right to left, as if to ward off danger.

Half an hour later I looked from my window toward the house in the pines. Far down the south road, its muzzle pointed to the moon, the bright-furred animal crouched and poured out a lament to the night. And its cry was like the wail of a child in pain.

Far into the night I paced my room, like a condemned convict when the vigil of the death watch is on him. Reason and memory struggled for the mastery; one urging me to give over my wild act, the other bidding me obey my promise to Mildred.

Toward morning I dropped into a chair, exhausted with my objectless marching. I must have fallen asleep, for when I started up the stars were dimming in the zenith, and bands of slate, shading to amethyst slanted across the horizon.

A moment I paused, laughing cynically at my fool's errand, then, seizing cap and book, I bolted down the stairs, and ran through the paling dawn to the house in the pines.

There was something ominous and terrifying in the two-toned pastel of the house that morning. Its windows stared at me with blank malevolence, like the half-closed eyes of one stricken dead in mortal sin. The little patches of hoarfrost on the lawn were like leprous spots on some unclean thing. From the trees behind the clearing an owl hooted mournfully, as if to say, "Beware, beware!" and the wind soughing through the black pine boughs echoed the refrain ceaselessly.

Three mounds, sunken and weed-grown, lay in the unkempt thicket behind the corncrib. I paused beside them, throwing off my cap and adjusting my stole hastily. Thumbing the pages to the committal service, I held the book close, that I might see the print through the morning shadows, and commenced: "I know that my redeemer liveth. . . ."

Almost beside me, under the branches of the pines, there

rose such a chorus of howls and yelps I nearly dropped my book. Like all the hounds in the kennels of hell, the sheep-killers clamored at me, rage and fear and mortal hatred in their cries. Through the bestial cadences, too, there seemed to run a human note; the sound of voices heard before beneath these very trees. Deep and throaty, and raging mad, two of the voices came to me, and, like the tremolo of a violin lightly played in an orchestra of brass, the shriller cry of a third beast sounded.

As the infernal hubbub rose at my back, I half turned to fly. Next instant I grasped my book more firmly and resumed my office, for like a beacon in the dark, Mildred's words flashed on my memory: *"Look back for nothing; heed no sound behind you."*

Strangely, too, the din approached no nearer; but as though held by an invisible bar, stayed at the boundary of the clearing.

"Man that is born of a woman hath but a short time to live and is full of misery . . . deliver us from all our offenses . . . O, Lord, deliver us not into the bitter pains of eternal death . . ." and to such an accompaniment, surely, as no priest ever before chanted the office, I pressed through the brief service to the final *Amen.*

Tiny grouts of moisture stood out on my forehead, my breath struggled in my throat as I gasped out the last word. My nerves were frayed to shreds and my strength nearly gone as I let fall my book, and turned upon the beasts among the trees.

They were gone. Abruptly as it had begun, their clamor stopped, and only the rotting pine needles, lightly gilded by the morning sun, met my gaze. A light touch fell in the palm of my open hand, as if a pair of cool, sweet lips had laid a kiss there.

A vapor like swamp-fog enveloped me. The outbuildings, the old, stone-curbed well where I had drunk the night I first saw Mildred, the house itself—all seemed fading into mist and swirling away in the morning breeze.

"Eh, eh, eh; but *M'sieur* will do himself an injury, sleeping on the wet earth!" Old Geronte bent over me, his arm beneath my shoulders. Behind him, great Boris, the mastiff, stood wagging his tail, regarding me with doggish good humor.

"Pierre," I muttered thickly, "how came you here?"

"This morning, going to my tasks, I saw *M'sieur* run down the road like a thing pursued. I followed quickly, for the woods hold terrors in the dark, *M'sieur*."

I looked toward the farmhouse. Only a pair of chimneys, rising stark and bare from a crumbling foundation were there. Fence, well, barn—all were gone, and in their place a thicket of sumac and briars, tangled and overgrown as though undisturbed for thirty years.

"The house, Pierre! Where is the house?" I croaked, sinking my fingers into his withered arm.

" 'Ouse?" he echoed. "Oh, but of course. There is no 'ouse here. *M'sieur;* nor has there been for years. This is an evil place, *M'sieur;* it is best we quit it, and that quickly. There be evil things that run by night—"

"No more," I answered, staggering toward the road, leaning heavily on him. "I brought them peace, Pierre."

He looked dubiously at the English prayer book I held. A Protestant clergyman is a thing of doubtful usefulness to the orthodox French-Canadian. Something of the heartsick misery in my face must have touched his kind old heart, for at last he relented, shaking his head pityingly and patting my shoulder gently, as one would soothe a sorrowing child.

"Per'aps, *M'sieur*," he conceded. "Per'aps; who shall say no? Love and sorrow are the purchase price of peace. Yes. Did not *le bon Dieu* so buy the peace of the world?"

It is a striking testimony to the progress of aviation in less than one lifetime that I can remember reading this story in a magazine. We have learned a great deal about flying since then; but our astronauts know no more about what may be waiting in outer space than Joyce-Armstrong knew about his air-jungle.

THE HORROR OF THE HEIGHTS
Arthur Conan Doyle
(Which includes the manuscript known as the Joyce-Armstrong Fragment)

THE IDEA THAT THE EXTRAORDINARY NARRATIVE WHICH HAS BEEN called the Joyce-Armstrong Fragment is an elaborate practical joke evolved by some unknown person, cursed by a perverted and sinister sense of humour, has now been abandoned by all who have examined the matter. The most *macabre* and imaginative of plotters would hesitate before linking his morbid fancies with the unquestioned and tragic facts which reinforce the statement. Though the assertions contained in it are amazing and even monstrous, it is none the less forcing itself upon the general intelligence that they are true, and that we must readjust our ideas to the new situation. This world of ours appears to be separated by a slight and precarious margin of safety from a most singular and unexpected danger. I will endeavour in this narrative, which reproduces the original document in its necessarily somewhat fragmentary form, to lay before the reader the whole of the facts up to date, prefacing my statement by saying that, if there be any who doubt the narrative of Joyce-Armstrong, there can be no question at all as to the facts concerning Lieutenant Myrtle, R.N., and Mr. Hay Connor, who undoubtedly met their end in the manner described.

The Joyce-Armstrong Fragment was found in the field which is called Lower Haycock, lying one mile to the westward of the village of Withyham, upon the Kent and Sussex border. It was on the fifteenth of September last that an agricultural labourer, James Flynn, in the employment of Mathew Dodd, farmer, of the Chauntry Farm, Withyham, perceived a briar pipe lying near the footpath which skirts the hedge in Lower Haycock. A few paces farther on he picked up a pair of broken binocular glasses. Finally, among some nettles in the ditch, he caught sight of a flat, canvas-backed book, which proved to be a note-book with detachable leaves, some of which had come loose and were fluttering along the base of the hedge. These he collected, but some, including the first, were never recovered, and leave a deplorable hiatus in this all-important statement. The note-book was taken by the labourer to his master, who in turn showed it to Dr. J. H. Atherton, of Hartfield. This gentleman at once recognized the need for an expert examination, and the manuscript was forwarded to the Aero Club in London, where it now lies.

The first two pages of the manuscript are missing. There is also one torn away at the end of the narrative, though none of these affect the general coherence of the story. It is conjectured that the missing opening is concerned with the record of Mr. Joyce-Armstrong's qualifications as an aeronaut, which can be gathered from our sources and are admitted to be unsurpassed among the air-pilots of England. For many years he has been looked upon as among the most daring and the most intellectual of flying men, a combination which has enabled him to both invent and test several new devices, including the common gyroscope attachment which is known by his name. The main body of the manuscript is written neatly in ink, but the last few lines are in pencil and are so ragged as to be hardly legible—exactly, in fact, as they might be expected to appear if they were scribbled off hurriedly from the seat of a moving aeroplane. There are, it may be added, several stains, both on the last page and on the outside cover which has been pronounced by the Home Office experts to be blood—probably human and certainly mammalian. The fact that something closely resembling the organism of malaria was discovered in this blood, and that

Joyce-Armstrong is known to have suffered from intermittent fever, is a remarkable example of the new weapons which modern science has placed in the hands of our detectives.

And now a word as to the personality of the author of this epoch-making statement. Joyce-Armstrong, according to the few friends who really knew something of the man, was a poet and a dreamer, as well as a mechanic and an inventor. He was a man of considerable wealth, much of which he had spent in the pursuit of his aeronautical hobby. He had four private aeroplanes in his hangars near Devizes, and is said to have made no fewer than one hundred and seventy ascents in the course of last year. He was a retiring man with dark moods, in which he would avoid the society of his fellows. Captain Dangerfield, who knew him better than anyone, says that there were times when his eccentricity threatened to develop into something more serious. His habit of carrying a shot-gun with him in his aeroplane was one manifestation of it.

Another was the morbid effect which the fall of Lieutenant Myrtle had upon his mind. Myrtle, who was attempting the height record, fell from an altitude of something over thirty thousand feet. Horrible to narrate, his head was entirely obliterated, though his body and limbs preserved their configuration. At every gathering of airmen, Joyce-Armstrong, according to Dangerfield, would ask, with an enigmatic smile: "And where, pray, is Myrtle's head?"

On another occasion after dinner, at the mess of the Flying School on Salisbury Plain, he started a debate as to what will be the most permanent danger which airmen will have to encounter. Having listened to successive opinions as to air-pockets, faulty construction, and over-banking, he ended by shrugging his shoulders and refusing to put forward his own views, though he gave the impression that they differed from any advanced by his companions.

It is worth remarking that after his own complete disappearance it was found that his private affairs were arranged with a precision which may show that he had a strong premonition of disaster. With these essential explanations I will now give the narrative exactly as it stands, beginning at page three of the blood-soaked notebook:

"Nevertheless, when I dined at Rheims with Coselli and Gustav Raymond I found that neither of them was aware of any particular danger in the higher layers of the atmosphere. I did not actually say what was in my thoughts, but I got so near to it that if they had any corresponding idea they could not have failed to express it. But then they are two empty, vainglorious fellows with no thought beyond seeing their silly names in the newspaper. It is interesting to note that neither of them had ever been much beyond the twenty-thousand-foot level. Of course, men have been higher than this both in balloons and in the ascent of mountains. It must be well above that point that the aeroplane enters the danger zone—always presuming that my premonitions are correct.

"Aeroplaning has been with us now for more than twenty years, and one might well ask: Why should this peril be only revealing itself in our day? The answer is obvious. In the old days of weak engines, when a hundred horse-power Gnome or Green was considered ample for every need, the flights were very restricted. Now that three hundred horse-power is the rule rather than the exception, visits to the upper layers have become easier and more common. Some of us can remember how, in our youth, Garros made a world-wide reputation by attaining nineteen thousand feet, and it was considered a remarkable achievement to fly over the Alps. Our standard now has been immeasurably raised, and there are twenty high flights for one in former years. Many of them have been undertaken with impunity. The thirty-thousand-foot level has been reached time after time with no discomfort beyond cold and asthma. What does this prove? A visitor might descend upon this planet a thousand times and never see a tiger. Yet tigers exist, and if he chanced to come down into a jungle he might be devoured. There are jungles of the upper air, and there are worse things than tigers which inhabit them.

I believe in time they will map these jungles accurately out. Even at the present moment I could name two of them. One of them lies over the Pau-Biarritz district of France. Another is just over my head as I write here in my house in Wiltshire. I rather think there is a third in the Homburg-Wiesbaden district.

"It was the disappearance of the airmen that first set me thinking. Of course, everyone said that they had fallen into the sea, but that did not satisfy me at all. First, there was Verrier in France; his machine was found near Bayonne, but they never got his body. There was the case of Baxter also, who vanished, though his engine and some of the iron fixings were found in a wood in Leicestershire. In that case, Dr. Middleton, of Amesbury, who was watching the flight with a telescope, declares that just before the clouds obscured the view he saw the machine, which was at an enormous height, suddenly rise perpendicularly upwards in a succession of jerks in a manner that he would have thought to be impossible. That was the last seen of Baxter. There was a correspondence in the papers, but it never led to anything. There were several other similar cases, and then there was the death of Hay Connor. What a cackle there was about an unsolved mystery of the air, and what columns in the halfpenny papers, and yet how little was ever done to get to the bottom of the business! He came down in a tremendous vol-plané from an unknown height. He never got off his machine and died in his pilot's seat. Died of what? 'Heart disease,' said the doctors. Rubbish! Hay Connor's heart was as sound as mine is. What did Venables say? Venables was the only man who was at his side when he died. He said that he was shivering and looked like a man who had been badly scared. 'Died of fright,' said Venables, but could not imagine what he was frightened about. Only said one word to Venables, which sounded like 'Monstrous.' They could make nothing of that at the inquest. But I could make something of it. Monsters! That was the last word of poor Harry Hay Connor. And he *did* die of fright, just as Venables thought.

"And then there was Myrtle's head. Do you really believe— does anybody really believe—that a man's head could be driven clean into his body by the force of a fall? Well, perhaps it may be possible, but I, for one, have never believed that it was so with Myrtle. And the grease upon his clothes—'all slimy with grease,' said somebody at the inquest. Queer that nobody got thinking after that! I did—but, then, I had been thinking for a good long time. I've made three ascents—how Dangerfield used to chaff me about my shot-gun—but I've never been high enough. Now, with this new, light Paul Veroner machine and its one hundred and seventy-five Robur, I should easily touch the thirty thousand tomorrow. I'll have a shot at the record. Maybe I shall have a shot at something else as well. Of course, it's dangerous. If a fellow wants to avoid danger he had best keep out of flying altogether and subside finally into flannel slippers and a dressing-gown. But I'll visit the air-jungle to-morrow—and if there's anything there I shall know it. If I return, I'll find myself a bit of a celebrity. If I don't, this note-book may explain what I am trying to do, and how I lost my life in doing it. But no drivel about accidents or mysteries, if *you* please.

"I chose my Paul Veroner monoplane for the job. There's nothing like a monoplane when real work is to be done. Beaumont found that out in very early days. For one thing it doesn't mind damp, and the weather looks as if we should be in the clouds all the time. It's a bonny little model and answers my hand like a tender-mouthed horse. The engine is a ten-cylinder rotary Robur working up to one hundred and seventy-five. It has all the modern improvements—enclosed fuselage, high-curved landing skids, brakes, gyroscopic steadiers, and three speeds, worked by an alteration of the angle of the planes upon the Venetian-blind principle. I took a shot-gun with me and a dozen cartridges filled with buck-shot. You should have seen the face of Perkins, my old mechanic, when I directed him to put them in. I was dressed like an Arctic explorer, with two jerseys under my overalls, thick socks inside my padded boots, a storm-cap with flaps, and my talc goggles. It was stifling outside the hangars, but I was going for the summit of the Himalayas, and had to dress for the part. Perkins knew there was something on and implored me to take him with me. Perhaps I should if I were using the biplane, but a monoplane is a one-man show—if you want to get the last foot of lift out of it. Of course, I took an oxygen bag; the man who goes for the altitude record without one will either be frozen or smothered—or both.

"I had a good look at the planes, the rudder-bar, and the elevating lever before I got in. Everything was in order so far as I could see. Then I switched on my engine and found that she was running sweetly. When they let her go she rose almost at once upon the lowest speed. I circled my home field once or twice just to warm her up, and then, with a wave to Perkins and the others, I flattened out my planes and put her on her highest. She skimmed like a swallow down wind for eight or ten miles until I turned her nose up a little and she began to climb in a great spiral for the cloud-bank above me. It's all important to rise slowly and adapt yourself to the pressure as you go.

"It was a close, warm day for an English September, and there was the hush and heaviness of impending rain. Now and then there came sudden puffs of wind from the south-west—one of them so gusty and unexpected that it caught me napping and turned me half-round for an instant. I remember the time when gusts and whirls and air-pockets used to be things of danger—before we learned to put an overmastering power into our engines. Just as I reached the cloud-banks, with the altimeter marking three thousand, down came the rain. My word, how it poured! It drummed upon my wings and lashed against my face, blurring my glasses so that I could hardly see. I got down on to a low speed, for it was painful to travel against it. As I got higher it became hail, and I had to turn tail to it. One of my cylinders was out of action—a dirty plug, I should imagine, but still I was rising steadily with plenty of power. After a bit the trouble passed, whatever it was, and I heard the full, deep-throated purr —the ten singing as one. That's where the beauty of our modern silencers comes in. We can at last control our engines by ear. How they squeal and squeak and sob when they are in trouble! All those cries for help were wasted in the old days, when every sound was swallowed up by the monstrous racket of the machine. If only the early aviators could come back to see the beauty and perfection of the mechanism which have been bought at the cost of their lives!

"About nine-thirty I was nearing the clouds. Down below me, all blurred and shadowed with rain, lay the vast expanse of Salisbury Plain. Half a dozen flying machines were doing hackwork at the thousand-foot level, looking like little black swallows against the green background. I dare say they were wondering what I was doing up in cloud-land. Suddenly a grey curtain drew across beneath me and the wet folds of vapours were swirling round my face. It was clammily cold and miserable. But I was above the hail-storm, and that was something gained. The cloud was as dark and thick as a London fog. In my anxiety to get clear, I cocked her nose up until the automatic alarm-bell rang, and I actually began to slide backwards. My sopped and dripping wings had made me heavier than I thought, but presently I was in lighter cloud, and soon had cleared the first layer. There was a second—opal-coloured and fleecy—at a great height above my head, a white, unbroken ceiling above, and a dark, unbroken floor below, with the monoplane labouring upwards upon a vast spiral between them. It is deadly lonely in these cloud-spaces. Once a great flight of some small water-birds went past me, flying very fast to the westwards. The quick whir of their wings and their musical cry were cheery to my ear. I fancy that they were teal, but I am a wretched zoologist. Now that we humans have become birds we must really learn to know our brethren by sight.

"The wind down beneath me whirled and swayed the broad cloud-plain. Once a great eddy formed in it, a whirlpool of vapour, and through it, as down a funnel, I caught sight of the distant world. A large white biplane was passing at a vast depth beneath me. I fancy it was the morning mail service betwixt Bristol and London. Then the drift swirled inwards again and the great solitude was unbroken.

"Just after ten I touched the lower edge of the upper cloud-stratum. It consisted of fine diaphanous vapour drifting swiftly from the westward. The wind had been steadily rising all this time and it was now blowing a sharp breeze—twenty-eight an hour by my gauge. Already it was very cold, though my altimeter only marked nine thousand. The engines were working beautifully, and we went droning steadily upwards. The cloud-bank was thicker than I had expected, but at last it thinned out into a golden mist before me, and then in an instant I had shot out from it, and there was an unclouded sky and a brilliant sun above my head—all blue and gold above, all shining silver below, one vast, glimmering plain as far as my eyes could reach. It was a quarter past ten o'clock, and the barograph needle pointed to twelve thousand, eight hundred. Up I went and up, my ears concentrated upon the deep purring of my motor, my eyes busy always with the watch, the revolution indicator, the petrol lever, and the oil pump. No wonder aviators are said to be a fearless race. With so many things to think of there is no time to trouble about oneself. About this time I noted how unreliable is the compass when above a certain height from earth. At fifteen thousand feet mine was pointing east and a point south. The sun and the wind gave me my true bearings.

"I had hoped to reach an eternal stillness in these high altitudes, but with every thousand feet of ascent the gale grew stronger. My machine groaned and trembled in every joint and rivet as she faced it, and swept away like a sheet of paper when I banked her on the turn, skimming down wind at a greater pace, perhaps, than ever mortal man has moved. Yet I had always to turn again and tack up in the wind's eye, for it was not merely a height record that I was after. By all my calculations it was above little Wiltshire that my air-jungle lay, and all my labour might be lost if I struck the outer layers at some farther point.

"When I reached the nineteen-thousand-foot level, which was about midday, the wind was so severe that I looked with some anxiety to the stays of my wings, expecting momentarily to see them snap or slacken. I even cast loose the parachute behind me, and fastened its hook into the ring of my leathern belt, so as to be ready for the worst. Now was the time when a bit of scamped work by the mechanic is paid for by the life of the aeronaut. But she held together bravely. Every cord and strut was humming and vibrating like so many harp-strings, but it was glorious to see how, for all the beating and the buffeting, she was still the conqueror of Nature and the mistress of the sky. There is surely something divine in man himself that he should rise so superior to the limitations which Creation seemed to impose—rise, too, by such unselfish, heroic devotion as this air-conquest has shown. Talk of human degeneration! When has such a story as this been written in the annals of our race?

"These were the thoughts in my head as I climbed that monstrous, inclined plane with the wind sometimes beating in my face and sometimes whistling behind my ears, while the cloud-land beneath me fell away to such a distance that the folds and hummocks of silver had all smoothed out into one flat, shining plain. But suddenly I had a horrible and unprecedented experience. I have known before what it is to be in what our neighbours have called a *tourbillon*, but never on such a scale as this. That huge, sweeping river of wind of which I have spoken had, as it appears, whirlpools within it which were as monstrous as itself. Without a moment's warning I was dragged suddenly into the heart of one. I spun around for a minute or two with such velocity that I almost lost my senses, and then fell suddenly, left wing foremost, down the vacuum funnel in the centre. I dropped like a stone, and lost nearly a thousand feet. It was only my belt that kept me in my seat, and the shock and breathlessness left me hanging half-insensible over the side of the fuselage. But I am always capable of a supreme effort—it is my one great merit as an aviator. I was conscious that the descent was slower. The whirlpool was a cone rather than a funnel, and I had come to the apex. With a terrific wrench, throwing my weight all to one side, I levelled my planes and brought her head away from the wind. In an instant I had shot out of the eddies and was skimming down the sky. Then, shaken but victorious, I turned her nose up and began once more my steady grind on the upward spiral. I took a large sweep to avoid the danger-spot of the whirl-pool, and soon I was safely above it. Just after one o'clock I was twenty-one thousand feet above the sea-level. To my great joy I had topped the gale, and with every hundred feet of ascent the air grew stiller. On the other hand, it was very cold, and I was conscious of that peculiar nausea which goes with rarefac-tion of the air. For the first time I unscrewed the mouth of my oxygen bag and took an occasional whiff of the glorious gas. I could feel it running like a cordial through my veins, and I was exhilarated almost to the point of drunkenness. I shouted and sang as I soared upwards into the cold, still outer world.

"It is very clear to me that the insensibility which came upon Glaisher, and in a lesser degree upon Coxwell, when, in 1862, they ascended in a balloon to the height of thirty thousand feet, was due to the extreme speed with which a perpendicular ascent is made. Doing it at an easy gradient and accustoming oneself to the lessened barometric pressure by slow degrees, there are no such dreadful symptoms. At the same great height I found that even without my oxygen inhaler I could breathe without undue distress. It was bitterly cold, however, and my thermometer was at zero, Fahrenheit. At one-thirty I was nearly seven miles above the surface of the earth, and still ascending steadily. I found, however, that the rarefied air was giving markedly less support to my planes, and that my angle of ascent had to be considerably lowered in consequence. It was already clear that even with my light weight and strong engine-power there was a point in front of me where I should be held. To make matters worse, one of my sparking-plugs was in trouble again and there was intermit-tent misfiring in the engine. My heart was heavy with the fear of failure.

"It was about that time that I had a most extraordinary experi-ence. Something whizzed past me in a trail of smoke and ex-ploded with a loud, hissing sound, sending forth a cloud of steam. For the instant I could not imagine what had happened. Then I remembered that the earth is for ever being bombarded by meteor stones, and would be hardly inhabitable were they not in nearly every case turned to vapour in the outer layers of the atmosphere. Here is a new danger for the high-altitude man, for two others passed me when I was nearing the forty-thousand-foot mark. I cannot doubt that at the edge of the earth's envelope the risk would be a very real one.

"My barograph needle marked forty-one thousand three hundred when I became aware that I could go no farther. Physically, the strain was not as yet greater than I could bear, but my machine had reached its limit. The attenuated air gave no firm support to the wings, and the least tilt developed into side-slip, while she seemed sluggish on her controls. Possibly, had the engine been at its best, another thousand feet might have been within our capacity, but it was still misfiring, and two out of the ten cylinders appeared to be out of action. If I had not already reached the zone for which I was searching then I should never see it upon this journey. But was it not possible that I had attained it? Soaring in circles like a monstrous hawk upon the forty-thousand-foot level I let the monoplane guide herself, and with my Mannheim glass I made a careful observation of my surroundings. The heavens were perfectly clear; there was no indication of those dangers which I had imagined.

"I have said that I was soaring in circles. It struck me suddenly that I would do well to take a wider sweep and open up a new air-tract. If the hunter entered an earth-jungle he would drive through it if he wished to find his game. My reasoning had led me to believe that the air-jungle which I had imagined lay somewhere over Wiltshire. This should be to the south and west of me. I took my bearings from the sun, for the compass was hopeless and no trace of earth was to be seen—nothing but the distant, silver cloud-plain. However, I got my direction as best I might and kept her head straight to the mark. I reckoned that my petrol supply would not last for more than another hour or so, but I could afford to use it to the last drop, since a single magnificant volplané could at any time take me to the earth.

"Suddenly I was aware of something new. The air in front of me had lost its crystal clearness. It was full of long, ragged wisps of something which I can only compare to very fine cigarette-smoke. It hung about in wreaths and coils, turning and twisting slowly in the sunlight. As the monoplane shot through it, I was aware of a faint taste of oil upon my lips, and there was a greasy scum upon the woodwork of the machine. Some infinitely fine organic matter appeared to be suspended in the atmosphere. There was no life there. It was inchoate and diffuse, extending for many square acres and then fringing off into the void. No, it was not life. But might it not be the remains of life? Above all, might it not be the food of life, of monstrous life, even as the humble grease of the ocean is the food for the mighty whale? The thought was in my mind when my eyes looked upward and I saw the most wonderful vision that ever man has seen. Can I hope to convey it to you even as I saw it myself last Thursday?

"Conceive a jelly-fish such as sails in our summer seas, bell-shaped and of enormous size—far larger, I should judge, than the dome of St. Paul's. It was of a light pink colour veined with a delicate green, but the whole huge fabric so tenuous that it was but a fairy outline against the dark blue sky. It pulsated with a delicate and regular rhythm. From it there depended two long, drooping, green tentacles, which swayed slowly backwards and forwards. This gorgeous vision passed gently with noiseless dignity over my head, as light and fragile as a soap-bubble, and drifted upon its stately way.

"I had half-turned my monoplane, that I might look after this beautiful creature, when, in a moment, I found myself amidst a perfect fleet of them, of all sizes, but none so large as the first. Some were quite small, but the majority about as big as an average balloon, and with much the same curvature at the top. There was in them a delicacy of texture and colouring which reminded me of the finest Venetian glass. Pale shades of pink and green were the prevailing tints, but all had a lovely iridescence where the sun shimmered through their dainty forms. Some hundreds of them drifted past me, a wonderful fairy squadron of strange, unknown argosies of the sky—creatures whose forms and substance were so attuned to these pure heights that one could not conceive anything so delicate within actual sight or sound of earth.

"But soon my attention was drawn to a new phenomenon— the serpents of the outer air. These were long, thin, fantastic coils of vapour-like material, which turned and twisted with great speed, flying round and round at such a pace that the eyes could hardly follow them. Some of these ghost-like creatures were twenty or thirty feet long, but it was difficult to tell their girth, for their outline was so hazy that it seemed to fade away into the air around them. These air-snakes were of a very light grey or smoke colour, with some darker lines within, which gave the impression of a definite organism. One of them whisked past my very face, and I was conscious of a cold, clammy contact, but their composition was so unsubstantial that I could not connect them with any thought of physical danger, any more than the beautiful bell-like creatures which had preceded them. There was no more solidity in their frames than in the floating spume from a broken wave.

"But a more terrible experience was in store for me. Floating downwards from a great height there came a purplish patch of vapour, small as I saw it first, but rapidly enlarging as it approached me, until it appeared to be hundreds of square feet in size. Though fashioned of some transparent, jelly-like substance, it was none the less of much more definite outline and solid consistence than anything which I had seen before. There were more traces, too, of a physical organization, especially two vast, shadowy, circular plates upon either side, which may have been eyes, and a perfectly solid white projection between them which was as curved and cruel as the beak of a vulture.

"The whole aspect of this monster was formidable and threatening, and it kept changing its colour from a very light mauve to a dark, angry purple so thick that it cast a shadow as it drifted between my monoplane and the sun. On the upper curve of its huge body there were three great projections which I can only describe as enormous bubbles, and I was convinced as I looked at them that they were charged with some extremely light gas which served to buoy up the misshapen and semi-solid mass in the rarefied air. The creature moved swiftly along, keeping pace easily with the monoplane, and for twenty miles or more it formed my horrible escort, hovering over me like a bird of prey which is waiting to pounce. Its method of progression—done so swiftly that it was not easy to follow—was to throw out a long, glutinous streamer in front of it, which in turn seemed to draw forward the rest of the writhing body. So elastic and gelatinous was it that never for two successive minutes was it the same shape, and yet each change made it more threatening and loathsome than the last.

"I knew that it meant mischief. Every purple flush of its hideous body told me so. The vague, goggling eyes which were turned always upon me were cold and merciless in their viscid hatred. I dipped the nose of my monoplane downwards to escape it. As I did so, as quick as a flash there shot out a long tentacle from this mass of floating blubber, and it fell as light and sinuous as a whip-lash across the front of my machine. There was a loud hiss as it lay for a moment across the hot engine, and it whisked itself into the air again, while the huge, flat body drew itself together as if in sudden pain. I dipped to a vol-piqué, but again a tentacle fell over the monoplane and was shorn off by the propeller as easily as it might have cut through a smoke wreath. A long, gliding, sticky, serpent-like coil came from behind and caught me round the waist, dragging me out of the fuselage. I tore at it, my fingers sinking into the smooth, glue-like surface, and for an instant I disengaged myself, but only to be caught round the boot by another coil, which gave me a jerk that tilted me almost on to my back.

"As I fell over I blazed off both barrels of my gun, though, indeed, it was like attacking an elephant with a pea-shooter to imagine that any human weapon could cripple that mighty bulk. And yet I aimed better than I knew, for, with a loud report, one of the great blisters upon the creature's back exploded with the puncture of the buck-shot. It was very clear that my conjecture was right, and that these vast, clear bladders were distended with some lifting gas, for in an instant the huge, cloud-like body turned sideways, writhing desperately to find its balance, while the white beak snapped and gaped in horrible fury. But already I had shot away on the steepest glide that I dared to attempt, my engine still full on, the flying propeller and the force of gravity shooting me downwards like an aerolite. Far behind me, I saw a dull, purplish smudge growing swiftly smaller and merging into the blue sky behind it. I was safe out of the deadly jungle of the outer air.

"Once out of danger I throttled my engine, for nothing tears a machine to pieces quicker than running on full power from a height. It was a glorious, spiral vol-plané from nearly eight miles of altitude—first, to the level of the silver cloud-bank, then to that of the storm-cloud beneath it, and finally, in beating rain, to the surface of the earth. I saw the Bristol Channel beneath me as I broke from the clouds, but, having still some petrol in my tank, I got twenty miles inland before I found myself stranded in a field half a mile from the village of Ashcombe. There I got three tins of petrol from a passing motor-car, and at ten minutes past six that evening I alighted gently in my own home meadow at Devizes, after such a journey as no mortal upon earth has ever yet taken and lived to tell the tale. I have seen the beauty and I have seen the horror of the heights—and greater beauty or greater horror than that is not within the ken of man.

"And now it is my plan to go once again before I give my results to the world. My reason for this is that I must surely have something to show by way of proof before I lay such a tale before my fellow-men. It is true that others will soon follow and will confirm what I have said, and yet I should wish to carry conviction from the first. Those lovely iridescent bubbles of the air should not be hard to capture. They drift slowly upon their way, and the swift monoplane could intercept their leisurely course. It is likely enough that they would dissolve in the heavier layers of the atmosphere, and that some small heap of amorphous jelly might be all that I should bring to earth with me. And yet something there would surely be, by which I could substantiate my story. Yes, I will go, even if I run a risk by doing so. These purple horrors would not seem to be numerous. It is probable that I shall not see one. If I do I shall dive at once. At the worst there is always the shot-gun and my knowledge of . . ."

Here a page of the manuscript is unfortunately missing. On the next page is written, in large, straggling writing:—

"Forty-three thousand feet. I shall never see earth again. They are beneath me, three of them. God help me; it is a dreadful death to die!"

Such in its entirety is the Joyce-Armstrong Statement. Of the man nothing has since been seen. Pieces of his shattered mono-plane have been picked up in the preserves of Mr. Budd-Lushington upon the borders of Kent and Sussex, within a few miles of the spot where the note-book was discovered. If the unfortunate aviator's theory is correct that this air-jungle, as he called it, existed only over the south-west of England, then it would seem that he had fled from it at the full speed of his mono-plane, but had been overtaken and devoured by these horrible creatures at some spot in the outer atmosphere above the place where the grim relics were found. The picture of that mono-plane skimming down the sky, with the nameless terrors flying as swiftly beneath it and cutting it off always from the earth while they gradually closed in upon their victim, is one upon which a man who valued his sanity would prefer not to dwell. There are many, I am aware, who still jeer at the facts which I have here set down, but even they must admit that Joyce-Armstrong has disappeared, and I would commend to them his own words: "This note-book may explain what I am trying to do, and how I lost my life in doing it. But no drivel about accidents or mysteries, if *you* please."

There is a short story, I believe by Kipling, about a small freighter which sights a sea serpent. One of the few passengers is a reporter, who thinks he has the scoop of all time; but the captain tells him they have sighted the sea serpent more than once, and have said nothing about it so as not to be thought either liars or crazy. The reporter sees the point, and holds his tongue about the monster.

Who knows what there is in the sea that you and I have not heard about?

THE THING ON OUTER SHOAL
P. Schuyler Miller

THE FIRST SHOCK MUST'VE COME ABOUT HALF PAST NINE. IT WAS in between the parts of that Sunday night concert Martha always listens to, during the talking, and I was up on a chair the way I always am at that time, winding the clock. I felt the chair sort of twist under me, and then the clock jumped off the mantel right into my face, and the two of us came down together with a bang.

I must've laid there stunned for a minute before Martha got to me, and I remember the feeling was like being up on a masthead in a high sea. It was like the whole earth was being sucked out from in under me, and then poured back, slow, like mud running into the hole where your foot has been. She had me by the arm, and I was getting my feet under me again when the second shock hit and both of us went down in a heap.

That was the bad one that smashed things all up and down the coast. We had the least of it, and we were high enough to miss the wave that came after it. It was different from the first one—grating and hard, like a ship driving on the rocks. The house jarred until the dishes flew off the shelves in the china closet and Martha's pots and pans came clattering down in a mess on the kitchen floor. The cat came flying through the room like it had fits and went scatting up the garret stairs, and then there was one last drop that nearly had my stomach out of me, and it was over.

I've been in quakes before, in Chile, and one time in Japan when I wasn't much more than a shaver, and I had a sort of notion there was more to come. I tried to put up the window, but the twisting the house had had made it stick, so I opened the front door and went out, with Martha right after me.

The fog was in. For two-three days it had been standing off shore and now it was in it was likely to stay. You couldn't see your hand on the end of your arm, but I knew that up on the point the way we are we'd be above anything that was apt to come.

We heard it, and then right away we smelled it—rank—full of the rotten muck it had raked up off the bottom of the sea, where things have been dying and settling into the mud for thousands and thousands of years. It sounded like the wind roaring, far away but coming closer, and the smell was enough to make a man gag. I could hear the buoy over Wilbur's Shoal clanging like mad, and I knew from the sound that it was adrift. Then the wave hit shore and I swear the whole point shook. The spray from it showered over us where we stood by the door, and then it struck again, not so hard, and that was the last except for the smell. We had that with us for a time.

We went back inside, because like I told Martha then, if any more was to come it wouldn't matter where we were, and a solid stone house like ours is a pretty safe place to be in come wind or high water. There's not many like it in the entire State of Maine.

I knew the first news would come over the Coast Guard station, so I turned the radio on to where they are on the dial and sure enough, they were at it a'ready. It didn't make nice hearing. Aside from the earthquake, which was as bad as we've ever had in these parts, the wave had done a pile of damage all up and down the coast. Down through Massachusetts the big beaches had been swept clean, but it was after the main season and there wasn't many killed compared to what there might have been.

After a little they began to fit things together. The first quake had been pretty well out to sea—maybe twenty-thirty miles—and north of us, but the second one, the big one, was right off Phillipsport and close inshore. I've fished that bottom all my life, and I figured I could place it pretty close. There's a deep place —never sounded to my way of knowing—between Dorner's Bank and Outer Shoal, and the way it sounded that was where it was.

The fog was in and it stayed for three days. Fog don't bother me any, or Martha neither, so we went down to town next morning but there wasn't any news we hadn't heard on the radio. The Coast Guard plane was waiting for the fog to clear before it went up, and they were getting ready to make new soundings in case the bottom had changed. Up in Alaska there's places where whole mountains have come up out of the sea overnight, and then dropped back again.

The smell was everywhere—rotten fish and rotten seaweed— worse than a keg of lobster bait. We got used to it before the fog lifted. Between 'em the quake and the tidal wave had fetched up the ocean bottom for miles around, and it took a while to settle.

Along Wednesday afternoon you could begin to see a little. The sea off our point was milky, and kind of phosphorescent after sundown. There was all sorts of stuff piled up along the rocks—pieces of sunk ships, buoys, weed, shells, dead fish, lobster pots—every kind of thing. There were lobsters there bigger than any that's been caught in the State of Maine since my grandfather Phillips' time. There was halibut that would weigh up to six-seven hundred pounds, and every kind of fish that was ever in the sea. By Wednesday the smell it made was enough to drive us out, and Martha made me go down with a fork and bury what I could of it.

Wednesday night was clear as a bell, with the moon out full, and I heard the Coast Guard plane up a couple of times. Thursday morning I was up and out with the sun. There wasn't much to see. Clear out to the horizon the sea was chalky with the stuff that had been riled up off the bottom, and there were little black spots of drift that wouldn't likely come in for days. I got out my grandfather Waters' glass and went up on the roof, but it didn't do much good. The buoy was gone off Wilbur's Shoal, like I thought, and so were all the channel markers. I heard in town that one of them fetched up on the veranda of the old Butler place, a good five miles back from the harbor up the inlet.

Out over Outer Shoal there was a kind of white cloud, and I watched it for a long time before I made out it was gulls—millions of 'em—swinging and swooping around over the shoal like they were following a school of mackerel. Then I heard the drone of a plane and picked it up, following the coast up from the south. It had Coast Guard markings, and pretty soon I heard our own plane sputter up off the water and swing over to meet it. They must've seen the gulls like I did, because they turned and circled out over the shoal. They were there a long time, swinging round and round like two big birds, and every now and then one of them would drop down to get a better look, but after a while they started back and I called to Martha and got my hat and went down to town to see what they had found out.

Well, sir, half the village was down to the Coast Guard station when I got there. The pilot from down the coast turned out to be a Phillipsport boy—Henry Anders' boy Jim—and when he saw me coming he let out a holler.

There was four-five people standing around the planes arguing—all of 'em men I'd been to sea with in my young days—and they were scratching their heads like chickens after corn. Fred Hibbard hailed me first.

"By gaggle," he shouted, "come down here! These boys has a puzzle none of us can answer. Tell him, Jim."

Jim grinned at me. He'd put on flesh since he joined up with the Coast Guard. "Hi there, Cap'n Waters," he said. "Maybe you can tell me more than these old salt-horses here. They claim what we saw on Outer Shoal isn't possible."

Tom Buck is our regular pilot here. "You were on the roof

when I swung over," he put in. "Likely you saw the gulls over the shoal. We figured maybe a ship had gone aground and broken up, so we went out there, but it's no ship. We don't know what it is."

Old Colonel Phillips may be ninety and he's my own father's uncle, but he's the cussedest old fool in Phillipsport. He creaks like a rusty gate when he talks, and his store teeth don't fit him any better than you'd expect of a mail-order set, but he's never satisfied until he's had his say.

"Blasted young lubbers!" he piped up. "Smart-Alecks! taint no mystery to me, or no need for one! I remember twice in my life there's been a whale grounded on that shoal, and you look in the town records and you'll find plenty more. That wave'd fetch in anything afloat!"

"How do you feel about that?" I asked them.

Jim Anders scratched his head. He has tow hair like his father's folks. They were Swedes, wrecked here and settled, back in my father's time—first-class seamen, every one of them. "Well," he admitted, "I suppose it could be. But if it is, it's the strangest whale I ever saw."

"We couldn't see much," Tom Buck explained. "The gulls have settled on it like flies on a lobster pot, and we couldn't drive 'em off. But it's big—big as any whale I ever laid eyes on— and it's funny shaped. And—it's white."

"What'd I tell you?" Colonel Phillips was just about prancing. "It's a white whale. Seen 'em many a time!"

"Belugas don't grow that big, Colonel," Buck told him. "And —the shape's wrong."

"Pish! Ever hear about Moby Dick? Ever hear about Killer Ned? There's white whales same as any animal, and most always they're big and mean. How is it now? Pretty ripe, ain't it? Any salvage to it?"

"We couldn't see," Jim told him. "It's no place to set down a plane, with all the drift afloat around the shoal. That quake brought up every derelict this side of the Azores. We've got days of work ahead, locating them. But if you old sea-horses can stand the stench, you might be able to pick up a little tobacco money out there. Whale oil's high."

I could tell then it wasn't only the old men who liked the idea, and I could tell it wasn't going by the board. We may be over sixty, some of us, but there are a few left who have shipped on whalers and know what to do and how to do it. When I went up to the store Henry Anders and Fred Hibbard and Welsh Peters and one or two others were with me, and found a couple-three more in Clem Potter's back room. Likewise, I saw that the younger men were drifting into Tony Spillani's garage across the street.

It was going to be a race for it, and I could feel my blood getting up at the thought. Likely the young fellers would try to hold off till night and then slip away. We couldn't pull out right in front of 'em, because they'd beat us hull down, but we had to get there first. Then we all of us thought of the colonel.

He knew it, too. He sat back there in Clem's old armchair with a satisfied smirk under his whiskers, waiting for us to ask him. But he couldn't wait long.

"Remembered me, ain't you?" he demanded. "Remembered I got three whaleboats off the old *Minnie P*, in my boathouse this minute, with engines in 'em and all the gear complete. Remembered I got casks and irons and everything you need over the other side of the point where there can't nobody tell what you're up to. Want 'em, don't you? Well—owner's third!"

The old skinflint had us, and it didn't matter much to any of us. It wasn't the oil we were after. It was wondering about the thing that had washed up on Outer Shoal—beating the young bucks at a game they figured we were too old for—having the kind of adventure that we all had thought was over and done with. It disappointed him a little when we took him up so quick. He just snorted and handed over the keys to the boathouse. Then an idea tickled him and he let out a cackle like a guinea hen. He poked Clem in the ribs with his cane.

"I'll fix those young squirts for you!" he vowed. "I know the way they're figgerin'. That man at the old livery stable has him a big new launch, an' that's the boat they'll use. That an' maybe Peters' and Crandall's. You gimme five pounds of sugar . . . no, by Jake, make it ten pounds . . . an' I'll go down sun myself a mite on the wharf while you're gettin' up a blackberryin' party over to my place. An' don't tell the wimmen!"

The old sculpin! There wasn't one of us would have thought of sugaring their gasoline.

The younger men were still in the garage with their heads together when we came out of the store. We split up—the colonel with his sugar sacks in his coat pockets headed for the wharf, and the rest of us scattering to meet along after dinner at the colonel's boathouse. That would give us the afternoon.

He was a shipshape old devil. Those three boats were as good as the day he got 'em, and the engines were tuned up fit to run a clock. Like as not he had some feller from out of town come and do it so's he wouldn't let on he cared how they were. There wasn't a speck of rust on his whaling irons, and his rope was new —brand new, but with the stiffness worked out of it. It was good gear, all of it. My point hid us from town and would until we were a good two miles out. The colonel's sugar would have to take care of things after that.

We manned two of the three boats. I was steersman in the first and the colonel took the second. We could reach the whale, mark it, and maybe cut a little blubber before nightfall. It was all any of us wanted—except maybe the colonel—the young folks could have the rest with our blessing, after they'd been put in their place.

They'd started up a game of baseball by the time the colonel left town, just to keep our suspicions down, but they must have posted a watch or else someone's wife blabbed. We weren't more than half a mile off the point when we heard the launch start up, and there they came, three boats of them, swinging across to cut us off. I could see the grin on Fred Hibbard's face as he monkeyed with our engine and made it cough and splutter like it wasn't going good. Let 'em be cocky while they could.

They passed us hooting and hollering like wild Indians, and

after a time we passed them, lying in the swell, tinkering with their engines. The three boats were strung out over a mile or so of sea, and some of the boys were turning a little green. By that time we could see the shoal.

The smell of the thing and the cackle of the gulls reached us long before we sighted it. It was ripe, but it didn't smell like whale to me. It had that seabottom rankness that the quake had brought up, and I began to remember yarns I'd heard about sea serpents and the like of that.

There must have been all the gulls in Maine over that reef. The sea was white with them, bobbing around in the oil slick that had spread from the thing on the shoal. They were stuffed too full to fly, but they covered the thing from the water's edge to where it lay awash until it was one big, stinking mountain of white feathers, sixty feet long if it was a yard. From the boats we couldn't tell much about how it looked, but it was—queer.

My boat was first, and we circled around it and came in from the seaward side, down wind. The gulls didn't rise until the boat was almost touching it, and when they did, I looked at the men and they looked at me. Their faces were funny-colored and I guess mine was, too, because it was a man.

The gulls had been at it for better than a day, but you could see it was a man. It was sixty feet from head to feet, more than fifteen feet across the shoulders, and it was a man. There was a layer of thick white blubber on it under a gray kind of skin. Big blue gills flared out where its neck should have been. And as the boat bumped against it a hand came floating up through the water beside me—wrinkled with the water, and webbed all the way to the tips of the fingers. It was a man.

A cloud had gone over the sun, and the wind was kind of cold on me. The smell of the thing choked me, and the screaming, wheeling birds overhead made my head swim. I reversed the engine and pulled us off a couple of lengths.

The gulls had been at it. All along its barrel of a body they had torn big, jagged holes through its skin and blubber and raw red meat, down to the white ribs. It lay on its face on the shoal, its back, where there was skin left, dull gray-white like a shark's belly. On its feet it would have looked kind of stubby, I guess, because it looked awful broad for its length, with big, powerful long arms made for swimming, and long, thick legs with webbed feet. Its face was under water, but it had no ears unless the gulls had torn them off, and its head was round and covered with stringy hair like a wad of dirty hemp.

It was a giant man out of deep part of the sea—the part that no man of our kind ever sees or hears tell of, except in sailors' yarns. The earthquake had vomited it up out of the sea to die here on Outer Shoal. The marks of the deep were on it, in the way Nature had made it to stand the pressure down there thousands of fathoms below, and in the great round scars that were on its back and sides. I knew those marks, and so did most of the others with me—we'd seen them often enough on whales. The Kraken had left them—the giant white squid that lives down in the cold and the black of the sea bottom where only whales go—and things like this.

Then I heard the colonel shout. He had climbed up on the dead thing's body and stood there between its gnarled shoulders looking down at us. Another figure bobbed up alongside him— Doc Higbee—and the two of them stooped down to study the thing they were standing on. Then the colonel straightened up as if he'd had a kink in his back and I heard him screech.

We had pulled off into the deep water that goes down like the side of a mountain off Outer Shoal. We had all been watching the two on the thing's back, but now we turned to look.

Out of the water a hundred feet away rose a face. Long hanks of grizzled hair hung over it, and out between them stared two huge, black, goggling eyes. There was a smear of white flesh between them where it should have had a nose. Its mouth stretched halfway across its head right under those staring eyes, and it was filled with little sharp pegs of teeth. The gills began below—a purple frill of flesh, opening and closing as it breathed. As it rose higher its mouth gaped open to suck in air, and I could see that it had no tongue.

It found footing on the shelving edge of the shoal, a boat's length away, before I had sense enough to move. Then I grabbed for the gas lever and we were hipering out of its way. But it didn't pay us any heed. The water was just under its armpits as it stood there, with its webbed hands floating on the water in front of it. It climbed higher—it was the sea-man's mate come after him out of the deeps!

The two men on the carcass were scrambling down the other side into their boat. The colonel made it, but Higbee slipped and splashed into the water. By now the woman-thing was standing kneedeep in the sea beside her mate. I wondered how she could support that monstrous body out of water, but she had giant's muscles. Her great saucer eyes stared at the dead thing, and one webbed hand took it by the shoulder and turned it over.

Then she saw the other boat. It had waited to pick up the doctor, and the men were struggling frantically over the engine with the little colonel hopping and cursing in the bow. She made a lunge toward it and stumbled over the carcass of her mate. The wash as she smashed into the sea nearly overset the boat, but they righted it and suddenly we heard the engine start. It sputtered a moment and stopped.

Henry Anders was harpooner on my father's whaler and he was bow man in my boat now. He got to his feet, picking up the heavy blubber spade at his side, as we came within range of the thing. It was never meant for throwing, but he hurled that iron like a lance. It struck the sea-woman's shoulder and sliced deep into the thick flesh, so that I could see the purplish blood running. She stopped, shoulder deep, and turned to face us.

Then, close by the colonel's boat and almost within reach of her groping hand the sea went suddenly white and smooth. A great, twisting tentacle went snaking out over the surface of the water and touched its thwart. Like a flash it clamped over the bow, inches from the colonel. A second followed it, and then the monster's body rose slowly out of the waves—two evil black pools of ink for eyes—a great white parrot beak—and surrounding them a nest of corpse-white tentacles. The Kraken!

It gave off a sickly kind of scent, and the sea-woman smelled it. She seemed to hunch down into the sea. They stared at each other for the space of a minute, and I saw its huge arm uncoiling from around the boat as it watched her. It was wary, but there was no fear in it—or her. Then, like lightning, she pounced; like coiling ropes its tentacles twined round her body, biting deep in the blubber.

Her strength was terrible. Her webbed fingers dug into the Kraken's rubbery flesh; the mucles swelled along her arms and across her naked back, and she tore the monster's body in her hands as if she was tearing rags. But it had its grip; its tentacles sucking and ripping at her leathery skin. One arm was bound fast to her body, and the tip of one tentacle was prying at her heaving gills.

Her legs were spread, her back bent; the muscles under her coat of blubber stood up in long, low ridges across her back as she set her fingers in the great squid's flesh and tore it loose. Those webbed fingers closed over its staring eyes and gaping beak and squeezed, and the flailing tentacles went limp.

She stood there, thigh-deep in the bloody sea, staring at the dead thing in her hands. She dropped it and her bulbous eyes swung slowly from one boat to the other. Suddenly she lunged forward and the water closed over her head. Then panic struck us.

We may have made ten boat lengths before she reached us. Out of the sea at my elbow the curve of her enormous shoulder rose against the boat. Her groping hand closed over the bow and pulled it under, hurling us over the side into the sea. As I came up, struggling for breath, I could hear the wood splinter in her fist. She dropped it and looked around her for us.

I hadn't heard the plane till then. We were too close for Jim Anders to use his gun, but he zoomed up past her face and she flinched back and batted at him like a kitten at a string. Her head swung around on her shoulders to watch him, and as he dived again she began to flounder away toward the shoal and the body of her dead mate.

That gave him an idea. The rap of his machine gun sounded over the whine of the diving plane—every Coast Guard plane had been armed since that trouble off Nantucket. Gouts of flesh spurted where the bullets struck the dead thing's pulpy form. The sea-woman was swimming frantically away from us. She found her footing again and pulled herself erect, her arms stretched up at the attacking plane. And Jim Anders dived for the third time and shot her down.

There was enough life left in her even then to carry her back into the deep out of which she came. Sometimes it seems that I can see her, swimming painfully down into the blackness and the cold and the quiet, until the last of her life flows out of her and she sinks down into the everlasting darkness where she was born. It was too bad it had to happen like it did.

We came out of it all right. Not even the colonel had more than a week's layup with his blood pressure. Of course we had to take a tongue-lashing from the womenfolks, but we'd figured on that anyway.

The boys in the launches were scared stiff. They'd seen the whole thing, but they couldn't raise a finger to help. The colonel had done a bang-up job on that gasoline.

We don't talk about it much in Phillipsport. Everyone in town knows about it, and it's no secret, but we don't like to talk about it much. It wasn't the kind of thing that sets well with a man.

It happened, though—no mistake about that. I have the proof. The pictures Tom Buck made before they bombed the thing to bits and let the sea have it again didn't come out. The gulls were back, and you can't see much but the shape of it. Far as I know, I have the only other proof there is. I got that from Doc Higbee the winter before he died.

Doc had had time, when he and the colonel landed on the thing, to slice off a chunk of skin and blubber and a mite of the flesh underneath. He kept them by him, even in the water, and stowed them away in alcohol when he got back.

The piece of skin he got shows one of the great round scars that the Kraken left. Maybe they feed on each other, down there miles under the sea where nothing but whales ever get to. Doc said it was human skin. He said the blood in it is human blood, only just about as salty as sea water is today. He showed me a book where it tries to figure out when our first ancestors crawled out of the sea, millions of years back, by measuring the amount of salt in our blood and figuring the amount of salt there was in the sea then. He said they were supposed to match, otherwise things couldn't keep alive.

Suppose some of those things that turned into men stayed in the sea when our ancestors came out on land, Doc said. Suppose they went right on living in the sea, changing the same way the things on land did, growing big enough and strong enough to stand the pressure and the cold down there. They might change into things like the ones we saw, Doc said. There couldn't be many of them, he thought. There wouldn't be enough to eat, except for squids and whales and dead things that sank down from above.

There was a reporter from Boston, a year or two back, got wind of the story some way and tried to pump it out of us. He spent near a week here, I guess, talking to this one and that one. The way he had it, it was a sea serpent that was washed up on the shoal. Well, sir, after a while it got around to the colonel, and I never did hear the like of the yarn he told that man. It was too good. I guess the feller figured it was all lies, which it mostly was, and judged the rumor was the same. Anyway, we've never been bothered about it since—until now.

The late Howard Phillips Lovecraft might almost be called his own most fantastic creation. He was born in Providence in 1895. He never knew his father, who was hospitalized for paresis, and died when his son was five. He grew up under the dominance of his mother and his two aunts, in an old house that contained the libraries of both his grandfathers. He steeped himself in these, to such an extent that he wrote of himself that he was more at home in the eighteenth century than in the world of today, that eighteenth-century spelling came naturally to him, and that he would prefer eighteenth-century dress. When he was about ten the family fortunes began to decline. He never entered the world of competition, but lived most of his life on a tiny inherited income of about fifteen dollars a week, and devoted himself to literature, writing fantastic stories which were published chiefly in the now defunct magazine Weird Tales. *He was married briefly, and during the period of his married life lived in Brooklyn; but his marriage was soon terminated by mutual consent, and little is known of it. Essentially he was a recluse; often, like Balzac, he wrote all night and closed the shutters by day. But evidently he had a strong capacity for affection, which found an outlet in his voluminous correspondence. The unusual nature of his stories led to his receiving many letters from strangers, especially aspiring writers, and to them he was unfailingly generous, pouring out advice and written talk in letters of many pages of tiny handwriting. Many writers have expressed their gratitude and affection for him. One of them, August Derleth, rescued Lovecraft's stories from the obscurity of a pulp-magazine file, and published them in a book which is now a collector's item.*

Lovecraft died in 1937. He has a sure place in the literature of the fantastic. "The Outsider" is one of the most original monster stories ever written.

———————

THE OUTSIDER

H. P. Lovecraft

That night the Baron dreamt of many a wo;
And all his warrior-guests, with shade and form
Of witch, and demon, and large coffin-worm,
Were long be-nightmared.

—KEATS

UNHAPPY IS HE TO WHOM THE MEMORIES OF CHILDHOOD BRING only fear and sadness. Wretched is he who looks back upon lone hours in vast and dismal chambers with brown hangings and maddening rows of antique books, or upon awed watches in twilight groves of grotesque, gigantic, and vine-encumbered trees that silently wave twisted branches far aloft. Such a lot the gods gave to me—to me, the dazed, the disappointed; the barren, the broken. And yet I am strangely content and cling desperately to those sere memories, when my mind momentarily threatens to reach beyond that to *the other*.

I know not where I was born, save that the castle was infinitely old and infinitely horrible, full of dark passages and having high ceilings where the eye could find only cobwebs and shadows. The stones in the crumbling corridors seemed always hideously damp, and there was an accursed smell everywhere, as of the piled-up corpses of dead generations. It was never light, so that I used sometimes to light candles and gaze steadily at them for relief, nor was there any sun outdoors, since the terrible trees grew high above the topmost accessible tower. There was one black tower which reached above the trees into the unknown outer sky, but that was partly ruined and could not be ascended save by a well-nigh impossible climb up the sheer wall, stone by stone.

I must have lived years in this place, but I can not measure the time. Beings must have cared for my needs, yet I can not recall any person except myself, or anything alive but the noiseless rats and bats and spiders. I think that whoever nursed me must have been shockingly aged, since my first conception of a living person was that of something mockingly like myself, yet distorted, shriveled, and decaying like the castle. To me there was nothing grotesque in the bones and skeletons that strewed some of the stone crypts deep down among the foundations. I fantastically associated these things with everyday events, and thought them more natural than the colored pictures of living beings which I found in many of the moldy books. From such books I learned all that I know. No teacher urged or guided me, and I do not recall hearing any human voice in all those years—not even my own; for although I had read of speech, I had never thought to try to speak aloud. My aspect was a matter equally unthought of, for there were no mirrors in the castle, and I merely regarded myself by instinct as akin to the youthful figures I saw drawn and painted in the books. I felt conscious of youth because I remembered so little.

Outside, across the putrid moat and under the dark mute trees, I would often lie and dream for hours about what I read in the books; and would longingly picture myself amidst gay crowds in the sunny world beyond the endless forest. Once I tried to escape from the forest, but as I went farther from the castle the shade grew denser and the air more filled with brooding fear; so that I ran frantically back lest I lose my way in a labyrinth of nighted silence.

So through endless twilights I dreamed and waited, though I knew not what I waited for. Then in the shadowy solitude my longing for light grew so frantic that I could rest no more, and I lifted entreating hands to the single black ruined tower that reached above the forest into the unknown outer sky. And at last I resolved to scale that tower, fall though I might; since it were better to glimpse the sky and perish, than to live without ever beholding day.

In the dank twilight I climbed the worn and aged stone stairs till I reached the level where they ceased, and thereafter clung perilously to small footholds leading upward. Ghastly and terrible was that dead, stairless cylinder of rock; black, ruined, and deserted, and sinister with startled bats whose wings made no noise. But more ghastly and terrible still was the slowness of my progress; for climb as I might, the darkness overhead grew no thinner, and a new chill as of haunted and venerable mold assailed me. I shivered as I wondered why I did not reach the light, and would have looked down had I dared. I fancied that night had come suddenly upon me, and vainly groped with one free hand for a window embrasure, that I might peer out and above, and try to judge the height I had attained.

All at once, after an infinity of awesome, sightless crawling up that concave and desperate precipice, I felt my head touch a solid thing, and knew I must have gained the roof, or at least some kind of floor. In the darkness I raised my free hand and tested the barrier, finding it stone and immovable. Then came a deadly circuit of the tower, clinging to whatever holds the slimy wall could give; till finally my testing hand found the barrier yielding, and I turned upward again, pushing the slab or door with my head as I used both hands in my fearful ascent. There was no light revealed above, and as my hands went higher I knew that my climb was for the nonce ended; since the slab was the trap-door of an aperture leading to a level stone surface of greater circumference than the lower tower, no doubt the floor of some lofty and capacious observation chamber. I crawled through carefully, and tried to prevent the heavy slab from falling back into place, but failed in the latter attempt. As I lay exhausted on the stone floor I heard the eery echoes of its fall, but hoped when necessary to pry it up again.

Believing I was now at a prodigious height, far above the accursed branches of the wood, I dragged myself up from the floor and fumbled about for windows, that I might look for the first time upon the sky, and the moon and stars of which I had read. But on every hand I was disappointed; since all that I found were vast shelves of marble, bearing odious oblong boxes of disturbing size. More and more I reflected, and wondered what hoary secrets might abide in this high apartment so many eons cut off from the castle below. Then unexpectedly my hands came upon a doorway, where hung a portal of stone, rough with strange chiseling. Trying it, I found it locked; but with a supreme burst of strength I overcame all obstacles and dragged it open inward. As I did so there came to me the purest ecstasy I have ever known; for shining tranquilly through an ornate grating of iron, and down a short stone passageway of steps that ascended from the newly found doorway, was the radiant full moon, which I had never before seen save in dreams and in vague visions I dared not call memories.

Fancying now that I had attained the very pinnacle of the castle, I commenced to rush up the few steps beyond the door; but the sudden veiling of the moon by a cloud caused me to stumble, and I felt my way more slowly in the dark. It was still very dark when I reached the grating—which I tried carefully and found unlocked, but which I did not open for fear of falling from the amazing height to which I had climbed. Then the moon came out.

Most demoniacal of all shocks is that of the abysmally unexpected and grotesquely unbelievable. Nothing I had before undergone could compare in terror with what I now saw; with the bizarre marvels that sight implied. The sight itself was as simple as it was stupefying, for it was merely this: instead of a dizzying prospect of treetops seen from a lofty eminence, there stretched around me on the level through the grating nothing less than *the solid ground,* decked and diversified by marble slabs and columns, and overshadowed by an ancient stone church, whose ruined spire gleamed spectrally in the moonlight.

Half unconscious, I opened the grating and staggered out upon the white gravel path that stretched away in two directions. My mind, stunned and chaotic as it was, still held the frantic craving for light; and not even the fantastic wonder which had happened could stay my course. I neither knew nor cared whether my experience was insanity, dreaming, or magic; but was determined to gaze on brilliance and gayety at any cost. I knew not who I was or what I was, or what my surroundings might be; though as I continued to stumble along I became conscious of a kind of fearsome latent memory that made my progress not wholly fortuitous. I passed under an arch out of that region of slabs and columns, and wandered through the open country; sometimes following the visible road, but sometimes leaving it curiously to tread across meadows where only occasional ruins bespoke the ancient presence of a forgotten road. Once I swam across a swift river where crumbling, mossy masonry told of a bridge long vanished.

Over two hours must have passed before I reached what seemed to be my goal, a venerable ivied castle in a thickly wooded park, maddeningly familiar, yet full of perplexing strangeness to me. I saw that the moat was filled in, and that some of the well-known towers were demolished; whilst new wings existed to confuse the beholder. But what I observed with chief interest and delight were the open windows—gorgeously ablaze with light and sending forth sound of the gayest revelry. Advancing to one of these I looked in and saw an oddly dressed company, indeed; making merry, and speaking brightly to one another. I had never, seemingly, heard human speech before and could guess only vaguely what was said. Some of the faces seemed to hold expressions that brought up incredibly remote recollections, others were utterly alien.

I now stepped through the low window into the brilliantly lighted room, stepping as I did so from my single bright moment of hope to my blackest convulsion of despair and realization. The nightmare was quick to come, for as I entered, there occurred immediately one of the most terrifying demonstrations I had ever conceived. Scarcely had I crossed the sill when there descended upon the whole company a sudden and unheralded fear of hideous intensity, distorting every face and evoking the most horrible screams from nearly every throat. Flight was universal, and in the clamor and panic several fell in a swoon and were dragged away by their madly fleeing companions. Many covered their eyes with their hands, and plunged blindly and awkwardly in their race to escape, overturning furniture and stumbling against the walls before they managed to reach one of the many doors.

The cries were shocking; and as I stood in the brilliant apartment alone and dazed, listening to their vanishing echoes, I trembled at the thought of what might be lurking near me unseen. At a casual inspection the room seemed deserted, but when I moved toward one of the alcoves I thought I detected a presence there—a hint of motion beyond the golden-arched doorway leading to another and somewhat similar room. As I approached the arch I began to perceive the presence more clearly; and then, with the first and last sound I ever uttered— a ghastly ululation that revolted me almost as poignantly as its noxious cause—I beheld in full, frightful vividness the inconceivable, indescribable, and unmentionable monstrosity which had by its simple appearance changed a merry company to a herd of delirious fugitives.

I can not even hint what it was like, for it was a compound of all that is unclean, uncanny, unwelcome, abnormal, and detestable. It was the ghoulish shade of decay, antiquity, and desolation; the putrid, dripping eidolon of unwholesome revelation, the awful baring of that which the merciful earth should always hide. God knows it was not of this world—or no longer of this world—yet to my horror I saw in its eaten-away and bone-revealing outlines a leering, abhorrent travesty on the human shape; and in its moldy, disintegrating apparel an unspeakable quality that chilled me even more.

I was almost paralyzed, but not too much so to make a feeble effort toward flight; a backward stumble which failed to break the spell in which the nameless, voiceless monster held me. My eyes, bewitched by the glassy orbs which stared loathsomely into them, refused to close; though they were mercifully blurred, and showed the terrible object but indistinctly after the first shock. I tried to raise my hand to shut out the sight, yet so stunned were my nerves that my arm could not fully obey my will. The attempt, however, was enough to disturb my balance; so that I had to stagger forward several steps to avoid falling. As I did so I became suddenly and agonizingly aware of the *nearness* of the carrion thing, whose hideous hollow breathing I half fancied I could hear. Nearly mad, I found myself yet able to throw out a hand to ward off the fetid apparition which pressed so close; when in one cataclysmic second of cosmic nightmarishness and hellish accident *my fingers touched the rotting outstretched paw of the monster beneath the golden arch.*

I did not shriek, but all the fiendish ghouls that ride the night-wind shrieked for me as in that same second there crashed down upon my mind a single and fleeting avalanche of soul-annihilating memory. I knew in that second all that had been; I remembered beyond the frightful castle and the trees, and recognized the altered edifice in which I now stood; I recognized, most terrible of all, the unholy abomination that stood leering before me as I withdrew my sullied fingers from its own.

But in the cosmos there is balm as well as bitterness, and that balm is nepenthe. In the supreme horror of that second I forgot what had horrified me, and the burst of black memory vanished in a chaos of echoing images. In a dream I fled from that haunted and accursed pile, and ran swiftly and silently in the moonlight. When I returned to the churchyard place of marble and went down the steps I found the stone trap-door immovable; but I was not sorry, for I had hated the antique castle and the trees. Now I ride with the mocking and friendly ghouls on the night wind, and play by day amongst the catacombs of Nephren-Ka in the sealed and unknown valley of Hadoth by the Nile. I know that light is not for me, save that of the moon over the rock tombs of Neb, nor any gayety save the unnamed feasts of Nitokris beneath the Great Pyramid; yet in my new wildness and freedom I almost welcome the bitterness of alienage.

For although nepenthe has calmed me, I know always that I am an outsider; a stranger in this century and among those who are still men. This I have known ever since I stretched out my fingers to the abomination within that great gilded frame; stretched out my fingers and touched *a cold and unyielding surface of polished glass.*

*"Lands are swayea by a king on his throne,
But the sea has no king but God alone,"*

*says Rosetti. For twenty years the Loch Ness monster has been
reported, yet it is still not certain whether it actually exists, or
what its shape is—and the sea is incomparably vaster than Loch
Ness. It was only in 1938, that there was discovered a living fish
called the coelacanth, which was supposed to have been extinct
for seventy million years—since the time of the last dinosaurs.
And, who knows what there is in the sea that we have never
heard of?*

SECOND NIGHT OUT

Frank Belknap Long

IT WAS PAST MIDNIGHT WHEN I LEFT MY STATEROOM. THE UPPER
promenade deck was entirely deserted and thin wisps of fog
hovered about deck chairs and curled and uncurled about the
gleaming rails. There was no air stirring. The ship moved
forward sluggishly through a quiet, fog-enshrouded sea.

But I did not object to the fog. I leaned against the rail and
inhaled the damp, murky air with a positive greediness. The
almost unendurable nausea, the pervasive physical and mental
misery had departed, leaving me serene and at peace. I was again
capable of experiencing sensuous delight, and the aroma of the
brine was not to be exchanged for pearls and rubies. I had paid
in exorbitant coinage for what I was about to enjoy—for the
five brief days of freedom and exploration in glamorous, sea-
splendid Havana which I had been promised by an enterprising
and, I hoped, reasonably honest tourist agent. I am in all respects
the antithesis of a wealthy man, and I had drawn so heavily
upon my bank balance to satisfy the greedy demands of The
Loriland Tours, Inc., that I had been compelled to renounce
such really indispensable amenities as after-dinner cigars and
ocean-privileged sherry and chartreuse.

But I was enormously content. I paced the deck and inhaled the moist, pungent air. For thirty hours I had been confined to my cabin with a sea illness more debilitating than bubonic plague or malignant sepsis, but having at length managed to squirm from beneath its iron heel I was free to enjoy my prospects. They were enviable and glorious. Five days in Cuba, with the privilege of driving up and down the sun-drenched Malecon in a flamboyantly upholstered limousine, and an opportunity to feast my discerning gaze on the pink walls of the Cabanas and the Columbus Cathedral and La Fuerza, the great storehouse of the Indies. Opportunity, also, to visit sunlit patios, and saunter by iron-barred rejas, and to sip refrescos by moonlight in open-air cafes, and to acquire, incidentally, a Spanish contempt for Big Business and the Strenuous Life. Then on to Haiti, dark and magical, and the Virgin Islands, and the quaint, incredible Old World harbor of Charlotte Amalie, with its chimneyless, red-roofed houses rising in tiers to the quiet stars—the natural Sargasso, the inevitable last port of call for rainbow fishes, diving boys and old ships with sun-bleached funnels and incurably drunken skippers. A flaming opal set in an amphitheater of malachite—its allure blazed forth through the gray fog and dispelled my northern spleen. I learned against the rail and dreamed also of Martinique, which I would see in a few days, and of the Indian and Chinese wenches of Trinidad. And then, suddenly, a dizziness came upon me. The ancient and terrible malady had returned to plague me.

Seasickness, unlike all other major afflictions, is a disease of the individual. No two people are ever afflicted with precisely the same symptoms. The manifestations range from a slight malaise to a devastating impairment of all one's faculties. I was afflicted with the gravest symptoms imaginable. Choking and gasping, I left the rail and sank helplessly down into one of the three remaining deck chairs.

Why the steward had permitted the chairs to remain on deck was a mystery I couldn't fathom. He had obviously shirked a duty, for passengers did not habitually visit the promenade deck in the small hours, and foggy weather plays havoc with the wicker-work of steamer chairs. But I was too grateful for the benefits which his negligence had conferred upon me to be excessively critical. I lay sprawled at full length, grimacing and gasping and trying fervently to assure myself that I wasn't nearly as sick as I felt. And then, all at once, I became aware of an additional source of discomfiture.

The chair exuded an unwholesome odor. It was unmistakable. As I turned about, as my cheek came to rest against the damp, varnished wood my nostrils were assailed by an acrid and alien odor of a vehement, cloying potency. It was at once stimulating and indescribably repellent. In a measure, it assuaged my physical unease, but it also filled me with the most overpowering revulsion, with a sudden, hysterical and almost frenzied distaste.

I tried to rise from the chair, but the strength was gone from my limbs. An intangible presence seemed to rest upon me and weigh me down. And then the bottom seemed to drop out of everything. I am not being facetious. Something of the sort actually occurred. The base of the sane, familiar world vanished, was swallowed up. I sank down. Limitless guilfs seemed open beneath me, and I was immersed, lost in a gray void. The ship, however, did not vanish. The ship, the deck, the chair continued to support me, and yet, despite the retention of these outward symbols of reality, I was afloat in an unfathomable void. I had the illusion of falling, of sinking helplessly down through an eternity of space. It was as though the chair which supported me had passed into another dimension without ceasing to leave the familiar world—as though it floated simultaneously both in our three-dimensional world and in another world of alien, unknown dimensions. I became aware of strange shapes and shadows all about me. I gazed through illimitable dark gulfs at continents and islands, lagoons, atolls, vast gray waterspouts. I sank down into the great deep. I was immersed in dark slime. The boundaries of sense were dissolved away, and the breath of an active corruption blew through me, gnawing at my vitals and filling me with extravagant torment. I was alone in the great deep. And the shapes that accompanied me in my utter abysmal isolation were shriveled and black and dead, and they cavorted deliriously with little monkey-heads with streaming, sea-drenched viscera and putrid, pupil-less eyes.

And then, slowly, the unclean vision dissolved. I was back again in my chair and the fog was as dense as ever, and the ship moved forward steadily through the quiet sea. But the odor was still present—acrid, overpowering, revolting. I leaped from the chair, in profound alarm. . . . I experienced a sense of having emerged from the bowels of some stupendous and unearthly encroachment, of having in a single instant exhausted the resources of earth's malignity, and drawn upon untapped and intolerable reserves.

I have gazed without flinching at the turbulent, demon-seething, utterly benighted infernos of the Italian and Flemish primitives. I have endured with calm vision the major inflictions of Hieronymus Bosch and Lucas Cranach, and I have not quailed even before the worst perversities of the elder Breughel, whose outrageous gargoyles and ghouls and cacodemons are so self-contained that they fester with an over-brimming malignancy, and seem about to burst asunder and dissolve hideously in a black and intolerable froth. But not even Signorelli's "Soul of the Damned," or Goya's "Los Caprichos," or the hideous, ooze-encrusted sea-shapes with half-assembled bodies and dead, pupil-less eyes which drag themselves sightlessly through Segrelles' blue worlds of fetor and decay were as unnerving and ghastly as the flickering visual sequence which had accompanied my perception of the odor. I was vastly and terribly shaken.

I got indoors somehow, into the warm and steamy interior of the upper saloon, and waited, gasping, for the deck steward to come to me. I had pressed a small button labeled "Deck Steward" in the wainscoting adjoining the central stairway, and I frantically hoped that he would arrive before it was too late, before the odor outside percolated into the vast, deserted saloon.

The steward was a daytime official, and it was a cardinal crime to fetch him from his berth at one in the morning, but I had to have some one to talk to, and as the steward was responsible for the chairs I naturally thought of him as the logical target for my interrogations. He would know. He would be able to explain. The odor would not be unfamiliar to him. He would be able to explain about the chairs . . . about the chairs . . . I was growing hysterical and confused.

I wiped the perspiration from my forehead with the back of my hand, and waited with relief for the steward to approach. He had come suddenly into view above the top of the central stairway, and he seemed to advance toward me through a blue mist.

He was extremely solicitous, extremely courteous. He bent above me and laid his hand concernedly upon my arm. "Yes, sir. What can I do for you, sir? A bit under the weather, perhaps. What can I do?"

Do? Do? It was horribly confusing. I could only stammer: "The chairs, steward. On the deck. Three chairs. Why did you leave them there? Why didn't you take them inside?"

It wasn't what I had intended asking him. I had intended questioning him about the odor. But the strain, the shock had confused me. The first thought that came into my mind on seeing the steward standing above me, so solicitous and concerned, was that he was a hypocrite and a scoundrel. He pretended to be concerned about me and yet out of sheer perversity he had prepared the snare which had reduced me to a pitiful and helpless wreck. He had left the chairs on deck deliberately, with a cruel and crafty malice, knowing all the time, no doubt, that something would occupy them.

But I wasn't prepared for the almost instant change in the man's demeanor. It was ghastly. Befuddled as I had become I could perceive at once that I had done him a grave, a terrible injustice. He hadn't known. All the blood drained out of his cheeks and his mouth fell open. He stood immobile before me, completely inarticulate, and for an instant I thought he was about to collapse, to sink helplessly down upon the floor.

"You saw—chairs?" he gasped at last.

I nodded.

The steward leaned toward me and gripped my arm. The flesh of his face was completely destitute of luster. From the parchment-white oval his two eyes, tumescent with fright, stared wildly down at me.

"It's the black, dead thing," he muttered. "The monkey-face. I knew it would come back. It always comes aboard at midnight on the second night out."

He gulped and his hand tightened on my arm.

"It's always on the second night out. It knows where I keep the chairs, and it takes them on deck and sits in them. I saw it last time. It was squirming about in the chair—lying stretched out and squirming horribly. Like an eel. It sits in all three of the chairs. When it saw me it got up and started toward me. But I got away. I came in here, and shut the door. But I saw it through the window."

The steward raised his arm and pointed.

"There. Through that window there. Its face was pressed against the glass. It was all black and shriveled and eaten away. A monkey-face, sir. So help me, the face of a dead, shriveled monkey. And wet—dripping. I was so frightened I couldn't breathe. I just stood and groaned, and then it went away."

He gulped.

"Doctor Blodgett was mangled, clawed to death at ten minutes to one. We heard his shrieks. The thing went back, I guess, and sat in the chairs for thirty or forty minutes after it left the window. Then it went down to Doctor Blodgett's stateroom and took his clothes. It was horrible. Doctor Blodgett's legs were missing, and his face was crushed to a pulp. There were claw-marks all over him. And the curtains of his berth were drenched with blood.

"The captain told me not to talk. But I've got to tell someone. I can't help myself, sir. I'm afraid—I've got to talk. This is the third time it's come aboard. It didn't take anybody the first time, but it sat in the chairs. It left them all wet and slimy, sir—all covered with black stinking slime."

I stared in bewilderment. What was the man trying to tell me? Was he completely unhinged? Or was I too confused, too ill myself to catch all that he was saying?

He went on wildly: "It's hard to explain, sir, but this boat is visited. Every voyage, sir—on the second night out. And each time it sits in the chairs. Do you understand?"

I didn't understand, clearly, but I murmured a feeble assent. My voice was appallingly tremulous and it seemed to come from the opposite side of the saloon.

"Something out there," I gasped. "It was awful. Out there, you hear? An awful odor. My brain. I can't imagine what's come over me, I feel as though something were pressing on my brain. Here."

I raised my fingers and passed them across my forehead.

"Something here—something—"

The steward appeared to understand perfectly. He nodded and helped me to my feet. He was still self-engrossed, still horribly wrought up, but I could sense that he was also anxious to re-assure and assist me.

"Stateroom 16 D? Yes, of course. Steady, sir."

The steward had taken my arm and was guiding me toward the central stairway. I could scarcely stand erect. My decrepitude was so apparent, in fact, that the steward was moved by compassion to the display of an almost heroic attentiveness. Twice I stumbled and would have fallen had not the guiding arm of my companion encircled my shoulders and levitated my sagging bulk.

"Just a few more steps, sir. That's it. Just take your time. There isn't anything will come of it, sir. You'll feel better when you're inside, with the fan going. Just take your time, sir."

At the door of my stateroom I spoke in a hoarse whisper to the man at my side. "I'm all right now. I'll ring if I need you. Just—let me—get inside. I want to lie down. Does this door lock from the inside?"

"Why, yes. Yes, of course. But maybe I'd better get you some water."

"No, don't bother. Just leave me—please."

"Well—all right, sir." Reluctantly the steward departed, after making certain that I had a firm grip on the handle of the door.

The stateroom was extremely dark. I was so weak that I was compelled to lean with all my weight against the door to close it. It shut with a slight click and the key fell out upon the floor. With a groan I went down on my knees and groveled apprehensively with my fingers on the soft carpet. But the key eluded me.

I cursed and was about to rise when my hand encountered something fibrous and hard. I started back, gasping. Then, frantically, my fingers slid over it, in a hectic effort at appraisal. It was—yes, undoubtedly a shoe. And sprouting from it, an ankle. The shoe reposed firmly on the floor of the stateroom. The flesh of the ankle, beneath the sock which covered it, was very cold.

In an instant I was on my feet, circling like a caged animal about the narrow dimensions of the stateroom. My hands slid over the walls, the ceiling. If only, dear God, the electric light button would not continue to elude me!

Eventually my hands encountered a rubbery excrescence on the smooth panels. I pressed, resolutely, and the darkness vanished to reveal a man sitting upright on a couch in the corner— a stout, well-dressed man holding a grip and looking perfectly composed. Only his face was invisible. His face was concealed by a handkerchief—a large handkerchief which had obviously been placed there intentionally, perhaps as a protection against the rather chilly air currents from the unshuttered port. The man was obviously asleep. He had not responded to the tugging of my hands on his ankles in the darkness, and even now he did not stir. The glare of the electric light bulbs above his head did not appear to annoy him in the least.

I experienced a sudden and overwhelming relief. I sat down beside the intruder and wiped the sweat from my forehead. I was still trembling in every limb, but the calm appearance of the man beside me was tremendously reassuring. A fellow-passenger, no doubt, who had entered the wrong compartment. It should not be difficult to get rid of him. A mere tap on the shoulder, followed by a courteous explanation, and the intruder would vanish. A simple procedure, if only I could summon the strength to act with decision. I was so horribly enfeebled, so incredibly weak and ill. But at last I mustered sufficient energy to reach out my hand and tap the intruder on the shoulder.

"I'm sorry, sir," I murmured, "but you've got into the wrong stateroom. If I wasn't a bit under the weather I'd ask you to stay and smoke a cigar with me, but you see I"—with a distorted effort at a smile I tapped the stranger again nervously—"I'd rather be alone, so if you don't mind—sorry I had to wake you."

Immediately I perceived that I was being premature. I had not waked the stranger. The stranger did not budge, did not so much as agitate by his breathing the handkerchief which concealed his features.

I experienced a resurgence of my alarm. Tremulously I stretched forth my hand and seized a corner of the handkerchief. It was an outrageous thing to do, but I had to know. If the intruder's face matched his body, if it was composed and familiar all would be well, but if for any reason—

The fragment of physiognomy revealed by the uplifted corner was not reassuring. With a gasp of affright I tore the handkerchief completely away. For a moment, a moment only, I stared at the dark and repulsive visage, with its stary, corpse-white eyes, viscid and malignant, its flat simian nose, hairy ears, and thick black tongue that seemed to leap up at me from out of the mouth. The face moved as I watched it, wriggled and squirmed revoltingly, while the head itself shifted its position, turning slightly to one side and revealing a profile more bestial and gangrenous and unclean than the brunt of its countenance.

I shrank back against the door, in frenzied dismay. I suffered as an animal suffers. My mind, deprived by shock of all capacity to form concepts, agonized instinctively, at a brutish level of consciousness. Yet through it all one mysterious part of myself remained horribly observant. I saw the tongue snap back into the mouth; saw the lines of the features shrivel and soften until presently from the slavering mouth and white sightless eyes there began to trickle thin streams of blood. In another moment the mouth was a red slit in a splotched horror of countenance—a red slit rapidly widening and dissolving in an amorphous crimson flood. The horror was hideously and repellently dissolving into the basal sustainer of all life.

It took the steward nearly ten minutes to restore me. He was compelled to force spoonfuls of brandy between my tightly-locked teeth, to bathe my forehead with ice-water and to massage almost savagely my wrists and ankles. And when, finally, I opened my eyes he refused to meet them. He quite obviously wanted me to rest, to remain quiet, and he appeared to distrust his own emotional equipment. He was good enough, however, to enumerate the measures which had contributed to my restoration, and to enlighten me in respect to the remnants:

"The clothes were all covered with blood—drenched, sir. I burned them."

On the following day he became more loquacious. "It was wearing the clothes of the gentleman who was killed last voyage, sir—it was wearing Doctor Blodgett's things. I recognized them instantly."

"But why—"

The steward shook his head. "I don't know, sir. Maybe your going up on deck saved you. Maybe it couldn't wait. It left a little after one the last time, sir, and it was later than that when I saw you to your stateroom. The ship may have passed out of its zone, sir. Or maybe it fell asleep and couldn't get back in time, and that's why it—dissolved. I don't think it's gone for good. There was blood on the curtains in Doctor Blodgett's cabin, and I'm afraid it always goes that way. It will come back next voyage, sir. I'm sure of it."

He cleared his throat.

"I'm glad you rang for me. If you'd gone right down to your stateroom it might be wearing your clothes next voyage."

Havana failed to restore me. Haiti was a black horror, a repellent quagmire of menacing shadows and alien desolation, and in Martinique I did not get a single hour of undisturbed sleep in my room at the hotel.

When Samson discovered a swarm of bees in the carcass of a lion, he set the Philistines a riddle: "Out of the eater came forth meat; out of the strong came forth sweetness." Samson, like everybody else for a couple of thousand years, was a believer in spontaneous generation.

When I was a boy, country boys still believed that horsehairs in a jar of pond water would turn into water wigglers; and there were generally enough embryonic wigglers of some kind in the pond water to convince them that they were right. Almost until within the memory of men living it was believed that rotting meat of itself produced blow-flies; that dirt and sweat produced lice. In the vivid imagination of the Elizabethans, corpses, even sealed up in lead coffins, themselves produced grave-worms.

Pasteur freed us from that nightmare; and yet—who knows exactly what conditions once brought forth life?

IT

Theodore Sturgeon

IT WALKED IN THE WOODS.

It was never born. It existed. Under the pine needles the fires burn, deep and smokeless in the mold. In heat and in darkness and decay there is growth. It grew, but it was not alive. It walked unbreathing through the woods, and thought and saw and was hideous and strong, and it was not born and it did not live. It grew and moved about without living.

It crawled out of the darkness and hot damp mold into the cool of a morning. It was huge. It was lumped and crusted with its own hateful substances, and pieces of it dropped off as it went its way, dropped off and lay writhing, and stilled, and sank putrescent into the forest loam.

It had no mercy, no laughter, no beauty. It had strength and great intelligence. And—perhaps it could not be destroyed. It crawled out of its mound in the wood and lay pulsing in the sunlight for a long moment. Patches of it shone wetly in the golden glow, parts of it were nubbled and flaked. And whose dead bones had given it the form of a man?

It scrabbled painfully with its half-formed hands, beating the ground and the bole of a tree. It rolled and lifted itself up on its crumbling elbows, and it tore up a great handful of herbs and shredded them against its chest, and it paused and gazed at the gray-green juices with intelligent calm. It wavered to its feet, and seized a young sapling and destroyed it, folding the slender trunk back on itself again and again, watching attentively the useless, fibered splinters. And it squealed, snatching up a fear-frozen field creature, crushing it slowly, letting blood and pulpy flesh and fur ooze from between its fingers, run down and rot on the forearms.

It began searching.

Kimbo drifted through the tall grasses like a puff of dust, his bushy tail curled tightly over his back and his long jaws agape. He ran with an easy lope, loving his freedom and the power of his flanks and furry shoulders. His tongue lolled listlessly over his hips. His lips were black and serrated, and each tiny pointed liplet swayed with his doggy gallop. Kimbo was all dog, all healthy animal.

He leaped high over a boulder and landed with a startled yelp as a long-eared cony shot from its hiding place under the rock. Kimbo hurtled after it, grunting with each great thrust of his legs. The rabbit bounced just ahead of him, keeping its distance, its ears flattened on its curving back and its little legs nibbling away at a distance hungrily. It stopped, and Kimbo pounced, and the rabbit shot away at a tangent and popped into a hollow log. Kimbo yelped again and rushed snuffling at the log, and knowing his failure, curvetted but once around the stump and ran on into the forest. The thing that watched from the wood raised its crusted arms and waited for Kimbo.

Kimbo sensed it there, standing dead-still by the path. To him it was a bulk which smelled of carrion not fit to roll in, and he snuffled distastefully and ran to pass it.

The thing let him come abreast and dropped a heavy twisted fist on him. Kimbo saw it coming and curled up tight as he ran, and the hand clipped stunningly on his rump, sending him rolling and yipping down the slope. Kimbo straddled to his feet, shook his head, shook his body with a deep growl, came back to the silent thing with green murder in his eyes. He walked stiffly, straight-legged, his tail as low as his lowered head and a ruff of fury round his neck. The thing raised its arms again, waited.

Kimbo slowed, then flipped himself through the air at the monster's throat. His jaws closed on it; his teeth clicked together through a mass of filth, and he fell choken and snarling at its feet. The thing leaned down and struck twice, and after the dog's back was broken, it sat beside him and began to tear him apart.

"Be back in an hour or so," said Alton Drew, picking up his rifle from the corner behind the wood box. His brother laughed.

"Old Kimbo 'bout runs your life, Alton," he said.

"Ah, I know the ol' devil," said Alton. "When I whistle for him for half an hour and he don't show up, he's in a jam or he's treed something wuth shootin' at. The ol' son of a gun calls me by not answerin'."

Cory Drew shoved a full glass of milk over to his nine-year-old daughter and smiled. "You think as much o' that houn'-dog o' yours as I do of Babe here."

Babe slid off her chair and ran to her uncle. "Gonna catch me the bad fella, Uncle Alton?" she shrilled. The "bad fella" was Cory's invention—the one who lurked in corners ready to pounce on little girls who chased the chickens and played around mowing machines and hurled green apples with a powerful young arm at the sides of the hogs, to hear the synchronized thud and grunt; little girls who swore with an Austrian accent like an ex-hired man they had had; who dug caves in haystacks till they tipped over, and kept pet crawfish in tomorrow's milk cans, and rode work horses to a lather in the night pasture.

"Get back here and keep away from Uncle Alton's gun!" said Cory. "If you see the bad fella, Alton, chase him back here. He has a date with Babe here for that stunt of hers last night." The preceding evening, Babe had kind-heartedly poured pepper on the cows' salt block.

"Don't worry, kiddo," grinned her uncle, "I'll bring you the bad fella's hide if he don't get me first."

Alton Drew walked up the path toward the wood, thinking about Babe. She was a phenomenon—a pampered farm child. Ah well—she had to be. They'd both loved Clissa Drew, and she'd married Cory, and they had to love Clissa's child. Funny thing, love. Alton was a man's man, and thought things out that way; and his reaction to love was a strong and frightened one. He knew what love was because he felt it still for his brother's wife and would feel it as long as he lived for Babe. It led him through his life, and yet he embarrassed himself by thinking of it. Loving a dog was an easy thing, because you and the old devil could love one another completely without talking about it. The smell of gun smoke and the smell of wet fur in the rain were perfume enough for Alton Drew, a grunt of satisfaction and the scream of something hunted and hit were poetry enough. They weren't like love for a human, that choked his throat so he could not say words he could not have thought of anyway. So Alton loved his dog Kimbo and his Winchester for all to see, and let his love for his brother's women, Clissa and Babe, eat at him quietly and unmentioned.

His quick eyes saw the fresh indentations in the soft earth behind the boulder, which showed where Kimbo had turned and leaped with a single surge, chasing the rabbit. Ignoring the tracks, he looked for the nearest place where a rabbit might hide, and strolled over to the stump. Kimbo had been there, he saw, and had been there too late. "You're an ol' fool," muttered Alton. "Y' can't catch a cony by chasin' it. You want to cross him up some way." He gave a peculiar trilling whistle, sure that Kimbo was digging frantically under some nearby stump for a rabbit that was three counties away by now. No answer. A little puzzled, Alton went back to the path. "He never done this before," he said softly. There was something about this he didn't like.

He cocked his .32-40 and cradled it. At the county fair someone had once said of Alton Drew that he could shoot at a handful of salt and pepper thrown in the air and hit only the pepper. Once he split a bullet on the blade of a knife and put two candles out. He had no need to fear anything that could be shot at. That's what he believed.

The thing in the woods looked curiously down at what it had done to Kimbo, and moaned the way Kimbo had before he died. It stood a minute storing away facts in its foul, unemotional mind. Blood was warm. The sunlight was warm. Things that moved and bore fur had a muscle to force the thick liquid through tiny tubes in their bodies. The liquid coagulated after a time. The liquid on rooted green things was thinner and the loss of a limb did not mean loss of life. It was very interesting, but the thing, the mold with a mind, was not pleased. Neither was it displeased. Its accidental urge was a thirst for knowledge, and it was only—interested.

It was growing late, and the sun reddened and rested awhile on the hilly horizon, teaching the clouds to be inverted flames. The thing threw up its head suddenly, noticing the dusk. Night was ever a strange thing, even for those of us who have known it in life. It would have been frightening for the monster had it been capable of fright, but it could only be curious; it could only reason from what it had observed.

What was happening? It was getting harder to see. Why? It threw its shapeless head from side to side. It was true—things were dim, and growing dimmer. Things were changing shape, taking on a new and darker color. What did the creatures it had crushed and torn apart see? How did they see? The larger one, the one that had attacked, had used two organs in its head. That must have been it, because after the thing had torn off two of the dog's legs it had struck at the hairy muzzle; and the dog, seeing the blow coming, had dropped folds of skin over the organs—closed its eyes. Ergo, the dog saw with its eyes. But then after the dog was dead, and its body still, repeated blows had had no effect on the eyes. They remained open and staring. The logical conclusion was, then, that a being that had ceased to live and breathe and move about lost the use of its eyes. It must be that to lose sight was, conversely, to die. Dead things did not walk about: They lay down and did not move. Therefore the thing in the wood concluded that it must be dead, and so it lay down by the path, not far away from Kimbo's scattered body, lay down and believed itself dead.

Alton Drew came up through the dusk to the wood. He was frankly worried. He whistled again, and then called, and there was still no response, and he said again, "The ol' flea-bus never done this before," and shook his heavy head. It was past milking time, and Cory would need him. "Kimbo!" he roared. The cry echoed through the shadows, and Alton flipped on the safety catch of his rifle and put the butt on the ground beside the path. Leaning on it, he took off his cap and scratched the back of his head, wondering. The rifle butt sank into what he thought was soft earth; he staggered and stepped into the chest of the thing that lay beside the path. His foot went up to the ankle in its yielding rottenness, and he swore and jumped back.

"*Whew!* Sompn sure dead as hell there! Ugh!" He swabbed at his boot with a handful of leaves while the monster lay in the growing blackness with the edges of the deep footprint in its chest sliding into it, filling it up. It lay there regarding him dimly out of its muddy eyes, thinking it was dead because of the darkness, watching the articulation of Alton Drew's joints, wondering at this new uncautious creature.

Alton cleaned the butt of his gun with more leaves and went on up the path, whistling anxiously for Kimbo.

Clissa Drew stood in the door of the milk shed, very lovely in red-checked gingham and a blue apron. Her hair was clean yellow, parted in the middle and stretched tautly back to a heavy braided knot. "Cory! Alton!" she called a little sharply.

"Well?" Cory responded gruffly from the barn, where he was stripping off the Ayrshire. The dwindling streams of milk plopped pleasantly into the froth of a full pail.

"I've called and called," said Clissa. "Supper's cold, and Babe won't eat until you come. Why—where's Alton?"

Cory grunted, heaved the stool out of the way, threw over the stanchion lock and slapped the Ayrshire on the rump. The cow backed and filled like a towboat, clattered down the line and out into the barnyard. "Ain't back yet."

"Not back?" Clissa came in and stood beside him as he sat by the next cow, put his forehead against the warm flank. "But, Cory, he said he'd—"

"Yeh, yeh, I know. He said he'd be back fer the milkin'. I heard him. Well, he ain't."

"And you have to— Oh, Cory, I'll help you finish up. Alton would be back if he could. Maybe he's—"

"Maybe he's treed a blue jay," snapped her husband. "Him an' that damn dog." He gestured hugely with one hand while the other went on milking. "I got twenty-six head o' cows to milk. I got pigs to feed an' chickens to put to bed. I got to toss hay for the mare and turn the team out. I got harness to mend and a wire down in the night pasture. I got wood to split an' carry." He milked for a moment in silence, chewing on his lip. Clissa stood twisting her hands together, trying to think of something to stem the tide. It wasn't the first time Alton's hunting had interfered with the chores. "So I got to go ahead with it. I can't interfere with Alton's spoorin'. Every damn time that hound o' his smells out a squirrel I go without my supper. I'm gettin' sick an'—"

"Oh, I'll help you!" said Clissa. She was thinking of the spring, when Kimbo had held four hundred pounds of raging black bear at bay until Alton could put a bullet in its brain, the time Babe had found a bearcub and started to carry it home, and had fallen into a freshet, cutting her head. You can't hate a dog that has saved your child for you, she thought.

"You'll do nothin' of the kind!" Cory growled. "Get back to the house. You'll find work enough there. I'll be along when I can. Dammit, Clissa, don't cry! I didn't mean to— Oh, shucks!" He got up and put his arms around her. "I'm wrought up," he said. "Go on now. I'd no call to speak that way to you. I'm sorry. Go back to Babe. I'll put a stop to this for good tonight. I've had enough. There's work here for four farmers an' all we've got is me an' that . . . that huntsman. Go on now, Clissa."

"All right," she said into his shoulder. "But, Cory, hear him out first when he comes back. He might be unable to come back this time. Maybe he . . . he—"

"Ain't nothin' kin hurt my brother that a bullet will hit. He can take care of himself. He's got no excuse good enough this time. Go on, now. Make the kid eat."

Clissa went back to the house, her young face furrowed. If Cory quarreled with Alton now and drove him away, what with the drought and the creamery about to close and all, they just couldn't manage. Hiring a man was out of the question. Cory'd have to work himself to death, and he just wouldn't be able to make it. No one man could. She sighed and went into the house. It was seven o'clock, and the milking not done yet. Oh, why did Alton have to—

Babe was in bed at nine when Clissa heard Cory in the shed, slinging the wire cutters into a corner. "Alton back yet?" they both said at once as Cory stepped into the kitchen; and as she shook her head he clumped over to the stove, and lifting a lid, spat into the coals. "Come to bed," he said.

She lay down her stitching and looked at his broad back. He was twenty-eight, and he walked and acted like a man ten years older, and looked like a man five years younger. "I'll be up in a while," Clissa said.

Cory glanced at the corner behind the wood box where Alton's rifle usually stood, then made an unspellable, disgusted sound and sat down to take off his heavy muddy shoes.

"It's after nine," Clissa volunteered timidly. Cory said nothing, reaching for house slippers.

"Cory, you're not going to—"

"Not going to what?"

"Oh, nothing. I just thought that maybe Alton—"

"Alton!" Cory flared. "The dog goes hunting field mice. Alton goes hunting the dog. Now you want me to go hunting Alton. That's what you want?"

"I just— He was never this late before."

"I won't do it! Go out lookin' for him at nine o'clock in the night? I'll be damned! He has no call to use us so, Clissa."

Clissa said nothing. She went to the stove, peered into the wash boiler, set it aside at the back of the range. When she turned around, Cory had his shoes and coat on again.

"I knew you'd go," she said. Her voice smiled though she did not.

"I'll be back durned soon," said Cory. "I don't reckon he's strayed far. It is late. I ain't feared for him, but—" He broke his 12-gauge shotgun, looked through the barrels, slipped two shells in the breech and a box of them into his pocket. "Don't wait up," he said over his shoulder as he went out.

"I won't," Clissa replied to the closed door, and went back to her stitching by the lamp.

The path up the slope to the wood was very dark when Cory went up it, peering and calling. The air was chill and quiet, and a fetid odor of mold hung in it. Cory blew the taste of it out through impatient nostrils, drew it in again with the next breath, and swore. "Nonsense," he muttered. "Houn'-dog. Huntin', at ten in th' night, too. Alton!" he bellowed. "Alton Drew!" Echoes answered him, and he entered the wood. The huddled thing he passed in the dark heard him and felt the vibrations of his footsteps and did not move because it thought it was dead.

Cory strode on, looking around and ahead and not down since his feet knew the path.

"Alton!"

"That you, Cory?"

Cory Drew froze. That corner of the wood was thickly set and as dark as a burial vault. The voice he heard was choked, quiet, penetrating.

"Alton?"

"I found Kimbo, Cory."

"Where the hell have you been?" shouted Cory furiously. He disliked this pitch-blackness; he was afraid at the tense hopelessness of Alton's voice, and he mistrusted his ability to stay angry at his brother.

"I called him, Cory. I whistled at him, an' the ol' devil didn't answer."

"I can say the same for you, you . . . you louse. Why weren't you to milkin'? Where are you? You caught in a trap?"

"The houn' never missed answerin' me before, you know," said the tight, monotonous voice from the darkness.

"Alton! What the devil's the matter with you? What do I care if your mutt didn't answer? Where—"

"I guess because he ain't never died before," said Alton, refusing to be interrupted.

"You *what?*" Cory clicked his lips together twice and then said, "Alton, you turned crazy? What's that you say?"

"Kimbo's dead."

"Kim . . . oh! Oh!" Cory was seeing that picture again in his mind—Babe sprawled unconscious in the freshet, and Kimbo raging and snapping against a monster bear, holding her back until Alton could get there. ",What happened, Alton?" he asked more quietly.

"I aim to find out. Someone tore him up."

"Tore him up?"

"There ain't a bit of him left tacked together, Cory. Every damn joint in his body tore apart. Guts out of him."

"Good God! Bear, you reckon?"

"No bear, nor nothin' on four legs. He's all here. None of him's been et. Whoever done it just killed him an'—tore him up."

"Good God!" Cory said again. "Who could've—" There was a long silence, then. "Come 'long home," he said almost gently. "There's no call for you to set up by him all night."

Cory would fill him so full of holes he'd look like a tumbleweed. Alton was lazy, shiftless, selfish, and one or two other things of questionable taste but undoubted vividness. Babe knew her father. Uncle Alton would never be safe in this county.

She bounced out of bed in the enviable way of the very young, and ran to the window. Cory was trudging down to the night pasture with two bridles over his arm, to get the team. There were kitchen noises from downstairs.

Babe ducked her head in the washbowl and shook off the water like a terrier before she toweled. Trailing clean shirt and dungarees, she went to the head of the stairs, slid into the shirt, and began her morning ritual with the trousers. One step down was a step through the right leg. One more, and she was into the left. Then, bouncing step by step on both feet, buttoning one button per step, she reached the bottom fully dressed and ran into the kitchen.

"Didn't Uncle Alton come back a-tall, Mum?"

"Morning, Babe. No, dear." Clissa was too quiet, smiling too much, Babe thought shrewdly. Wasn't happy.

"Where'd he go, Mum?"

"We don't know, Babe. Sit down and eat your breakfast."

"What's a misbegotten, Mum?" the Babe asked suddenly. Her mother nearly dropped the dish she was drying. "Babe! You must never say that again!"

"Oh. Well, why is Uncle Alton, then?"

"Why is he what?"

Babe's mouth muscled around an outsize spoonful of oatmeal. "A misbe—"

"Babe!"

"All right, Mum," said Babe with her mouth full. 'Well, why?"

"I told Cory not to shout last night," Clissa said half to herself.

"Well, whatever it means, he isn't," said Babe with finality. "Did he go hunting again?"

"He went to look for Kimbo, darling."

"Kimbo? Oh Mummy, is Kimbo gone, too? Didn't he come back either?"

"No, dear. Oh, please, Babe, stop asking questions!"

"All right. Where do you think they went?"

"Into the north woods. Be quiet."

Babe gulped away at her breakfast. An idea struck her; and as she thought of it she ate slower and slower, and cast more and more glances at her mother from under the lashes of her tilted eyes. It would be awful if daddy did anything to Uncle Alton. Someone ought to warn him.

Babe was halfway to the woods when Alton's .32-40 sent echoes giggling up and down the valley.

Cory was in the south thirty, riding a cultivator and cussing at the team of grays when he heard the gun. "Hoa," he called to the horses, and sat a moment to listen to the sound. "One-two-three. Four," he counted. "Saw someone, blasted away at him. Had a chance to take aim and give another, careful. My God!" He threw up the cultivator points and steered the team into the shade of three oaks. He hobbled the gelding with swift tosses of a spare strap, and headed for the woods. "Alton a killer," he murmured, and doubled back to the house for his gun. Clissa was standing just outside the door.

"Get shells!" he snapped and flung into the house. Clissa followed him. He was strapping his hunting knife on before she could get a box off the shelf. "Cory—"

"Hear that gun, did you? Alton's off his nut. He don't waste lead. He shot at someone just then, and he wasn't fixin' to shoot pa'tridges when I saw him last. He was out to get a man. Gimme my gun."

"Cory, Babe—"

"You keep her here. Oh, God, this is a helluva mess! I can't stand much more." Cory ran out the door.

Clissa caught his arm. "Cory, I'm trying to tell you. Babe isn't here. I've called, and she isn't here."

Cory's heavy, young-old face tautened. "Babe— Where did you last see her?"

"Breakfast." Clissa was crying now.

"She say where she was going?"

"No. She asked a lot of questions about Alton and where he'd gone."

"Did you say?"

Clissa's eyes widened, and she nodded, biting the back of her hand.

"You shouldn't ha' done that, Clissa," he gritted, and ran toward the woods. Clissa looked after him, and in that moment she could have killed herself.

Cory ran with his head up, straining with his legs and lungs and eyes at the long path. He puffed up the slope to the woods, agonized for breath after the forty-five minutes' heavy going. He couldn't even notice the damp smell of mold in the air.

He caught a movement in a thicket to his right, and dropped. Struggling to keep his breath, he crept forward until he could see clearly. There was something in there, all right. Something black, keeping still. Cory relaxed his legs and torso completely to make it easier for his heart to pump some strength back into them, and slowly raised the 12-gauge until it bore on the thing hidden in the thicket.

"Come out!" Cory said when he could speak.

Nothing happened.

"Come out or by God I'll shoot!" rasped Cory.

There was a long moment of silence, and his finger tightened on the trigger.

"You asked for it," he said, and as he fired the thing leaped sideways into the open, screaming.

It was a thin little man dressed in sepulchral black, and bearing the rosiest little baby-face Cory had ever seen. The face was twisted with fright and pain. The little man scrambled to his feet and hopped up and down saying over and over, "Oh, my hand! Don't shoot again! Oh, my hand! Don't shoot again!" He stopped after a bit, when Cory had climbed to his feet, and he regarded the farmer out of sad, china-blue eyes. "You shot me," he said reproachfully, holding up a little bloody hand. "Oh, my goodness!"

Cory said, "Now, who the hell are you?"

The man immediately became hysterical, mouthing such a flood of broken sentences that Cory stepped back a pace and half-raised his gun in self-defense. It seemed to consist mostly of "I lost my papers," and "I didn't do it," and "It was horrible. Horrible. Horrible," and "The dead man," and "Oh, don't shoot again!"

Cory tried twice to ask him a question, and then he stepped over and knocked the man down. He lay on the ground writhing and moaning and blubbering and putting his bloody hand to his mouth where Cory had hit him.

The man rolled over and sat up. "I didn't do it!" he sobbed. "I didn't! I was walking along and I heard the gun and I heard some swearing and an awful scream and I went over there and peeped and I saw the dead man and I ran away and you came and I hid and you shot me and—"

"*Shut up!*" The man did, as if a switch had been thrown. "Now," said Cory, pointing along the path, "you say there's a dead man up there?"

The man nodded and began crying in earnest. Cory helped him up. "Follow this path back to my farmhouse," he said. "Tell my wife to fix up your hand. *Don't* tell her anything else. And wait there until I come. Hear?"

"Yes. Thank you. Oh, thank you. *Snff.*"

"Go on now." Cory gave him a gentle shove in the right direction and went alone, in cold fear, up the path to the spot where he had found Alton the night before.

He found him here now, too, and Kimbo. Kimbo and Alton had spent several years together in the deepest friendship; they had hunted and fought and slept together, and the lives they owed each other were finished now. They were dead together.

It was terrible that they died the same way. Cory Drew was a strong man, but he gasped and fainted dead away when he saw what the thing of the mold had done to his brother and his brother's dog.

The little man in black hurried down the path, whimpering and holding his injured hand as if he rather wished he could limp with it. After a while the whimper faded away, and the hurried stride changed to a walk as the gibbering terror of the last hour receded. He drew two deep breaths, said, "My goodness!" and felt almost normal. He bound a linen handkerchief around his wrist, but the hand kept bleeding. He tried the elbow, and that made it hurt. So he stuffed the handkerchief back in his pocket and simply waved the hand stupidly in the air until the blood clotted.

It wasn't much of a wound. Two of the balls of shot had struck him, one passing through the fleshy part of his thumb and the other scoring the side. As he thought of it, he became a little proud that he had borne a gunshot wound. He strolled along in the midmorning sunlight, feeling a dreamy communion with the boys at the front. "The whine of shot and shell—" Where had he read that? Ah, what a story this would make! "And there beside the"—what was the line?—"the embattled farmer stood." Didn't the awfulest things happen in the nicest places? This was a nice forest. No screeches and snakes and deep dark menaces. Not a story-book wood at all. Shot by a gun. How exciting! He was now—he strutted—a gentleman adventurer. He did not see the great moist horror that clumped along behind him, though his nostrils crinkled a little with its foulness.

The monster had three little holes close together on its chest, and one little hole in the middle of its slimy forehead. It had three close-set pits in its back and one on the back of its head. These marks were where Alton Drew's bullets had struck and passed through. Half of the monster's shapeless face was sloughed away, and there was a deep indentation on its shoulder. This was what Alton Drew's gun butt had done after he clubbed it and struck at the thing that would not lie down after he put his four bullets through it. When these things happened the monster was not hurt or angry. It only wondered why Alton Drew acted that way. Now it followed the little man without hurrying at all, matching his stride step by step and dropping little particles of muck behind it.

The little man went on out of the wood and stood with his back against a big tree at the forest's edge, and he thought. Enough had happened to him here. What good would it do to stay and face a horrible murder inquest, just to continue this silly, vague quest? There was supposed to be the ruin of an old, old hunting lodge deep in this wood somewhere, and perhaps it would hold the evidence he wanted. But it was a vague report—vague enough to be forgotten without regret. It would be the height of foolishness to stay for all the hick-town red tape that would follow that ghastly affair back in the wood. Ergo, it would be ridiculous to follow that farmer's advice, to go to his house and wait for him. He would go back to town.

The monster was leaning against the other side of the big tree.

The little man snuffled disgustedly at a sudden overpowering odor of rot. He reached for his handkerchief, fumbled and dropped it. As he bent to pick it up, the monster's arm *whuffed* heavily in the air where his head had been—a blow that would certainly have removed that baby-faced protuberance. The man stood up and would have put the handkerchief to his nose had it not been so bloody. The creature behind the tree lifted its arms again just as the little man tossed the handkerchief away and stepped out into the field, heading across country to the distant highway that would take him back to town. The monster pounced on the handkerchief, picked it up, studied it, tore it across several times and inspected the tattered edges. Then it gazed vacantly at the disappearing figure of the little man, and finding him no longer interesting, turned back into the woods.

Babe broke into a trot at the sound of the shots. It was important to warn Uncle Alton about what her father had said, but it was more interesting to find out what he had bagged. Oh, he'd bagged it, all right. Uncle Alton never fired without killing. This was about the first time she had ever heard him blast away like that. Must be a bear, she thought excitedly, tripping over a root, sprawling, rolling to her feet again, without noticing the tumble. She'd love to have another bearskin in her room. Where would she put it? Maybe they could line it and she could have it for a blanket. Uncle Alton could sit on it and read to her in the evening— Oh, no. No. Not with this trouble between him and dad. Oh, if she could only do something! She tried to run faster, worried and anticipating, but she was out of breath and went more slowly instead.

At the top of the rise by the edge of the woods she stopped and looked back. Far down in the valley lay the south thirty. She scanned it carefully, looking for her father. The new furrows and the old were sharply defined, and her keen eyes saw immediately that Cory had left the line with the cultivator and had angled the team over to the shade trees without finishing his row. That wasn't like him. She could see the team now, and Cory's pale-blue denim was not in sight.

A little nearer was the house; and as her gaze fell on it she moved out of the cleared pathway. Her father was coming; she had seen his shotgun and he was running. He could really cover ground when he wanted to. He must be chasing her, she thought immediately. He'd guessed that she would run toward the sound of the shots, and he was going to follow her tracks to Uncle Alton and shoot him. She knew that he was as good a woodsman as Alton; he would most certainly see her tracks. Well, she'd fix him.

She ran along the edge of the wood, being careful to dig her heels deeply into the loam. A hundred yards of this, and she angled into the forest and ran until she reached a particularly thick grove of trees. Shinnying up like a squirrel, she squirmed from one close-set tree to another until she could go no farther back toward the path, then dropped lightly to the ground and crept on her way, now stepping very gently. It would take him an hour to beat around for her trail, she thought proudly, and by that time she could easily get to Uncle Alton. She giggled to herself as she thought of the way she had fooled her father. And the little sound of laughter drowned out, for her, the sound of Alton's hoarse dying scream.

She reached and crossed the path and slid through the brush beside it. The shots came from up around here somewhere. She stopped and listened several times, and then suddenly heard something coming toward her, fast. She ducked under cover, terrified, and a little baby-faced man in black, his blue eyes wide with horror, crashed blindly past her, the leather case he carried catching on the branches. It spun a moment and then fell right in front of her. The man never missed it.

Babe lay there for a long moment and then picked up the case and faded into the woods. Things were happening too fast for her. She wanted Uncle Alton, but she dared not call. She stopped again and strained her ears. Back toward the edge of the wood she heard her father's voice, and another's—probably the man who had dropped the brief case. She dared not go over there. Filled with enjoyable terror, she thought hard, then snapped her fingers in triumph. She and Alton had played Injun many times up here; they had a whole repertoire of secret signals. She had practiced birdcalls until she knew them better than the birds themselves. What would it be? Ah—blue jay. She threw back her head and by some youthful alchemy produced a nerve-shattering screech that would have done justice to any jay that ever flew. She repeated it, and then twice more.

The response was immediate—the call of a blue jay, four times, spaced two and two. Babe nodded to herself happily. That was the signal that they were to meet immediately at The Place. The Place was a hide-out that he had discovered and shared with her, and not another soul knew of it; an angle of rock beside a stream not far away. It wasn't exactly a cave, but almost. Enough so to be entrancing. Babe trotted happily away toward the brook. She had just known that Uncle Alton would remember the call of the blue jay, and what it meant.

In the tree that arched over Alton's scattered body perched a large jay bird, preening itself and shining in the sun. Quite unconscious of the presence of death, hardly noticing the Babe's realistic cry, it screamed again four times, two and two.

It took Cory more than a moment to recover himself from what he had seen. He turned away from it and leaned weakly against a pine, panting. Alton. That was Alton lying there, in—parts.

"God! God, God, God—"

Gradually his strength returned, and he forced himself to turn again. Stepping carefully, he bent and picked up the .32-40. Its barrel was bright and clean, but the butt and stock were smeared with some kind of stinking rottenness. Where had he seen the stuff before? Somewhere—no matter. He cleaned it off absently, throwing the befouled bandanna away afterward. Through his mind ran Alton's words—was that only last night?—*"I'm goin' to start trackin'. An' I'm goin' to keep trackin' till I find the one done this job on Kimbo."*

Cory searched shrinkingly until he found Alton's box of shells. The box was wet and sticky. That made it—better, somehow. A bullet wet with Alton's blood was the right thing to use. He went away a short distance, circled around till he found heavy footprints, then came back.

"I'm a-trackin' for you, Bud," he whispered thickly, and began. Through the brush he followed its wavering spoor, amazed at the amount of filthy mold about, gradually associating it with the thing that had killed his brother. There was nothing in the world for him any more but hate and doggedness. Cursing himself for not getting Alton home last night, he followed the tracks to the edge of the woods. They led him to a big tree there, and there he saw something else—the footprints of the little city man. Nearby lay some tattered scraps of linen, and—what was that?

Another set of prints—small ones. Small, stub-toed ones. Babe's.

"Babe!" Cory screamed. "Babe!"

No answer. The wind sighed. Somewhere a blue jay called.

Babe stopped and turned when she heard her father's voice, faint with distance, piercing.

"Listen at him holler," she crooned delightedly. "Gee, he sounds mad." She sent a jay bird's call disrespectfully back to him and hurried to The Place.

It consisted of a mammoth boulder beside the brook. Some upheaval in the glacial age had cleft it, cutting out a huge V-shaped chunk. The widest part of the cleft was at the water's edge, and the narrowest was hidden by bushes. It made a little ceilingless room, rough and uneven and full of pot-holes and cavelets inside, and yet with quite a level floor. The open end was at the water's edge.

Babe parted the bushes and peered down the cleft.

"Uncle Alton!" she called softly. There was no answer. Oh, well, he'd be along. She scrambled in and slid down to the floor.

She loved it here. It was shaded and cool, and the chattering little stream filled it with shifting golden lights and laughing gurgles. She called again, on principle, and then perched on an outcropping to wait. It was only then she realized that she still carried the little man's brief case.

She turned it over a couple of times and then opened it. It was divided in the middle by a leather wall. On one side were a few papers in a large yellow envelope, and on the other some sandwiches, a candy bar, and an apple. With a youngster's complacent acceptance of manna from heaven, Babe fell to. She saved one sandwich for Alton, mainly because she didn't like its highly spiced bologna. The rest made quite a feast.

She was a little worried when Alton hadn't arrived, even after she had consumed the apple core. She got up and tried to skim some flat pebbles across the roiling brook, and she stood on her hands, and she tried to think of a story to tell herself, and she tried just waiting. Finally, in desperation, she turned again to the brief case, took out the papers, curled up by the rocky wall and began to read them. It was something to do, anyway.

There was an old newspaper clipping that told about strange

wills that people had left. An old lady had once left a lot of money to whoever would make the trip from the Earth to the Moon and back. Another had financed a home for cats whose masters and mistresses had died. A man left thousands of dollars to the first man who could solve a certain mathematical problem and prove his solution. But one item was blue-penciled. It was:

One of the strangest of wills still in force is that of Thaddeus M. Kirk, who died in 1920. It appears that he built an elaborate mausoleum with burial vaults for all the remains of his family. He collected and removed caskets from all over the country to fill the designated niches. Kirk was the last of his line; there were no relatives when he died. His will stated hat the mausoleum was to be kept in repair permanently, and that a certain sum was to be set aside as a reward for whoever could produce the body of his grandfather, Roger Kirk, whose niche is still empty. Anyone finding this body is eligible to receive a substantial fortune.

Babe yawned vaguely over this, but kept on reading because there was nothing else to do. Next was a thick sheet of business correspondence, bearing the letterhead of a firm of lawyers. The body of it ran:

In regard to your query regarding the will of Thaddeus Kirk, we are authorized to state that his grandfather was a man about five feet, five inches, whose left arm had been broken and who had a triangular silver plate set into his skull. There is no information as to the whereabouts of his death. He disappeared and was declared legally dead after the lapse of fourteen years.

The amount of the reward as stated in the will, plus accrued interest, now amounts to a fraction over sixty-two thousand dollars. This will be paid to anyone who produces the remains, providing that said remains answer descriptions kept in our private files.

There was more, but Babe was bored. She went on to the little black notebook. There was nothing in it but penciled and highly abbreviated records of visits to libraries; quotations from books with titles like *History of Angelina and Tyler Counties* and *Kirk Family History*. Babe threw that aside, too. Where could Uncle Alton be?

She began to sing tunelessly, "Tumalumalum tum, ta ta ta," pretending to dance a minuet with flowing skirts like a girl she had seen in the movies. A rustle of the bushes at the entrance to The Place stopped her. She peeped upward, saw them being thrust aside. Quickly she ran to a tiny cul-de-sac in the rock wall, just big enough for her to hide in. She giggled at the thought of how surprised Uncle Alton would be when she jumped out at him.

She heard the newcomer come shuffling down the steep slope of the crevice and land heavily on the floor. There was something about the sound—what was it? It occurred to her that though it was a hard job for a big man like Uncle Alton to get through the little opening in the bushes, she could hear no heavy breathing. She heard no breathing at all!

Babe peeped out into the main cave and squealed in utmost horror. Standing there was, not Uncle Alton, but a massive caricature of a man: a huge thing like an irregular mud doll, clumsily made. It quivered and parts of it glistened and parts of it were dried and crumby. Half of the lower left part of its face was gone, giving it a lopsided look. It had no perceptible mouth or nose, and its eyes were crooked, one higher than the other, both a dingy brown with no whites at all. It stood quite still looking at her, its only movement a steady unalive quivering of its body.

It wondered about the queer little noise Babe had made.

Babe crept far back against a little pocket of stone, her brain running round and round in tiny circles of agony. She opened her mouth to cry out, and could not. Her eyes bulged and her face flamed with the strangling effort, and the two golden ropes of her braided hair twitched and twitched as she hunted hopelessly for a way out. If only she were out in the open—or in the wedge-shaped half-cave where the thing was—or home in bed!

The thing clumped toward her, expressionless, moving with a slow inevitability that was the sheer crux of horror. Babe lay wide-eyed and frozen, mounting pressure of terror stilling her lungs, making her heart shake the whole world. The monster came to the mouth of the little pocket, tried to walk to her and was stopped by the sides. It was such a narrow little fissure; and it was all Babe could do to get in. The thing from the wood stood straining against the rock at its shoulders, pressing harder and harder to get to Babe. She sat up slowly, so near to the thing that its odor was almost thick enough to see, and a wild hope burst through her voiceless fear. It couldn't get in! It couldn't get in because it was too big!

The substance of its feet spread slowly under the tremendous strain, and at its shoulder appeared a slight crack. It widened as the monster unfeelingly crushed itself against the rock, and suddenly a large piece of the shoulder came away and the being twisted slushily three feet farther in. It lay quietly with its muddy eyes fixed on her, and then brought one thick arm up over its head and reached.

Babe scrambled in the inch farther she had believed impossible, and the filthy clubbed hand stroked down her back, leaving a trail of muck on the blue denim of the shirt she wore. The monster surged suddenly and, lying full length now, gained the last precious inch. A black hand seized one of her braids, and for Babe the lights went out.

When she came to, she was dangling by her hair from that same crusted paw. The thing held her high, so that her face and its featureless head were not more than a foot apart. It gazed at her with a mild curiosity in its eyes, and it swung her slowly back and forth. The agony of her pulled hair did what fear could not do—gave her a voice. She screamed. She opened her mouth and puffed up her powerful young lungs, and she sounded off. She held her throat in the position of the first scream, and her chest labored and pumped more air through the frozen throat. Shrill and monotonous and infinitely piercing, her screams.

The thing did not mind. It held her as she was, and watched.

When it had learned all it could from this phenomenon, it dropped her jarringly, and looked around the half-cave, ignoring the stunned and huddled Babe. It reached over and picked up the leather brief case and tore it twice across as if it were tissue. It saw the sandwich Babe had left, picked it up, crushed it, dropped it.

Babe opened her eyes, saw that she was free, and just as the thing turned back to her she dove between its legs and out into the shallow pool in front of the rock, paddled across and hit the other bank screaming. A vicious little light of fury burned in her; she picked up a grapefruit-sized stone and hurled it with all her frenzied might. It flew low and fast, and struck squashily on the monster's ankle. The thing was just taking a step toward the water; the stone caught it off balance, and its unpracticed equilibrium could not save it. It tottered for a long, silent moment at the edge and then splashed into the stream. Without a second look Babe ran shrieking away.

Cory Drew was following the little gobs of mold that somehow indicated the path of the murderer, and he was nearby when he first heard her scream. He broke into a run, dropping his shotgun and holding the .32-40 ready to fire. He ran with such deadly panic in his heart that he ran right past the huge cleft rock and was a hundred yards past it before she burst out through the pool and ran up the bank. He had to run hard and fast to catch her, because anything behind her was that faceless horror in the cave, and she was living for the one idea of getting away from there. He caught her in his arms and swung her to him, and she screamed on and on and on.

Babe didn't see Cory at all, even when he held her and quieted her.

The monster lay in the water. It neither liked nor disliked the new element. It rested on the bottom, its massive head a foot beneath the surface, and it curiously considered the facts that it had garnered. There was the little humming noise of Babe's voice that sent the monster questing into the cave. There was the black material of the brief case that resisted so much more than green things when he tore it. There was the little two-legged one who sang and brought him near, and who screamed when he came. There was this new cold moving thing he had fallen into. It was washing his body away. That had never happened before. That was interesting. The monster decided to stay and observe this new thing. It felt no urge to save itself; it could only be curious.

The brook came laughing down out of its spring, ran down from its source beckoning to the sunbeams and embracing freshets and helpful brooklets. It shouted and played with streaming little roots, and nudged the minnows and pollywogs about in its tiny backwaters. It was a happy brook. When it came to the pool by the cloven rock it found the monster there, and plucked at it. It soaked the foul substances and smoothed and melted the molds, and the waters below the thing eddied darkly with its diluted matter. It was a thorough brook. It washed all it touched, persistently. Where it found filth, it removed filth; and if there were layer on layer of foulness, then layer by foul layer it was removed. It was a good brook. It did not mind the poison of the monster, but took it up and thinned it and spread it in little rings around rocks downstream, and let it drift to the rootlets of water plants, that they might grow greener and lovelier. And the monster melted.

"I am smaller," the thing thought. "That is interesting. I could not move now. And now this part of me which thinks is going, too. It will stop in just a moment, and drift away with the rest of the body. It will stop thinking and I will stop being, and that, too, is a very interesting thing."

So the monster melted and dirtied the water, and the water was clean again, washing and washing the skeleton that the monster had left. It was not very big, and there was a badly healed knot on the left arm. The sunlight flickered on the triangular silver plate set into the pale skull, and the skeleton was very clean now. The brook laughed about it for an age.

They found the skeleton, six grim-lipped men who came to find a killer. No one had believed Babe, when she told her story days later. It had to be days later because Babe had screamed for seven hours without stopping, and had lain like a dead child for a day. No one believed her at all, because her story was all about the bad fella, and they knew that the bad fella was simply a thing that her father had made up to frighten her with. But it was through her that the skeleton was found, and so the men at the bank sent a check to the Drews for more money than they had ever dreamed about. It was old Roger Kirk, sure enough, that skeleton, though it was found five miles from where he had died and sank into the forest floor where the hot molds builded around his skeleton and emerged—a monster.

So the Drews had a new barn and fine new livestock and they hired four men. But they didn't have Alton. And they didn't have Kimbo. And Babe screams at night and has grown very thin.

It is not giving anything away very far in advance to say the dancing partner of this story is what would now be called a robot, though the word had not been invented at the time the story was written.

The word robot, from a Czech root meaning to work, was coined by the playwright Carel Capek for his play R.U.R., which was a smash hit in several countries when it was first produced in 1922, and closed in four nights when it was revived in New York in 1942. Robots were an exciting novelty in 1922; by 1942, they were a commonplace of the imagination. R.U.R. stands for Rossum's Universal Robots. Rossum was an inventor who created a form of synthetic protoplasm and used it to make artificial workers.

Later writers on science fiction have tried to make a distinction between a robot and an android, the robot being a purely mechanical man, like Tik-Tok of Oz, deriving its power, like any machine, from an outside source, and the android being an artificial man like Frankenstein's monster, made out of organic material and capable of living and thinking independently.

Ironically, by this definition the original robots would be androids. But the distinction is of little value; in some of the later robot stories (those by Ray Bradbury, for instance) robots are indistinguishable from men—until the synthetic flesh is cut through to reveal the wheels and springs. A type halfway between the robot and the android is the golem of mediaeval Jewish legend, a figure made of clay and animated by Kabbalistic magic.

All three types are liable to get out of hand. The original robots of R.U.R. were submissive and obedient, manufactured with no qualities except those desirable in a worker. But the makers constantly improved them, making them stronger and more intelligent so as to be able to do harder and more complex tasks. At the beginning of the play they have just been given a sense of pain, because without that they have no motive to avoid injuries which send them to the scrap-heap sooner than would be caused by normal wear and tear. Inevitably, the robots revolt and massacre the human race. The play's next to last scene shows

*the last half-dozen humans left alive, barricaded in a room sur-
rounded by robots. I can still remember from the original pro-
duction the cold chill when one of the characters looks out at
the besieging robots and says, "We shouldn't have made their
faces all alike." The last scene, if you are curious, shows that the
robots have developed into beings that are essentially human; it
is to be hoped that they will do better with their humanity than
we have.*

*The golem, too, revolted. The best-known legends of the
golem center about the great Rabbi Loew of Prague, a historic
figure who lived during one of the periods of Jewish persecution.
He is said to have made a golem, to detect the informers of the
Inquisition and to defend the Jews. The rabbi warned his wife
not to use the golem for common tasks, but once in his absence
she set it to fetch water, and, just like the demon raised by the
Sorcerer's apprentice, it continued to fetch water until the house
was flooded. That time the rabbi came home in time to bring
the golem under control and all ended happily; but I well remember a Continental moving picture of the early nineteen
twenties called* The Golem, *in which a gigantic clay figure
(whether Rabbi Loew's or another I do not know) ran amuck,
trampling people underfoot; until a little girl, too innocent to
be fearful, climbed up to the golem's shoulders and pulled from
its mouth the slip of parchment with the unspeakable name of
God which gave it its life. And we all remember what happened
to Frankenstein.*

*All these stories are evidence of a deep, centuries-old fear in
the human race that we may release a force which we cannot
control. And we are now proving how well justified these fears
are. Our generation has let the jinn out of the bottle; it remains
to be seen what we can do with it.*

THE DANCING PARTNER
Jerome K. Jerome

"THIS STORY," COMMENCED MACSHAUGNASSY, "COMES FROM FURT-wangen, a small town in the Black Forest. There lived there a very wonderful old fellow named Nicholas Geibel. His business was the making of mechanical toys, at which work he had acquired an almost European reputation. He made rabbits that would emerge from the heart of a cabbage, flop their ears, smooth their whiskers, and disappear again; cats that would wash their faces, and mew so naturally that dogs would mistake them for real cats, and fly at them; dolls, with phonographs concealed within them, that would raise their hats and say, 'Good morning; how do you do?' and some that would even sing a song.

"But he was something more than a mere mechanic; he was an artist. His work was with him a hobby, almost a passion. His shop was filled with all manner of strange things that never would, or could, be sold—things he had made for the pure love of making them. He had contrived a mechanical donkey that would trot for two hours by means of stored electricity, and trot, too, much faster than the live article, and with less need for exertion on the part of the driver; a bird that would shoot up into the air, fly round and round in a circle, and drop to earth at the exact spot from where it started; a skeleton that, supported by an upright iron bar, would dance a hornpipe; a life-sized lady doll that could play the fiddle; and a gentleman with a hollow inside who could smoke a pipe and drink more lager beer than any three average German students put together, which is saying much.

"Indeed, it was the belief of the town that old Geibel could make a man capable of doing everything that a respectable man need want to do. One day he made a man who did too much, and it came about in this way:

"Young Doctor Follen had a baby, and the baby had a birthday. Its first birthday put Doctor Follen's household into somewhat of a flurry, but on the occasion of its second birthday, Mrs.

Doctor Follen gave a ball in honor of the event. Old Geibel and his daughter Olga were among the guests.

"During the afternoon of the next day some three or four of Olga's bosom friends, who had also been present at the ball, dropped in to have a chat about it. They naturally fell to discussing the men, and to criticizing their dancing. Old Geibel was in the room, but he appeared to be absorbed in his newspaper, and the girls took no notice of him.

" 'There seem to be fewer men who can dance at every ball you go to,' said one of the girls.

" 'Yes, and don't the ones who can give themselves airs,' said another; 'they make quite a favor of asking you.'

" 'And how stupidly they talk,' added a third. 'They always say exactly the same things: "How charming you are looking to-night." "Do you often go to Vienna? Oh, you should, it's delight-ful." "What a charming dress you have on." "What a warm day it has been." "Do you like Wagner?" I do wish they'd think of something new.'

" 'Oh, I never mind how they talk,' said a fourth. 'If a man dances well he may be a fool for all I care.'

" 'He generally is,' slipped in a thin girl, rather spitefully.

" 'I go to a ball to dance,' continued the previous speaker, not noticing the interruption. 'All I ask of a partner is that he shall hold me firmly, take me round steadily, and not get tired before I do.'

" 'A clockwork figure would be the thing for you,' said the girl who had interrupted.

" 'Bravo!' cried one of the others, clapping her hands, 'what a capital idea!'

" 'What's a capital idea?' they asked.

" 'Why, a clockwork dancer, or, better still, one that would go by electricity and never run down.'

"The girls took up the idea with enthusiasm.

" 'Oh, what a lovely partner he would make,' said one; 'he would never kick you, or tread on your toes.'

" 'Or tear your dress,' said another.

" 'Or get out of step.'

" 'Or get giddy and lean on you.'

" 'And he would never want to mop his face with his handkerchief. I do hate to see a man do that after every dance.'

" 'And wouldn't want to spend the whole evening in the supper room.'

" 'Why, with a phonograph inside him to grind out all the stock remarks, you would not be able to tell him from a real man,' said the girl who had first suggested the idea.

" 'Oh, yes, you would,' said the thin girl, 'he would be so much nicer.'

"Old Geibel had laid down his paper, and was listening with both his ears. On one of the girls glancing in his direction, however, he hurriedly hid himself again behind it.

"After the girls were gone, he went into his workshop, where Olga heard him walking up and down, and every now and then chuckling to himself; and that night he talked to her a good deal about dancing and dancing men—asked what they usually said and did—what dances were most popular—what steps were gone through, with many other questions bearing on the subject.

"Then for a couple of weeks he kept much to his factory, and was very thoughtful and busy, though prone at unexpected moments to break into a quiet low laugh, as if enjoying a joke that nobody else knew of.

"A month later another ball took place in Furtwangen. On this occasion it was given by old Wenzel, the wealthy timber merchant, to celebrate his niece's betrothal, and Geibel and his daughter were again among the invited.

"When the hour arrived to set out, Olga sought her father. Not finding him in the house, she tapped at the door of his workshop. He appeared in his shirt sleeves, looking hot but radiant.

" 'Don't wait for me,' he said, 'you go on, I'll follow you. I've got something to finish.'

"As she turned to obey he called after her, 'Tell them I'm going to bring a young man with me—such a nice young man, and an excellent dancer. All the girls will like him.' Then he laughed and closed the door.

"Her father generally kept his doings secret from everybody, but she had a pretty shrewd suspicion of what he had been planning, and so, to a certain extent, was able to prepare the guests for what was coming. Anticipation ran high, and the arrival of the famous mechanist was eagerly awaited.

"At length the sound of wheels was heard outside, followed by a great commotion in the passage, and old Wenzel himself, his jolly red face red with excitement and suppressed laughter, burst into the room and announced in stentorian tones:

" 'Herr Geibel—and a friend.'

"Herr Geibel and his 'friend' entered, greeted with shouts of laughter and applause, and advanced to the center of the room.

" 'Allow me, ladies and gentlemen,' said Herr Geibel, 'to introduce you to my friend, Lieutenant Fritz. Fritz, my dear fellow, bow to the ladies and gentlemen.'

"Geibel placed his hand encouragingly on Fritz's shoulder, and the lieutenant bowed low, accompanying the action with a harsh clicking noise in his throat, unpleasantly suggestive of a death rattle. But that was only a detail.

" 'He walks a little stiffly' (old Geibel took his arm and walked him forward a few steps. He certainly did walk stiffly.) 'but then, walking is not his forte. He is essentially a dancing man. I have only been able to teach him the waltz as yet, but at that he is faultless. Come, which of you ladies may I introduce him to as a partner? He keeps perfect time; he never gets tired; he won't kick you or tread on your dress; he will hold you as firmly as you like, and go as quickly or as slowly as you please; he never gets giddy; and he is full of conversation. Come, speak up for yourself, my boy.'

"The old gentleman twisted one of the buttons at the back of his coat, and immediately Fritz opened his mouth, and in thin tones that appeared to proceed from the back of his head, remarked suddenly, 'May I have the pleasure?' and then shut his mouth again with a snap.

"That Lieutenant Fritz had made a strong impression on the company was undoubted, yet none of the girls seemed inclined to dance with him. They looked askance at his waxen face, with his staring eyes and fixed smile, and shuddered. At last old Geibel came to the girl who had conceived the idea.

"'It is your own suggestion, carried out to the letter,' said Geibel, 'an electric dancer. You owe it to the gentleman to give him a trial.'

"She was a bright, saucy little girl, fond of a frolic. Her host added his entreaties, and she consented.

"Herr Geibel fixed the figure to her. Its right arm was screwed round her waist, and held her firmly; its delicately jointed left hand was made to fasten itself upon her right. The old toymaker showed her how to regulate its speed, and how to stop it and release herself.

"'It will take you round in a complete circle,' he explained; 'be careful that no one knocks against you, and alters its course.'

"The music struck up. Old Geibel put the current in motion, and Annette and her strange partner began to dance.

"For a while everyone stood watching them. The figure performed its purpose admirably. Keeping perfect time and step, and holding its little partner tight clasped in an unyielding embrace, it revolved steadily, pouring forth at the same time a constant flow of squeaky conversation, broken by brief intervals of grinding silence.

"'How charming you are looking tonight,' it remarked in its thin, faraway voice. 'What a lovely day it has been. Do you like dancing? How well our steps agree. You will give me another, won't you? Oh, don't be so cruel. What a charming gown you have on. Isn't waltzing delightful? I could go on dancing forever—with you. Have you had supper?'

"As she grew more familiar with the uncanny creature, the girl's nervousness wore off, and she entered into the fun of the thing.

"'Oh, he's just lovely,' she cried, laughing. 'I could go on dancing with him all my life.'

"Couple after couple now joined them, and soon all the danc-
ers in the room were whirling round behind them. Nicholas
Geibel stood looking on, beaming with childish delight at his
success.

"Old Wenzel approached him, and whispered something in
his ear. Geibel laughed and nodded, and the two worked their
way quietly toward the door.

" 'This is the young people's house tonight,' said Wenzel, so
soon as they were outside; 'you and I will have a quiet pipe and
a glass of hock, over in the counting house.'

"Meanwhile the dancing grew more fast and furious. Little
Annette loosened the screw regulating her partner's rate of
progress, and the figure flew round with her swifter and swifter.
Couple after couple dropped out exhausted, but they only went
the faster, till at length they remained dancing alone.

"Madder and madder became the waltz. The music lagged
behind: the musicians, unable to keep the pace, ceased, and sat
staring. The younger guests applauded, but the older faces
began to grow anxious.

" 'Hadn't you better stop, dear,' said one of the women,
'you'll make yourself so tired.'

"But Annette did not answer.

" 'I believe she's fainted,' cried out a girl who had caught
sight of her face as it was swept by.

"One of the men sprang forward and clutched at the figure,
but its impetus threw him down onto the floor, where its steel-
cased feet laid bare his cheek. The thing evidently did not in-
tend to part with its prize easily.

"Had anyone retained a cool head, the figure, one cannot
help thinking, might easily have been stopped. Two or three
men acting in concert might have lifted it bodily off the floor,
or have jammed it into a corner. But few human heads are
capable of remaining cool under excitement. Those who are
not present think how stupid must have been those who were;
those who are reflect afterward how simple it would have been

to do this, that, or the other, if only they had thought of it at the time.

"The women grew hysterical. The men shouted contradictory directions to one another. Two of them made a bungling rush at the figure, which had the result of forcing it out of its orbit in the center of the room, and sending it crashing against the walls and furniture. A stream of blood showed itself down the girl's white frock, and followed her along the floor. The affair was becoming horrible. The women rushed screaming from the room. The men followed them.

"One sensible suggestion was made: 'Find Geibel—fetch Geibel.'

"No one had noticed him leave the room, no one knew where he was. A party went in search of him. The others, too unnerved to go back into the ballroom, crowded outside the door and listened. They could hear the steady whir of the wheels upon the polished floor as the thing spun round and round; the dull thud as every now and again it dashed itself and its burden against some opposing object and richocheted off in a new direction

"And everlastlingly it talked in that thin ghostly voice, repeating over and over the same formula: 'How charming you are looking tonight. What a lovely day it has been. Oh, don't be so cruel. I could go on dancing forever—with you. Have you had supper?'

"Of course they sought for Geibel everywhere but where he was. They looked in every room in the house, then rushed off in a body to his own place, and spent precious minutes in waking up his deaf old housekeeper. At last it occurred to one of the party that Wenzel was missing also, and then the idea of the counting house across the yard presented itself to them, and there they found him.

"He rose up, very pale, and followed them; and he and old Wenzel forced their way through the crowd of guests gathered outside, and entered the room and locked the door behind them.

"From within there came the muffled sound of low voices and quick steps, followed by a confused scuffling noise, then silence, then the low voices again.

"After a time the door opened, and those near it pressed forward to enter, but old Wenzel's broad shoulders barred the way.

" 'I want you—and you, Bekler,' he said, addressing a couple of the elder men. His voice was calm, but his face was deadly white. 'The rest of you, please go—get the women away as quickly as you can.'

"From that day old Nicholas Geibel confined himself to the making of mechanical rabbits, and cats that mewed and washed their faces."

"The Damned Thing," first published in 1893, is one of the most famous of early science fiction stories. Ambrose Bierce, the author, was born in 1842; he served with distinction in the Civil War, the background for many of his stories, and later turned to writing and journalism. He mainly wrote short stories and books of epigrammatic reflections; his reflections are as remarkable for their bitterness, as his stories are for their horror. In 1913, he went to Mexico, then in a state of disturbance because of the insurrectionary activities of Pancho Villa. That is the last that was ever heard of him.

Regarded as science fiction, "The Damned Thing" has one fallacy. Can you spot it?

THE DAMNED THING

Ambrose Bierce

I

One Does Not Always Eat What Is on the Table

BY THE LIGHT OF A TALLOW CANDLE WHICH HAD BEEN PLACED ON one end of a rough table a man was reading something written in a book. It was an old account book, greatly worn; and the writing was not, apparently, very legible, for the man sometimes held the page close to the flame of the candle to get a stronger light on it. The shadow of the book would then throw into obscurity a half of the room, darkening a number of faces and figures; for besides the reader, eight other men were present. Seven of them sat against the rough log walls, silent, motionless, and the room being small, not very far from the table. By extending an arm any one of them could have touched the eighth man, who lay on the table, face upward, partly covered by a sheet, his arms at his sides. He was dead.

The man with the book was not reading aloud, and no one spoke; all seemed to be waiting for something to occur; the dead man only was without expectation. From the blank darkness outside came in, through the aperture that served for a window, all the ever unfamiliar noises of night in the wilderness—the long nameless note of a distant coyote; the stilly pulsing thrill of tireless insects in trees; strange cries of night birds, so different from those of the birds of day; the drone of great blundering beetles, and all that mysterious chorus of small sounds that seem always to have been but half heard when they have suddenly ceased, as if conscious of an indiscretion. But nothing of all this was noted in that company; its members were not overmuch addicted to idle interest in matters of no practical importance; that was obvious in every line of their rugged faces—obvious even in the dim light of the single candle. They were evidently men of the vicinity—farmers and woodsmen.

The person reading was a trifle different; one would have said of him that he was of the world, worldly, albeit there was that in his attire which attested a certain fellowship with the organisms of his environment. His coat would hardly have passed muster in San Francisco; his foot-gear was not of urban origin, and the hat that lay by him on the floor (he was the only one uncovered) was such that if one had considered it as an article of mere personal adornment he would have missed its meaning. In countenance the man was rather prepossessing, with just a hint of sternness; though that he may have assumed or cultivated, as appropriate to one in authority. For he was a coroner. It was by virtue of his office that he had possession of the book in which he was reading; it had been found among the dead man's effects —in his cabin, where the inquest was now taking place.

When the coroner had finished reading he put the book into his breast pocket. At that moment the door was pushed open and a young man entered. He, clearly, was not of mountain birth and breeding: he was clad as those who dwell in cities. His clothing was dusty, however, as from travel. He had, in fact, been riding hard to attend the inquest.

The coroner nodded; no one else greeted him.

"We have waited for you," said the coroner. "It is necessary to have done with this business to-night."

The young man smiled. "I am sorry to have kept you," he said. "I went away, not to evade your summons, but to post to my newspaper an account of what I suppose I am called back to relate."

The coroner smiled.

"The account that you posted to your newspaper," he said, "differs, probably, from that which you will give here under oath."

"That," replied the other, rather hotly and with a visible flush, "is as you please. I use manifold paper and have a copy of what I sent. It was not written as news, for it is incredible, but as fiction. It may go as a part of my testimony under oath."

"But you say it is incredible."

"That is nothing to you, sir, if I also swear that it is true."

The coroner was silent for a time, his eyes upon the floor. The men about the sides of the cabin talked in whispers, but seldom withdrew their gaze from the face of the corpse. Presently the coroner lifted his eyes and said: "We will resume the inquest."

The men removed their hats. The witness was sworn.

"What is your name?" the coroner asked.

"William Harker."

"Age?"

"Twenty-seven."

"You knew the deceased, Hugh Morgan?"

"Yes."

"You were with him when he died?"

"Near him."

"How did that happen—your presence, I mean?"

"I was visiting him at this place to shoot and fish. A part of my purpose, however, was to study him and his odd, solitary way of life. He seemed a good model for a character in fiction. I sometimes write stories."

"I sometimes read them."

"Thank you."

"Stories in general—not yours."

Some of the jurors laughed. Against a sombre background

humor shows high lights. Soldiers in the intervals of battle laugh easily, and a jest in the death chamber conquers by surprise.

"Relate the circumstances of this man's death," said the coroner. "You may use any notes or memoranda that you please."

The witness understood. Pulling a manuscript from his breast pocket he held it near the candle and, turning the leaves until he found the passage that he wanted, began to read.

II

What May Happen in a Field of Wild Oats

". . . The sun had hardly risen when we left the house. We were looking for quail, each with a shotgun, but we had only one dog. Morgan said that our best ground was beyond a certain ridge that he pointed out, and we crossed it by a trail through the *chaparral.* On the other side was comparatively level ground, thickly covered with wild oats. As we emerged from the *chaparral* Morgan was but a few yards in advance. Suddenly we heard, at a little distance to our right and partly in front, a noise as of some animal thrashing about in the bushes, which we could see were violently agitated.

" 'We've started a deer,' I said. 'I wish we had brought a rifle.'

"Morgan, who had stopped and was intently watching the agitated *chaparral,* said nothing, but had cocked both barrels of his gun and was holding it in readiness to aim. I thought him a trifle excited, which surprised me, for he had a reputation for exceptional coolness, even in moments of sudden and imminent peril.

" 'O, come,' I said. 'You are not going to fill up a deer with quail-shot, are you?'

"Still he did not reply; but catching a sight of his face as he turned it slightly toward me I was struck by the intensity of his look. Then I understood that we had serious business in hand and my first conjecture was that we had 'jumped' a grizzly. I advanced to Morgan's side, cocking my piece as I moved.

"The bushes were now quiet and the sounds had ceased, but Morgan was as attentive to the place as before.

" 'What is it? What the devil is it?' I asked.

" 'That Damned Thing!' he replied, without turning his head. His voice was husky and unnatural. He trembled visibly.

"I was about to speak further, when I observed the wild oats near the place of the disturbance moving in the most inexplicable way. I can hardly describe it. It seemed as if stirred by a streak of wind, which not only bent it, but pressed it down— crushed it so that it did not rise; and this movement was slowly prolonging itself directly toward us.

"Nothing that I had ever seen had affected me so strangely as this unfamiliar and unaccountable phenomenon, yet I am unable to recall any sense of fear. I remember—and tell it here because, singularly enough, I recollected it then—that once in looking carelessly out of an open window I momentarily mistook a small tree close at hand for one of a group of larger trees at a little distance away. It looked the same size of the others, but being more distinctly and sharply defined in mass and detail seemed out of harmony with them. It was a mere falsification of the law of aërial perspective, but it startled, almost terrified me. We so rely upon the orderly operation of familiar natural laws that any seeming suspension of them is noted as a menace to our safety, a warning of unthinkable calamity. So now the apparently causeless movement of the herbage and the slow, undeviating approach of the line of disturbance were distinctly disquieting. My companion appeared actually frightened, and I could hardly credit my senses when I saw him suddenly throw his gun to his shoulder and fire both barrels at the agitated grain! Before the smoke of the discharge had cleared away I heard a loud savage cry—a scream like that of a wild animal—and flinging his gun upon the ground Morgan sprang away and ran swiftly from the spot. At the same instant I was thrown violently to the ground by the impact of something unseen in the smoke—some soft, heavy substance that seemed thrown against me with great force.

"Before I could get upon my feet and recover my gun, which seemed to have been struck from my hands, I heard Morgan crying out as if in mortal agony, and mingling with his cries were such hoarse, savage sounds as one hears from fighting dogs. Inexpressibly terrified, I struggled to my feet and looked in the direction of Morgan's retreat; and may Heaven in mercy spare me from another sight like that! At a distance of less than thirty yards was my friend, down upon one knee, his head thrown back at a frightful angle, hatless, his long hair in disorder and his whole body in violent movement from side to side, backward and forward. His right arm was lifted and seemed to lack the hand—at least, I could see none. The other arm was invisible. At times, as my memory now reports this extraordinary scene, I could discern but a part of his body; it was as if he had been partly blotted out—I cannot otherwise express it—then a shifting of his position would bring it all into view again.

"All this must have occurred within a few seconds, yet in that time Morgan assumed all the postures of a determined wrestler vanquished by superior weight and strength. I saw nothing but him, and him not always distinctly. During the entire incident his shouts and curses were heard, as if through an enveloping uproar of such sounds of rage and fury as I had never heard from the throat of man or brute!

"For a moment only I stood irresolute, then throwing down my gun I ran forward to my friend's assistance. I had a vague belief that he was suffering from a fit, or some form of convulsion. Before I could reach his side he was down and quiet. All sounds had ceased, but with a feeling of such terror as even these awful events had not inspired I now saw again the mysterious movement of the wild oats, prolonging itself from the trampled area about the prostrate man toward the edge of a wood. It was only when it had reached the wood that I was able to withdraw my eyes and look at my companion. He was dead."

III
A Man Though Naked May Be in Rags

The coroner rose from his seat and stood beside the dead man. Lifting an edge of the sheet he pulled it away, exposing the entire body, altogether naked and showing in the candle-light a claylike yellow. It had, however, broad maculations of bluish black, obviously caused by extravasated blood from contusions. The chest and sides looked as if they had been beaten with a bludgeon. There were dreadful lacerations; the skin was torn in strips and shreds.

The coroner moved round to the end of the table and undid a silk handkerchief which had been passed under the chin and knotted on the top of the head. When the handkerchief was drawn away it exposed what had been the throat. Some of the jurors who had risen to get a better view repented their curiosity and turned away their faces. Witness Harker went to the open window and leaned out across the sill, faint and sick. Dropping the handkerchief upon the dead man's neck the coroner stepped to an angle of the room and from a pile of clothing produced one garment after another, each of which he held up a moment for inspection. All were torn, and stiff with blood. The jurors did not make a closer inspection. They seemed rather uninterested. They had, in truth, seen all this before; the only thing that was new to them being Harker's testimony.

"Gentlemen," the coroner said, "we have no more evidence, I think. Your duty has been already explained to you; if there is nothing you wish to ask you may go outside and consider your verdict."

The foreman rose—a tall, bearded man of sixty, coarsely clad.

"I should like to ask one question, Mr. Coroner," he said. "What asylum did this last witness escape from?"

"Mr. Harker," said the coroner, gravely and tranquilly, "from what asylum did you last escape?"

Harker flushed crimson again, but said nothing, and the seven jurors rose and solemnly filed out of the cabin.

"If you have done insulting me, sir," said Harker, as soon as he and the officer were left alone with the dead man, "I suppose I am at liberty to go?"

"Yes."

Harker started to leave, but paused, with his hand on the door latch. The habit of his profession was strong in him—stronger than his sense of personal dignity. He turned about and said:

"The book that you have there—I recognize it as Morgan's diary. You seemed greatly interested in it; you read in it while I was testifying. May I see it? The public would like—"

"The book will cut no figure in this matter," replied the official, slipping it into his coat pocket; "all the entries in it were made before the writer's death."

As Harker passed out of the house the jury reentered and stood about the table, on which the now covered corpse showed under the sheet with sharp definition. The foreman seated himself near the candle, produced from his breast pocket a pencil and scrap of paper and wrote rather laboriously the following verdict, which with various degrees of effort all signed:

"We, the jury, do find that the remains come to their death at the hands of a mountain lion, but some of us thinks, all the same, they had fits."

IV

An Explanation from the Tomb

In the diary of the late Hugh Morgan are certain interesting entries having, possibly, a scientific value as suggestions. At the inquest upon his body the book was not put in evidence; possibly the coroner thought it not worthwhile to confuse the jury. The date of the first of the entries mentioned cannot be ascertained; the upper part of the leaf is torn away; the part of the entry remaining follows:

". . . would run in a half-circle, keeping his head turned always toward the centre, and again he would stand still, barking furiously. At last he ran away into the brush as fast as he could go.

I thought at first that he had gone mad, but on returning to the house found no other alternation in his manner than what was obviously due to fear of punishment.

"Can a dog see with his nose? Do odors impress some cerebral centre with images of the thing that emitted them? . . .

"Sept. 2.—Looking at the stars last night as they rose above the crest of the ridge east of the house, I observed them successively disappear—from left to right. Each was eclipsed but an instant, and only a few at the same time, but along the entire length of the ridge all that were within a degree or two of the crest were blotted out. It was as if something had passed along between me and them; but I could not see it, and the stars were not thick enough to define its outline. Ugh! I don't like this." . . .

Several weeks' entries are missing, three leaves being torn from the book.

"Sept. 27.—It has been about here again—I find evidences of its presence every day. I watched again all last night in the same cover, gun in hand, double-charged with buckshot. In the morning the fresh footprints were there, as before. Yet I would have sworn that I did not sleep—indeed, I hardly sleep at all. It is terrible, insupportable! If these amazing experiences are real I shall go mad; if they are fanciful I am mad already.

"Oct. 3.—I shall not go—it shall not drive me away. No, this is *my* house, *my* land. God hates a coward. . . .

"Oct. 5.—I can stand it no longer; I have invited Harker to pass a few weeks with me—he has a level head. I can judge from his manner if he thinks me mad.

"Oct. 7.—I have the solution of the mystery; it came to me last night—suddenly, as by revelation. How simple—how terribly simple!

"There are sounds that we cannot hear. At either end of the scale are notes that stir no chord of that imperfect instrument, the human ear. They are too high or too grave. I have observed a flock of blackbirds occupying an entire tree-top—the tops of several trees—and all in full song. Suddenly—in a moment—at absolutely the same instant—all spring into the air and fly away.

How? They could not all see one another—whole tree-tops intervened. At no point could a leader have been visible to all. There must have been a signal of warning or command, high and shrill above the din, but by me unheard. I have observed, too, the same simultaneous flight when all were silent, among not only blackbirds, but other birds—quail, for example, widely separated by bushes—even on opposite sides of a hill.

"It is known to seamen that a school of whales basking or sporting on the surface of the ocean, miles apart, with the convexity of the earth between, will sometimes dive at the same instant—all gone out of sight in a moment. The signal has been sounded—too grave for the ear of the sailor at the masthead and his comrades on the deck—who nevertheless feel its vibrations in the ship as the stones of a cathedral are stirred by the bass of the organ.

"As with sounds, so with colors. At each end of the solar spectrum the chemist can detect the presence of what are known as 'actinic' rays. They represent colors—integral colors in the composition of light—which we are unable to discern. The human eye is an imperfect instrument; its range is but a few octaves of the real 'chromatic scale.' I am not mad; there are colors that we cannot see.

"And, God help me! the Damned Thing is of such a color!"

If the Damned Thing obscured the stars as it passed before them, and partially blotted out Morgan's figure, it would equally have blotted out everything else, and would have appeared as a constantly shifting, dead-black silhouette, somewhat like Nelson Bond's Monster from Nowhere. In Bierce's time ultra-violet and infra-red rays were just beginning to be talked about. If anything could be of such a color, it would apear to our eyes as absolute black; the only way for anything to be invisible, as H. G. Wells pointed out in The Invisible Man, *is to be completely transparent.*

It is entirely possible that this story isn't about vampires at all—but it does provide a place to mention them. You'll see why when you have read it. It is interesting that though the belief in human bloodsucking vampires is hundreds of years old, the vampire bat was discovered only in the nineteenth century. It was given its name by Charles Darwin, on account of its bloodsucking habits. It is highly probable, though not certain, that it was Bran Stoker in his novel Dracula *who first suggested that the human vampire might transform itself into the bat.*

SKELETON

Ray Bradbury

IT WAS PAST TIME FOR HIM TO SEE THE DOCTOR AGAIN. MR. HARRIS turned palely in at the stairwell, and on his way up the flight he saw Dr. Burleigh's name gilded over a pointing arrow. Would Dr. Burleigh sigh when he walked in? After all, this would make the tenth trip so far this year. But Burleigh shouldn't complain; after all, he was paid for the examinations!

The nurse looked Mr. Harris over and smiled, a bit amusedly, as she tiptoed to the glazed glass door, opened it, and put her head in. Harris thought he heard her say, "Guess who's here, Doctor?" And didn't the doctor's acid voice reply, faintly, "Oh, my God, *again?*" Harris swallowed uneasily.

When Harris walked in, Dr. Burleigh snorted thinly. "Aches in your bones again! Ah!!" He scowled at Harris and adjusted his glasses. "My dear Harris, you've been curried with the finest tooth combs and bacteria-brushes known to science. You're only nervous. Let's see your fingers. Too many cigarettes. Let me smell your breath. Too much protein. Let's see your eyes. Not enough sleep. My response? Go to bed, stop the protein, no smoking. Ten dollars, please."

Harris stood there, sulking.

The doctor glanced up from his papers. *"You* still here? You're a hypochondriac! That's *eleven* dollars, now."

"But why should my bones ache?" asked Harris.

Dr. Burleigh addressed him like a child. "You ever had a sore muscle, and kept at it, irritating it, fussing with it, rubbing it? It gets worse, the more you bother it. Then you leave it alone and the pain vanishes. You realize you caused most of the soreness, yourself. Well, son, that's what's with you. Leave yourself alone. Take a dose of salts. Get out of here and take that trip to Phoenix you've stewed about for months. Do you good to travel!"

Five minutes later, Mr. Harris riffled through a classified phone directory at the corner druggists. A fine lot of sympathy one got from blind fools like Burleigh! He passed his finger down a list of BONE SPECIALISTS, found one named M. Munigant. Munigant lacked an M.D., or any other academical lettering behind his name, but his office was conveniently near. Three blocks down, one block over. . . .

M. Munigant, like his office, was small and dark. Like his office, he smelled of iodoform, iodine, and other odd things. He was a good listener, though, and listened with eager, shiny moves of his eyes, and when he talked to Harris, he had an accent and seemed to whistle every word, undoubtedly due to imperfect dentures. Harris told all.

M. Munigant nodded. He had seen cases like this before. The bones of the body. Man was not aware of his bones. Ah, yes, the bones. The skeleton. Most difficult. Something concerning an imbalance, an unsympathetic coordination between soul, flesh and bone. Very complicated, softly whistled M. Munigant. Harris listened, fascinated. Now, *here* was a doctor who understood his illness! Psychological, said M. Munigant. He moved swiftly, delicately to a dingy wall and rattled down half a dozen X-rays and paintings of the human skeleton. He pointed at these. Mr. Harris must become aware of his problem, yes. He pointed at this and that bone, and these and those, and some others.

The pictures were quite awful. They had something of the grotesquerie and off-bounds horror of a Dali painting. Harris shivered.

M. Munigant talked on. Did Mr. Harris desire treatment for his bones?

"That all depends," said Harris.

M. Munigant could not help Harris unless Harris was in the proper mood. Psychologically, one had to *need* help, or the doctor was of no use. But (shrugging) M. Munigant would "try."

Harris lay on a table with his mouth open. The lights were switched off, the shades drawn. M. Munigant approached his patient.

Something touched Harris' tongue.

He felt his jawbones forced out. They cracked and made noises. One of those pictures on the dim wall seemed to leap. A violent shivering went through Harris and, involuntarily, his mouth snapped shut.

M. Munigant cried out. He had almost had his nose bitten off! It was no use. Now was not the time. M. Munigant raised the shades. He looked dreadfully disappointed. When Mr. Harris felt he could co-operate psychologically, when Mr. Harris really *needed* help and trusted M. Munigant to help him, then maybe something could be done. M. Munigant held out his little hand. In the meantime, the fee was only two dollars. Mr. Harris must begin to think. Here was a sketch for Mr. Harris to take home and study. It would acquaint him with his body. He must be aware of himself. He must be careful. Skeletons were strange, unwieldy things. M. Munigant's eyes glittered. Good day to Mr. Harris. Oh, and would he have a breadstick? He proffered a jar of long hard salty breadsticks to Harris, taking one himself to chew on, and saying that chewing breadsticks kept him in—ah—practice. See you soon, Mr. Harris. Mr. Harris went home.

The next day was Sunday. Mr. Harris started the morning by feeling all sorts of new aches and pains in his body. He spent some time glancing at the funny papers and then looking with new interest at the little painting, anatomically perfect, of a skeleton M. Munigant had given him.

His wife, Clarisse, startled him at dinner when she cracked her exquisitely thin knuckles, one by one, until he clapped his hands to his ears and cried, "Don't do that!"

The remainder of the day he quarantined himself in his room. Clarisse was seated at bridge in the living room with three other ladies, laughing and conversing. Harris himself spent his time fingering and weighing the limbs of his body with growing curiosity. After an hour of this he suddenly stood up and called:

"Clarisse!"

She had a way of dancing into any room, her body doing all sorts of soft, agreeable things to keep her feet from ever quite touching the nap of a rug. She excused herself from her friends and came to see him now, brightly. She found him reseated in a far corner and she saw that he was staring at that anatomical sketch. "Are you still brooding, darling?" she asked. "Please don't." She sat upon his knees.

Her beauty could not distract him, now, in his absorption. He juggled her lightness, he touched her knee-cap, suspiciously. It seemed to move under her pale, glowing skin. "Is it supposed to do that?" he asked, sucking in his breath.

"Is what supposed to do what?" she laughed. "You mean my knee-cap?"

"Is it supposed to run around on top your knee that way?"

She experimented. "So it *does*," she marveled. "Well, now, so it does. Icky." She pondered. "No. On the other hand—it doesn't. It's only an optical illusion. I think. The skin moves over the bone; not vice-versa. See?" She demonstrated.

"I'm glad yours slithers, too," he sighed. "I was beginning to worry."

"About what?"

He patted his ribs. "My ribs don't go all the way down, they stop *here*. And I found some confounded ones that dangle in mid-air!"

Beneath the curve of her small breasts, Clarisse clasped her hands.

"Of course, silly, everybody's ribs stop at a given point. And those funny little short ones are just floating ribs."

"I just hope they don't float around too much," he said, making an uneasy joke. Now, he desired that his wife leave him, he

had some important discovering to do with his own body and
he didn't want her laughing at him.

"I'll feel all right," he said. "Thanks for coming in, dear."

"Any time," she said, kissing him, rubbing her small pink nose
warm against his.

"I'll be damned!" He touched his nose with his fingers, then
hers. "Did you ever realize that the nose bone only comes down
so far and a lot of gristly tissue takes up from there on?"

She wrinkled hers. "So what?" And, dancing, she exited.

He felt the sweat rise from the pools and hollows of his face,
forming a salten tide to flow down his cheeks. Next on the
agenda was his spinal cord and column. He examined it in the
same manner as he operated the numerous push-buttons in his
office, pushing them to summon the messenger boys. But, in
these pushings of his spinal column, fear and terrors answered,
rushed from a million doors in Mr. Harris' mind to confront and
shake him. His spine felt awfully—bony. Like a fish, freshly
eaten and skeletonized, on a china platter. He fingered the little
rounded knobbins. "My God."

His teeth began to chatter. "God All-Mighty," he thought,
"why haven't I realized it all these years? All these years I've
gone around with a—SKELETON—inside me!" He saw his
fingers blur before him, like motion films triply speeded in their
quaking apprehension. "How is it that we take ourselves so much
for granted? How is it we never question our bodies and our
being?"

A skeleton. One of those jointed, snowy, hard things, one of
those foul, dry, brittle, gouge-eyed, skull-faced, shake-fingered,
rattling things that sway from neck-chains in abandoned webbed
closets, one of those things found on the desert all long and
scattered like dice!

He stood upright, because he could not bear to remain seated.
Inside me now, he grasped his stomach, his head, inside my head
is a—skull. One of those curved carapaces which holds my brain
like an electrical jelly, one of those cracked shells with the holes
in front like two holes shot through it by a double-barreled shot-

gun! With its grottoes and caverns of bone, its rivetments and placements for my flesh, my smelling, my seeing, my hearing, my thinking! A skull, encompassing my brain, allowing it exit through its brittle windows to see the outside world!

He wanted to dash into the bridge party, upset it, a fox in a chickenyard, the cards fluttering all around like chicken feathers burst upward in clouds! He stopped himself only with a violent, trembling effort. Now, now, man, control yourself. This is a revelation, take it for what it's worth, understand it, savor it. BUT A *SKELETON!* screamed his subconscious. I won't stand for it. It's vulgar, it's terrible, it's frightening. Skeletons are horrors; they clink and tinkle and rattle in old castles, hung from oaken beams, making long, indolently rustling pendulums on the wind. . . .

"Darling, will you come in and meet the ladies?" called his wife's sweet, clear voice.

Mr. Harris stood up. His SKELETON was holding him up. This thing inside him, this invader, this horror, was supporting his arms, legs, and head. It was like feeling someone just behind you who shouldn't be there. With every step he took he realized how dependent he was upon this other Thing.

"Darling, I'll be with you in a moment," he called weakly. To himself he said, "Come on, now, brace up. You've got to go back to work tomorrow. And Friday you've got to make that trip to Phoenix. It's a long drive. Hundreds of miles. Got to be in shape for that trip or you won't get Mr. Creldon to put his money into your ceramics business. Chin up, now."

Five minutes later he stood among the ladies being introduced to Mrs. Withers, Mrs. Abblematt, and Miss Kirthy, all of whom had skeletons inside them but took it very calmly, because nature had carefully clothed the bare nudity of clavicle, tibia, and femur with breasts, thighs, calves, with coiffure and eyebrow satanic, with bee-stung lips and—LORD! shouted Mr. Harris inwardly—when they talk or eat, part of their skeleton shows—their *teeth!* I never thought of that.

"Excuse me," he said, and ran from the room only in time to

drop his lunch among the petunias over the garden balustrade.

That night, seated on the bed as his wife undressed, he pared his toenails and fingernails scrupulously. These parts, too, were where his skeleton was showing, indignantly growing out. He must have muttered something concerning this theory, because next thing he knew his wife, in negligee, slithered on the bed in animal cuddlesomeness, yawning, "Oh, my darling, fingernails are *not* bone, they're only hardened skin growths."

He threw the scissors away with relief. "Glad to hear that. Feel better." He looked at the ripe curves of her body, marveling. "I hope all people are made the same way."

"If you aren't the darndest hypochondriac I ever saw," she said. She snuggled to him. "Come on. What's wrong? Tell mama."

"Something inside me," he said. "Something—I ate."

The next morning and all afternoon at his downtown office, Mr. Harris found that the sizes, shapes, and constructions of various bones in his body displeased him. At ten A.M. he asked to feel Mr. Smith's elbow one moment. Mr. Smith obliged, but scowled suspiciously. And after lunch Mr. Harris asked to touch Miss Laurel's shoulderblade and she immediately pushed herself back against him, purring like a kitten, shutting her eyes in the mistaken belief that he wished to examine a few other anatomical delicacies. "Miss Laurel!" he snapped. "Stop that!"

Alone, he pondered his neuroses. The war just over, the pressure of his work, the uncertainty of the future, probably had much to do with his mental outlook. He wanted to leave the office, get into his own business, for himself. He had more than a little talent at artistic things, had dabbled in ceramics and sculpture. As soon as possible he'd get over into Arizona and borrow that money from Mr. Creldon. It would build him his kiln and set up his own shop. It was a worry. What a case he was. But it was a good thing he had contacted M. Munigant, who had seemed to be eager to understand and help him. He would fight it out with himself, not go back to either Munigant or Dr. Burleigh unless he was forced to. The alien feeling would pass. He sat staring into nothing.

The alien feeling did not pass. It grew.

On Tuesday and Wednesday it bothered him terrifically that his outer dermis, epidermis, hair, and other appendages were of a high disorder, while the integumented skeleton of himself was a slick clean structure of efficient organization. Sometimes, in certain lights while his lips were drawn morosely downward, weighted with melancholy, he imagined he saw his skull grinning at him behind the flesh. *It had its nerve, it did!*

"Let go of me!" he cried. "Let go of me! You've caught me, you've captured me! My lungs, you've got them in a vise! Release them!"

He experienced violent gasps as if his ribs were pressing in, choking the breath from him.

"My brain; stop *squeezing* it!"

And terrible hot headaches caught his brain like a bivalve in the compressed clamp of skull-bones.

"My vitals! All my organs, let them be, for God's sake! Stay away from my heart!' His heart seemed to cringe from the fanning nearness of his ribs. Ribs like pale spiders crouched and fiddling with their prey.

Drenched with sweat, he lay upon the bed one night while Clarisse was out attending a Red Cross meet. He tried to gather his wits again, and always the conflict of his disorderly exterior and this cool calciumed thing inside him with all its exact symmetry.

His complexion: wasn't it oily and lined with worry?

Observe the flawless, snow-white perfection of the skull.

His nose: wasn't it too large?

Then observe the small tiny bones of the skull's nose before that monstrous nasal cartilage begins forming Harris' lopsided proboscis.

His body: wasn't it a bit plump?

Well, then, consider the skeleton; so slender, so svelte, so economical of line and contour. Like exquisitely carved oriental ivory it is, perfected and thin as a reed.

His eyes: weren't they protuberant and ordinary and numb looking?

Be so kind as to note the eye-sockets of the skeleton's skull; so deep and rounded, sombre, quiet, dark pools, all knowing, eternal. Gaze deeply into skull sockets and you never touch the bottom of their dark understanding with any plumb line. All irony; all sadism, all life, all everything is there in the cupped darkness.

Compare. Compare. Compare.

He raged for hours, glib and explosive. And the skeleton, ever the frail and solemn philosopher, quietly hung inside of Harris, saying not a word, quietly suspended like a delicate insect within a chrysalis, waiting and waiting.

Then it came to Harris.

"Wait a minute. Hold on a minute," he exclaimed. "You're helpless, too. I've got you, too. I can make you do anything I want you to! And you can't prevent it! I say put up your carpels, metacarpels, and phalanges and—sswtt—up they go, as I wave to someone!" He giggled.

"I order to the fibula and femur to locomote and *Hunn* two three four, *Hunn* two three four—we walk around the block. There."

Harris grinned.

"It's a fifty-fifty fight. Even steven. And we'll fight it out, we two, we shall. After all, I'm the part that *thinks!*" That was good, it was a triumph, he'd remember that. "Yes, by God, yes. I'm the part that thinks. If I didn't have you, even then I could still think!"

Instantly, he felt a pain strike his head. His cranium, crowding in slowly, began giving him some of his own treatment back.

At the end of the week he had postponed the Phoenix trip because of his health. Weighing himself on a penny scales he saw the slow glide of the red arrow as it pointed to: 164.

He groaned. "Why, I've weighed 175 for ten years. I can't have lost ten pounds." He examined his cheeks in the fly-dotted mirror. Cold primitive fear rushed over him in odd little shivers. "Hold on! I know what you're about, *you*."

He shook his finger at his bony face, particularly addressing his remarks to his superior maxillary, his inferior maxillary, to his cranium, and to his cervical vertebrae.

"You rum thing, you. Think you can starve me off, make me lose weight, eh? A victory for you, is that? Peel the flesh off, leave nothing but skin on bone. Trying to ditch me, so you can be supreme, ah? No, no!"

He fled into a cafeteria.

Ordering turkey, dressing, creamed potatoes, four vegetables, three desserts, he soon found he could not eat it, he was sick to his stomach. He forced himself. His teeth began to ache. "Bad teeth, is it?" he wanted to know, angrily. "I'll eat in spite of every tooth clanging and banging and rattling so they fall in my gravy. "

His head ached, his breathing came hard from a constricted chest, his teeth pulsed with pain, but he had one small victory. He was about to drink milk when he stopped and poured it into a vase of nasturtiums. "No calcium for you, my boy, no more calcium for you. Never again shall I eat foods with calcium or other bone-fortifying minerals. I'll eat for one of us, not both, my lad."

"One hundred and fifty pounds," he said, the following week to his wife. "Do you see how I've changed?"

"For the better," said Clarisse. "You were always a little plump for your height, darling." She stroked his chin. "I like your face, it's so much nicer, the lines of it are so firm and strong now."

"They're not *my* lines, they're his, damn him! You mean to say you like him better than you like me?" he demanded indignantly.

"Him? Who's '*him*'?"

In the parlor mirror, beyond Clarisse, his skull smiled back at him behind his fleshy grimace of hatred and despair.

Fuming, he popped malt tablets into his mouth. This was one way of gaining weight when you couldn't keep other foods down. Clarisse noticed the malt pellets. "But, darling, really, you don't have to gain the weight for me," she said.

"Oh, shut up!" he felt like saying.

She came to him and sat down and made him lie so his head was in her lap. "Darling," she said. "I've watched you lately. You're so—badly off. You don't say anything, but you look—hunted. You toss in bed at night. Maybe you should go to a psychiatrist. But I think I can tell you everything he would say. I've put it all together, from hints you've let escape you. I can tell you that you and your skeleton are one and the same, one nation, indivisible, with liberty and justice for all. United you stand, divided you fall. If you two fellows can't get along like an old married couple in the future, go back and see Dr. Burleigh. But, *first*, relax. You're in a vicious circle, the more you worry, the more your bones stick out, the more your bones stick out, the more you worry. After all, now, who picked this fight—you or that anonymous entity you claim is lurking around behind your alimentary canal?"

He closed his eyes. "*I* did. I guess I did. Oh, my darling, I love you so."

"You rest now," she said softly. "Rest and forget."

Mr. Harris felt buoyed up for half a day, then he began to sag again. It was all very well to say every thing was imagination, but this particular skeleton, by God, was fighting back.

Harris set out for M. Munigant's office late in the day. Walking for half an hour until he found the address, he caught sight of the name M. Munigant initialled in ancient, flaking gold on a glass plate outside the building. Then, his bones seemed to explode from their moorings, blasted and erupted with pain. He could hardly see in his wet, pain-filled eyes. So violent were the pains that he staggered away. When he opened his eyes again he had rounded a corner. M. Munigant's office was out of sight.

The pains ceased.

M. Munigant was the man to help him. He *must* be! If the sight of his gilt-lettered name could cause so titanic a reaction in the deepness of Harris' body, why, of course M. Munigant *must* be just the man.

But, not today. Each time he tried to return to that office, the terrible pains laid him low. Perspiring, he had to give up, and stagger into a cocktail bar for respite.

Moving across the dim room of the cocktail lounge, he wondered briefly if a lot of blame couldn't be put on M. Munigant's shoulders; after all, it was Munigant who'd first drawn such specific attention to his skeleton, and brought home the entire psychological impact of it! Could M. Munigant be using him for some nefarious purpose? But what purpose? Silly to even suspect him. Just a little doctor. Trying to be helpful. Munigant and his jar of bread-sticks. Ridiculous. M. Munigant was okay, okay.

There was a sight within the cocktail lounge to give him hope. A large fat man, round as a butterball, stood drinking consecutive beers at the bar. Now *there* was a successful man. Harris repressed a desire to go up, clap the fat man's shoulder, and inquire as to how he'd gone about impounding his bones. Yes, the fat man's skeleton was luxuriously closeted. There were pillows of fat here, resilient bulges of it there, with several round chandeliers of fat under his chin. The poor skeleton was lost, it could never fight clear of *that* blubber; it may have tried once—but now, overwhelmed, not a bony echo of the fat man's supporter remained.

Not without envy, Harris approached the fat man as one might cut across the bow of an ocean liner. Harris ordered a drink, drank it, and then dared to address the fat man:

"Glands?"

"You talking to me?" asked the fat man.

"Or is there a special diet?" wondered Harris. "I beg your pardon, but, as you see, I'm down. Can't seem to put on any weight. I'd like a stomach like that one of yours. Did you grow it because you were afraid of something?"

"You," announced the fat man, "are drunk. But—I like drunkards." He ordered more drinks. "Listen close. I'll tell you—"

"Layer by layer," said the fat man, "twenty years, man and boy, I built this." He held his vast stomach like a globe of the world, teaching his audience its gastronomical geography. "It was no overnight circus. The tent was not raised before dawn on the wonders installed within. I have cultivated my inner organs as if they were thoroughbred dogs, cats, and other animals. My stomach is a fat pink Persian tom slumbering, rousing at intervals to purr, mew, growl, and cry for chocolate titbits. I feed it well, it will almost sit up for me. And, my dear fellow, my intestines are the rarest pure-bred Indian anacondas you ever viewed in the sleekest, coiled, fine, and ruddy health. Keep 'em in prime, I do, all my pets. For fear of something? Perhaps."

This called for another drink for everybody.

"Gain weight?" The fat man savored the words on his tongue. "Here's what you do; get yourself a quarreling bird of a wife, a baker's dozen of relatives who can flush a covey of troubles out from behind the veriest molehill. Add to these a sprinkling of business associates whose prime motivation is snatching your last lonely quid, and you are well on your way to getting fat. How so? In no time you'll begin subconsciously building fat betwixt yourself and them. A buffer epidermal state, a cellular wall. You'll soon find that eating is the only fun on earth. But one needs to be bothered by outside sources. Too many people in this world haven't enough to worry about, then they begin picking on *themselves,* and they lose weight. Meet all of the vile, terrible people you can possibly meet, and pretty soon you'll be adding the good old fat!"

And with that advice, the fat man launched himself out into the dark tide of night, swaying mightily and wheezing.

"That's exactly what Dr. Burleigh told me, slightly changed," said Harris thoughtfully. "Perhaps that trip to Phoenix, now, at this time—"

The trip from Los Angeles to Phoenix was a sweltering one, crossing, as it did, the Mojave desert on a broiling yellow day. Traffic was thin and inconstant, and for long stretches there would not be a car on the road for miles ahead or behind. Harris twitched his fingers on the steering wheel. Whether or not Creldon, in Phoenix, lent him the money he needed to start his business, it was still a good thing to get away, to put distance behind.

The car moved in the hot sluice of desert wind. The one Mr. H. sat inside the other Mr. H. Perhaps both perspired. Perhaps both were miserable.

On a curve, the inside Mr. H. suddenly constricted the outer flesh, causing him to jerk forward on the hot steering wheel.

The car plunged off the road into deepest sand. It turned half over.

Night came on, a wind rose, the road was lonely and silent with little traffic. Those few cars that passed went swiftly on their way, their view obstructed. Mr. Harris lay unconscious until very late he heard a wind rising out of the desert, felt the sting of little sand needles on his cheeks, and opened his eyes.

Morning found him gritty-eyed and wandering in thoughtless, senseless circles, having, in his delirium, gotten away from the road. At noon he sprawled in the poor shade of a bush. The sun struck into him with a keen sword edge, cutting through to his —bones. A vulture circled.

Harris' parched lips cracked open, weakly. "So that's it?" he whimpered, red-eyed, bristle-cheeked. "One way or another you'll wreck me, walk me, starve me, thirst me, kill me." He swallowd dry burrs of dust. "Sun cook off my flesh so you can peek forth. Vultures lunch and breakfast from me, and then there you'll lie, grinning. Grinning with victory. Like a bleached xylophone strewn and played by vultures with an ear for odd music. You'd like that. Freedom."

He walked on through a landscape that shivered and bubbled in the direct pour of sunlight; stumbling, falling flat, lying to feed himself little mouths of flame. The air was blue alcohol flame, and vultures roasted and steamed and glittered as they flew in glides and circles. Phoenix. The road. Car. Water. Safety.

"Hey!"

Somebody called from way off in the blue alcohol flame.

Mr. Harris propped himself up.

"Hey!"

The call was repeated. A crunching of footsteps, quick.

With a cry of unbelievable relief, Harris rose, only to collapse again into the arms of someone in a uniform with a badge. . . .

The car tediously hauled, repaired, Phoenix reached, Harris found himself in such an unholy state of mind that the business transaction was more a numb pantomime than anything else. Even when he got the loan and held the money in his hand it meant nothing. This Thing within him like a hard white sword in a scabbard tainted his business, his eating, colored his love for Clarisse, made it unsafe to trust an automobile; all in all this Thing had to be put in its place before he could have love for business or anything. That desert incident had brushed too closely. Too near the bone, one might say with an ironic twist of one's mouth. Harris heard himself thanking Mr. Creldon, dimly, for the money. Then he turned his car and motored back across the long miles, this time cutting across to San Diego, so that he would miss that desert stretch between El Centro and Beaumont. He drove north along the coast. He didn't trust that desert. But —careful! Salt waves boomed, hissing on the beach outside Laguna. Sand, fish, and crustacia would cleanse his bones as swiftly as vultures. Slow down on the curves over the surf.

If anything happened, he wanted cremation. The two of them'd burn together that way. None of this graveyard burial stuff where little crawling things eat and leave nothing but un-mantled bone! No, they'd burn. Damn Him! He was sick. Where could he turn? Clarisse? Burleigh? Munigant? Bone specialist. Munigant. Well?

"Darling!" trilled Clarisse, kissing him, so he winced at the solidness of her teeth and jaw behind the passionate exchange.

"Darling," he said, slowly wiping his lips with his wrist, trembling.

"You look thinner; oh, darling, the business deal—?"

"It went through. Yeah, it went through. I guess. Yeah, it did," he said.

She enthused. She kissed him again. Lord, he couldn't even enjoy kisses any more because of this obsession. They ate a slow, falsely cheerful dinner, with Clarisse laughing and encouraging him. He studied the phone, several times he picked it up indeci-sively, then laid it down. His wife walked in, putting on her coat and hat. "Well, sorry, but I have to leave now," she laughed, and pinched him lightly on the cheek. "Come on now, cheer up! I'll be back from Red Cross in three hours. You lie around and snooze. I simply *have* to go."

When Clarisse was gone, Harris dialed the phone, nervously. "M. Munigant?"

The explosions and the sickness in his body after he set the phone down were unbelievable. His bones were racked with every kind of pain, cold and hot, he had ever thought of or ex-perienced in wildest nightmare. He swallowed all the aspirin he could find in an effort to stave off the assault; but when the doorbell finally rang an hour later, he could not move, he lay weak and exhausted, panting, tears streaming down his cheeks, like a man on a torture rack. Would M. Munigant go away if the door was not answered?

"Come in!" he tried to gasp it out. "Come in, for God's sake!"

M. Munigant came in. Thank God the door had been unlocked.

Oh, but Mr. Harris looked terrible. M. Munigant stood in the center of the living room, small and dark. Harris nodded at him. The pains rushed through him, hitting him with large iron hammers and hooks. M. Munigant's eyes glittered as he saw Harris' protuberant bones. Ah, he saw that Mr. Harris was now psychologically prepared for aid. Was it not so? Harris nodded again, feebly, sobbing. M. Munigant still whistled when he talked; something about his tongue and the whistling. No matter. Through his shimmering eyes Harris seemed to see M. Munigant shrink, get smaller. Imagination, of course. Harris sobbed out his story of the Phoenix trip. M. Munigant sympathized. This skeleton was a—a traitor! They would *fix* him for once and for all! "M. Munigant," sighed Harris, faintly. "I—I never noticed before. You have such an odd, odd tongue. Round. Tube-like. Hollow? Guess it's my eyes. Don't mind me. Delirious. I'm ready. What do I do?"

M. Munigant whistled softly, appreciatively, coming closer. If Mr. Harris would relax in his chair, and open his mouth? The lights were switched off. M. Munigant peered into Harris' dropped jaw. Wider, please? It had been so hard, that first visit, to help Harris, with both body and bone in rebellion. Now, he had cooperation from the flesh of the man, anyway, even if the skeleton was acting up somewhat. In the darkness, M. Munigant's voice got small, small, tiny, tiny. The whistling became high and shrill. Now. Relax, Mr. Harris. NOW!

Harris felt his jaw pressed violently in all directions, his tongue depressed as with a spoon, his throat clogged. He gasped for breath. Whistle. He couldn't breathe! He was corked. Something squirmed, cork-screwed his cheeks out, bursting his jaws. Like a hot water douche, something squirted into his sinuses, his ears clanged! "Ahhh!" shrieked Harris, gagging. His head, its carapaces riven, shattered, hung loose. Agony shot into his lungs, around.

Harris could breathe again, momentarily. His watery eyes sprang wide. He shouted. His ribs, like sticks picked up and bundled, were loosened in him. Pain! He fell to the floor, rocking, rolling, wheezing out his hot breath.

Light flickered in his senseless eyeballs, he felt his limbs swiftly cast loose and free, expertly. Through streaming eyes he saw the parlor.

The room was empty.

M. Munigant was gone.

"Help!"

Then he heard it.

Deep down in the subterranean fissures of his bodily well, he heard the minute, unbelievable noises; little smackings and twistings and little dry chippings and grindings and nuzzling sounds —like a tiny hungry mouse down in the red blooded dimness, gnawing ever so earnestly and expertly at what may have been, but was not, a submerged timber . . . !

Clarisse, walking along the sidewalk, held her head high and marched straight toward her house on Saint James Place. She was thinking of the Red Cross and a thousand other things as she turned the corner and almost ran into this little dark man who smelled of iodine.

Clarisse would have ignored him if it were not for the fact that as she passed he took something long, white and oddly familiar from his coat and proceeded to chew on it, as on a peppermint stick. Its end devoured, his extraordinary tongue darted within the white confection, sucking out the filling, making contented noises. He was still crunching his goodie as she proceeded up the sidewalk to her house, turned the doorknob and walked in.

"Darling?" she called, smiling around. "Darling, where are you?"

She shut the door, walked down the hall and into the living room.

"Darling. . . ."

She stared at the floor for twenty seconds, trying to understand. She screamed.

Outside in the sycamore darkness, the little man pierced a long white stick with intermittent holes; then, softly, sighing, lips puckered, played a little sad tune upon the improvised instrument to accompany the shrill and awful singing of Clarisse's voice as she stood in the living room.

Many times as a little girl Clarisse had run on the beach sands, stepped on a jelly fish and screamed. It was not so bad, finding an intact, gelatin-skinned jelly-fish in one's living room. One could step back from it.

It was when the jelly-fish *called you by name.* . . .

You may think that it is a very long coincidence that the Thing found the right conditions to enable it to live and grow; but then, scientists say that it is by a very long coincidence that life was able to arise; though they also say that, given enough worlds, the coincidence is bound to be repeated on some of them. So, perhaps, if we are given enough ponds—

THE THING IN THE POND
Paul Ernst

IT WAS LATE AFTERNOON WHEN GORDON SHARPE, TALL, LEAN, and bearded, got out of the hired car at the door of Professor Weidbold's country house. He lifted out his grips and his gun case.

"That must be a right sizable shootin' iron, mister," the driver drawled.

"It's stopped quite a few elephants in its time," replied Sharpe, with his steel-blue eyes twinkling.

The driver glanced oddly at him. "Well, there ain't any elephants around here, but this is a funny part of Florida, mister, just the same."

Sharpe's thick black beard stirred with a grin. "I read about it in the papers last night," he said. "Got a monster or something, down this way, haven't you?"

"That's what they say. Me—I don't take no stock in it."

The hired car rattled off. The door opened, and Weidbold's servant came out of the house. Sharpe stared at him. He was small, quiet, efficient. Quite different from old Sam Klegg, the sulky, not-too-clean loafer Weidbold had had working for him when Sharpe last visited here.

The man reached for the grips and the gun case.

"I'll carry that," said Sharpe. "Where's the professor?"

"He's out by the pond," replied the servant. "I'll show you to your room and then tell him you're here."

Sharpe went upstairs with the man. When he was alone, he stepped to the window.

His room was at the rear of the combined house and laboratory. Twenty acres of weeds and neglect stretched before his eyes from the house to a small, marshy puddle called Greer's Pond. Sharpe remembered this as a stagnant pool, fed by seepage, heated to blood warmth by the Florida sun. It was rather deep, and it teemed with small life.

He could see the sluggish glint of the water now, and, at one end, the stoop-shouldered, shambling figure of Professor Weidbold. Then he saw the servant start across the fields and noted his grim, precise walk. The man contrasted humorously with the surly ruffian, Sam Klegg, who had worked here ten years ago.

Sharpe went downstairs to the laboratory. Weidbold spent most of his waking hours here. He would expect to meet his ex-pupil there.

The tanned, powerful African explorer blinked as he entered the cool dimness of the laboratory. Then he saw that all was unchanged.

There was the delicate device for registering the minute quantities of electricity generated by a growing plant. There was the little glass case in which Weidbold had kept a bit of muscle from the heart of a chicken, a lump no larger than the head of a match, living and growing in a salt solution for sixteen years. Here was the complicated apparatus with which Weidbold increased the chlorophyll content in plants with ultra-violet rays. Then came cases of zoölogical monstrosities—newts with three eyes, salamanders with tails where their legs should be, and heads grafted on where their tails should be.

The door of the laboratory opened.

"Gordon!" exclaimed Professor Weidbold, coming in. "It's good to see you again. You're looking fine."

"Nothing seems changed," said Sharpe heartily. "I might have stepped out yesterday instead of ten years ago. The only new thing is your servant. You fired Sam Klegg at last, eh?"

"Yes," said the professor, a muscle twitching in his cheek. "A few weeks after you'd left. I wrote you about it, I think."

"You did. And you wrote me, too, that the sullen fellow took a mean revenge by dumping several casks of chemicals and some of your most valuable laboratory equipment into Greer's Pond."

The professor looked so distressed that Sharpe put his big arm affectionately over the thin shoulders.

"It's ancient history now," he said. Then: "Why on earth did you ask me to bring an elephant gun when I came for the visit? Are you going into ballistics now?"

Weidbold did not smile back. "Not exactly," he murmured, avoiding Sharpe's gaze.

"Then," Sharpe returned, laughing, "it must be you wanted me to use it on the monster in your pool."

Professor Weidbold did not smile at this, either. "So you've heard," he said.

"I've heard of little else in the last twenty-four hours," Sharpe responded, gazing at the professor with worried eyes. "The Associated Press got the story. The whole country is laughing at the hoax. You'll probably have pilgrims to Greer's Pond by the thousands in a few days."

"What did the papers say about the—the hoax?"

Sharpe lighted his pipe, his eyes continuing to probe Weidbold's. "The New York papers say there is a dinosaur alive down here. The Chicago sheets think it's a sea serpent. But of course nobody really believes there's anything cooped up in your spoonful of water. It's just another tall tale, like that of the monster in the Scottish loch some time."

Again the muscle twitched in Weidbold's cheek. Sharpe's fingers tightened on the bowl of his pipe. The old man looked as if he actually put credence in this silly story of a monster in Greer's Pond. He must have broken recently in mind as well as in health not to laugh with a scientist's skepticism at such talk.

A monster! In Greer's Pond!

"Of course there may actually be some big beast, like an alligator, in the pool," said Sharpe, keeping his tone light. "It'll be sport to find out. We'll go hunting tomorrow. We'll take your spaniel, Spot—"

"Spot's dead," Weidbold interrupted heavily.

Sharpe whistled. "Too bad! Run over by an automobile?"

"No," said Weidbold; "drowned. In Greer's Pond. It was three nights ago. I heard him barking as if his throat would split out by the pond. Then, suddenly, the barking ceased."

The professor stared abstractedly at a glass case in which a curious monstrosity, a newt with two heads, from an egg cell half divided in embryo, was preserved.

"I went back to sleep, thinking little of it. But next morning Spot didn't appear, so I wandered over to the pond. I saw his tracks in the soft mud next to the water's edge. They went into the water and disappeared."

"That sounds like a 'gator, all right," Sharpe nodded. "They go for dogs."

"An alligator?" mused Weidbold. "Possibly. But Raeburn, who owns the land behind mine, doesn't think so. He thinks that if a big alligator was in the pool, it would be seen often on the surface of the water or on the bank. And Raeburn has never actually seen anything. Nor have I."

"Why not drain the pond?" asked Sharpe.

Weidbold sighed. "I am a poor man. Due to the lie of the land, draining would cost more than my entire fortune." He cleared his throat. "Come on out and look around now, will you? I saw something rather interesting this noon. I was out looking at it again when you arrived."

"Certainly," said Sharpe. "Shall I take my gun?"

He had tried to make his voice careless, but some tone in it must have sounded wrong.

"You think I'm a little mad, don't you?" said Weidbold. "Well, no matter. Come along."

They went out by the laboratory door and started across the

neglected acreage behind the house to Greer's Pond. Far off was the country road. They saw several cars slow down as they passed.

"Sightseers will be swarming here pretty soon to look at the monster in the pond," predicted Sharpe.

Weidbold shivered as if he were cold. "I know. Dozens of people crowding around the edge of the pool— Something must be done at once."

They reached the scum-flecked pond. Sharpe remembered it well. He and Weidbold had seined out many a wriggling subject for laboratory experimentation. Oddly, he saw no small life now.

"Here," said Weidbold, in a low, strained tone. "This is what I wanted to show you."

Sharpe gazed where the old professor pointed. He saw cow tracks—ordinary cow tracks etched in the mud by the water. A fresh wave of pity for Weidbold grew in his breast.

Then he moistened his lips as he peered closer at the tracks, and he forgot to pity Weidbold so tolerantly.

The cow tracks led from the property on Raeburn's side of the pond to the edge of the pool. Indistinct till they reached the mud, they were only too clear there.

The tracks were deep. They were slurred and close-bunched. The animal that had made them had been pulling back frantically, straining back with deep-planted hoofs from the water and being inexorably hauled into it just the same.

"It must have been a monster 'gator," muttered Sharpe stubbornly. "It *must* have been—"

But there were no 'gator tracks anywhere to be seen. Instead, half effacing the cow tracks in some places, there was something the like of which he had never observed in all his big-game hunting days.

The mud around some of the cow tracks had been pressed flat and smooth as if a heavy, fat body had slithered across there.

"Here comes my neighbor," he heard Weidbold say.

He looked up and saw a man approaching them. He was a big, burly fellow in faded blue overalls. He was striding toward them aggressively, swiftly, glaring at the professor as he came.

"I might have knowed I should look here first for my cow," he shouted when he was still fifty yards from them. "Spent the hull day phoning around to see if she'd gone into some one else's barn. But I should have knowed where she'd disappeared to!"

He reached them with the last words and took just one look at the tracks. His black eyes glittered with rage.

"Perfessor," he grated, "what the hell's in this pond? What in tarnation"—he glared at the tracks—"can drag a full-grown Guernsey down into the water?"

"Who knows, Raeburn!" said Weidbold, his old voice trembling. "I lost my dog, you know, a few nights ago."

"It's probably a 'gator," Sharpe offered.

Raeburn whirled on him. "A 'gator! Whoever you are and wherever you come from, I reckon you must know better than that. You don't see any tracks, do you? And nobody's ever seen one sunnin' itself, have they? And what would one 'gator do with a hull cow?"

He whirled back to Weidbold, and his voice tensed Sharpe's muscles angrily.

"Perfessor, we've been mighty tolerant around here about the devil's work you do alone in that lab'atory of your'n. We ain't said nothing and we ain't done nothing, though we all knew your work was agin' nature. Now I reckon it's time to think of acting. You know—there has been folks lynched around this part of the country."

Sharpe's fists clenched, but he remembered that this man had just lost a valuable animal.

"Why do you talk like that to me?" faltered the old professor. "Whatever is in this pond—"

"Perfessor," Raeburn interrupted, "you know what's in that pond! I don't, and no one else does—but you do. I can see it in your face. I been seein' it there for a month."

"I assure you—" mumbled Weibold.

But Raeburn didn't stop to hear. He turned on his heel and walked away.

Sharpe gazed at Weidbold.

"You see," murmured the professor wearily, "I have something actual to fear, regardless of what may or may not be in that slimy water."

Sharpe's gaze held steady. "What *is* in there, professor?"

"I—I haven't the faintest idea. As a scientist I simply cannot admit that—"

"What?" Sharpe rapped out, as the old man stopped.

"Nothing." Weidbold sighed. And he would say no more.

Sharpe turned from him to stare at the pond again. Covered in spots with green scum, clear in spots like a black mirror, the surface of the opaque water lay without a ripple to feather it. The eye could not penetrate more than a foot or so down into the motionless, silt-filled pool.

Sharpe stared harder.

No movement? No ripples? But there were.

In the center of the pond a faint stir of water grew regularly into being—so faint that Sharpe had not caught it till now. It ringed out, wider and wider, barely stirring the scum, till it reached the shores.

In slow, rhythmic succession, the ripples ringed from the center of the pond to stir at last along the shore. As if something down under there was breathing, with a slow heave of sides or gills. Or as if a mighty heart was beating down there, with each slow pulsation registering on the recording surface of the pool. That was more apt. The water was stirring regularly, like a huge, slow pulse.

Sharpe's finger nails pressed into the palms of his hands; but his voice was even as he said: "Got any meat in your refrigerator?"

Weidbold glanced at him quickly. It was impossible to guess whether his old eyes had been alert enough to catch the steady stir of the water.

"I have a slab of bacon and some beef," he said.

"Good!" Sharpe's voice was incisive. "We won't wait till tomorrow to hunt. Visitors might be crowding in by then, and that might be—unhealthy. Would you mind stepping to the house and asking your man to bring my gun and the meat here to me?"

Weidbold nodded and turned away. Sharpe watched him shamble across the field, then turned back to watch the enigmatic surface of the pond. Down in its mysterious, black depths—

Weidbold brought the meat and gun back himself. Sharpe frowned at him.

"No need for you to stay around, sir. Nothing may rise to this bait at all, since the cow was dragged in so recently."

"I will stay," said the old professor.

"There might be danger—"

"I will stay, Gordon."

Sharpe shrugged, and loaded the big gun. They went to the edge of the pond, not speaking to each other, not looking at each other.

Sharpe threw the slab of bacon as near to the center of the pool as he could. It splashed in the green scum.

There was no answering splash. Ripples welled out from the disturbance and gradually subsided. That was all.

"It—it might be that the—the thing has such a low nervous organization that it can't tell when food or prey is near," faltered Weidbold. His face was white and his hands were shaking.

"We might ask the cow what her opinion is," said Sharpe.

He picked up the chunk of beef and sent it after the bacon. It hit the scum even nearer the center of the pool.

The slimy surface of the pond boiled a little near the meat. It seemed to hump up slightly. Grimly, silently, the commotion in the water grew. With strained intensity the two men stared.

Something broke the surface of the pond; something that was pallidly pink and smooth and glistening; something that was hollowed in the center like a gigantic cup.

The monstrous cup closed around the meat just as Sharpe's gun roared out. Both men saw a hole torn in the pink fringe of the cup. Both men saw the fringe continue to clamp down over the meat as if nothing had happened. Then the thing sank silently under the water. There was a soft sucking noise as an eddy whirled above. The eddy died down and there was nothing.

Sharpe wiped the palms of his hands on his trouser legs.

"It didn't even feel it!" he breathed, his eyes wide and staring. "A slug that would have stopped an elephant, and it didn't even feel it!"

Weidbold's trembling fingers were plucking at his lips.

"Like firing into a sofa cushion," Sharpe went on. "No chance for the explosive bullet to get in its work. It simply tore through—"

He stopped abruptly. Weidbold's hand clutched convulsively at his arm. The two glared at the water before them.

A commotion was growing there. Once again the green scum was humping upward as something sluggishly sought the surface. And the commotion rippled the stagnant, warm water in a straight line for the spot where Sharpe and Weidbold stood.

With a hoarse exclamation, Sharpe jerked his arm from the professor's clutch and ripped the bolt of his gun out and back. He leveled it toward the seething water.

The surface of the water broke at last, almost at their feet. Something pallidly pink shone wet and sleek above the green scum. It was coming steadily through the water toward them.

It reached the shore—rather, the front of it reached the shore. The rear of it trailed back out of sight in the black water. It began, with a queer hitching movement, to climb out onto the mud.

Something roughly oblong and flat, like an undulating pink blanket—something that was simply a blind, sluggish lump, without limbs or tentacles, exuding mucus to protect its tender-looking surface from twigs and pebbles in the mud.

As the thing crawled farther and farther up on the bank it seemed to slough off chunks of itself. But in an instant it was apparent that the chunks were half-dissolved bits of meat. A horn dropped, and some whitened bones, and the skull of a cow.

"Shoot!" cried the professor.

Sharpe only stood there, peering over his sights at the thing. It hitched toward them, progressing by humping itself up in folds and then straightening out—expanding and contracting in rhythmic waves of movement. And still its bulk trailed endlessly from the pond.

"Shoot!" screeched Weidbold.

Sharpe pressed the trigger.

Again the heavy-caliber gun roared out in the silent afternoon. Again a big bullet tore into the viscous, tender-looking pink mass. And again it sliced right through, with not enough resistance offered for the explosion of the bullet.

A jagged hole, oozing straw-colored fluid, yawned in the loathsome pinkish mass. The bulk of it stirred as the bullet exploded in the mud beneath. But it kept on coming.

Both men ran, sweat streaming down their faces—ran as if pursued by fiends.

A hundred yards away they stopped and looked back.

There was a subsiding commotion at the water's edge. Something flipped sluggishly up from the green scum and then sank.

"Maybe—it's dead," quavered Professor Weidbold.

Sharpe drew a long breath, and then began to stride purposefully toward the house.

"You know better than that," he said quietly. "That thing could never die. It could be blown to bits and still not die. Because it isn't alive; not as a complete organism, anyhow. It has no nervous system; it has no vital organs; it simply has cellular, multifarious life. Isn't that right, professor?"

Weidbold said nothing. He hurried to keep pace with Sharpe's long strides.

"What are you going to do, Gordon?" he asked as they neared the house.

"I'm going to do some telephoning," he said. "I am going to order some dynamite and about a carload of sulphuric acid, and I'm going to have a contractor come out first thing in the morning. We'll dynamite the pool at dawn. Then the contractor can put up a high fence. After that we'll sluice the pool with sulphuric acid and keep sluicing it. That's the only way I can think of to destroy utterly the thing in the pond. And if it isn't destroyed," he added grimly, "I see no reason why it shouldn't keep on growing indefinitely, till it's the size of a ten-story building. Do you?"

Weidbold only looked at him, miserably, imploringly.

Next morning, with pearl first streaking the east, the two went back to the pond. Sharpe walked carefully, carrying half a dozen sticks of dynamite tied in a bundle with a short fuse attached.

The pond looked like a great, green-flecked fire opal in the early morning. Sharpe stared at it. Off center a little, perhaps thirty yards from where they stood, a faint ripple formed regularly on the still surface, to ring the stagnant water and subside gently on the shores. Beat, beat, beat.

Sharpe lighted the fuse and threw the bundle of dynamite.

It fell with a splash in the center of the rhythmic ripples. Both men ran from the pool, covering their ears, holding their mouths open.

There was a thunderous roar before they had taken twenty steps. They were knocked from their feet.

Water and mud rained down on them. Water and mud, and something else—fragments of pallid pinkish substance that struck down on them like clammy hands, to plop off onto to the ground, and to begin at once, with queer, humping movements, to slide back to the boiling, half-emptied pond.

Alive, but not alive! Frightful, blind growth, as vital and indestructible as the living, primal ooze!

"No death for it but utter annihilation," muttered Sharpe. "But it will be weeks before any of the pieces can become dangerously big. Long before that we'll have the place burned out with acid.

The two got up slowly. Sharpe looked at the professor for a long time.

"I know what you're thinking," said Weidbold. "But it can't be true. It can't! By all the laws of biology it can't—"

"Professor," said Sharpe, "it was about ten years ago that your discharged servant got back at you by dumping that laboratory stuff into the pool, wasn't it?"

"Yes," said the old man, his lips twitching.

"Among the stuff was a lot of sodium, potassium, and calcium salts, and probably a barrel of sugar," guessed Sharpe.

"Y-yes," admitted Weidbold.

"Now, while I was here ten years ago you cut off a bit of that chicken-heart muscle you've kept living and pulsing for sixteen years in a solution of potassium, calcium, sodium, and sugar. I remember that distinctly. You've cut off several bits; otherwise the stuff would outgrow the nourishment-capacity of the case. What happened to that fragment?"

"I—it got lost, or something."

"It's conceivable that it was among the stuff your servant dumped into the pond, isn't it?"

"Such a fantastic accident—" mumbled Weidbold.

"All accidents are fantastic," said Sharpe curtly. "That's why they call them accidents. It's conceivable—isn't it?"

Weidbold nodded.

"And in this warm, life-filled pond," Sharpe pursued relentlessly, "the tiny bit of muscle substance flourished. It absorbed the chemicals freakishly dumped in with it, and finally all the small life. Then it began to reach out for more food in its voracious growth."

"I tell you it's impossible!" almost shrieked the professor. "It could not live outside a laboratory! Ask any scientist—"

"I'd prefer to ask Raeburn's cow or your dog," Sharpe cut in dryly.

Weidbold spread his hands in a defeated gesture. "Gordon," he said in a different tone, "I'm an old man. I have neither the money nor the energy to move to another part of the country and set up my laboratory all over again—which I'd have to do if the people around here believed that some experiment in my laboratory really was responsible for—this. Now—you see how impossible it is that a tiny bit of flesh from the heart of a dead chicken could grow to a thing like—like that, don't you?"

Sharpe watched the last of the small pink fragments fold over on itself on its way to the water of Greer's Pond. The little fragment slipped sluggishly under the green scum of the surface.

"We'll say it's impossible," he conceded at last.

In my anthology Deals with the Devil *I said, "No collection of
pacts with the Devil would be complete without one in the good
old-fashioned manner, with an old house and a ghost-story atmosphere." The same thing is true of monster stories.*

NEGOTIUM PERAMBULANS

E. F. Benson

THE CASUAL TOURIST IN WEST CORNWALL MAY JUST POSSIBLY HAVE
noticed, as he bowled along over the bare high plateau between
Penzance and the Land's End, a dilapidated signpost pointing
down a steep lane and bearing on its battered finger the faded
inscription "Polearn 2 miles," but probably very few have had
the curiosity to traverse those two miles in order to see a place
to which their guidebooks award so cursory a notice. It is
described there, in a couple of unattractive lines, as a small fishing village with a church of no particular interest except for
certain carved and painted wooden panels (originally belonging
to an earlier edifice) which form an altar-rail. But the church at
St. Creed (the tourist is reminded) has a similar decoration far
superior in point of preservation and interest, and thus even the
ecclesiastically disposed are not lured to Polearn. So meagre a
bait is scarce worth swallowing, and a glance at the very steep
lane which in dry weather presents a carpet of sharp-pointed
stones, and after rain a muddy watercourse, will almost certainly
decide him not to expose his motor or his bicycle to risks like
these in so sparsely populated a district. Hardly a house has met
his eye since he left Penzance, and the possible trundling of a
punctured bicycle for half a dozen weary miles seems a high
price to pay for the sight of a few painted panels.

Polearn, therefore, even in the high noon of the tourist season,
is little liable to invasion, and for the rest of the year I do not
suppose that a couple of folk a day traverse those two miles (long
ones at that) of steep and stony gradient. I am not forgetting
the postman in this exiguous estimate, for the days are few when,

leaving his pony and cart at the top of the hill, he goes as far as the village, since but a few hundred yards down the lane there stands a large white box, like a sea-trunk, by the side of the road, with a slit for letters and a locked door. Should he have in his wallet a registered letter or be the bearer of a parcel too large for insertion in the square lids of the sea-trunk, he must needs trudge down the hill and deliver the troublesome missive, leaving it in person on the owner, and receiving some small reward of coin or refreshment for his kindness. But such occasions are rare, and his general routine is to take out of the box such letters as may have been deposited there, and insert in their place such letters as he has brought. These will be called for, perhaps that day or perhaps the next, by an emissary from the Polearn post-office. As for the fishermen of the place, who, in their export trade, constitute the chief link of movement between Polearn and the outside world, they would not dream of taking their catch up the steep lane and so, with six miles farther of travel, to the market at Penzance. The sea route is shorter and easier, and they deliver their wares to the pier-head. Thus, though the sole industry of Polearn is sea-fishing, you will get no fish there unless you have bespoken your requirements to one of the fishermen. Back come the trawlers as empty as a haunted house, while their spoils are in the fish-train that is speeding to London.

Such isolation of a little community, continued, as it has been, for centuries, produces isolation in the individual as well, and nowhere will you find greater independence of character than among the people of Polearn. But they are linked together, so it has always seemed to me, by some mysterious comprehension: it is as if they had all been initiated into some ancient rite, inspired and framed by forces visible and invisible. The winter storms that batter the coast, the vernal spell of the spring, the hot, still summers, the season of rains and autumnal decay, have made a spell which, line by line, has been communicated to them, concerning the powers, evil and good, that rule the world, and manifest themselves in ways benignant or terrible. . . .

I came to Polearn first at the age of ten, a small boy, weak and sickly, and threatened with pulmonary trouble. My father's business kept him in London, while for me abundance of fresh air and a mild climate were considered essential conditions if I was to grow to manhood. His sister had married the vicar of Polearn, Richard Bolitho, himself native to the place, and so it came about that I spent three years, as a paying guest, with my relations. Richard Bolitho owned a fine house in the place, which he inhabited in preference to the vicarage, which he let to a young artist, John Evans, on whom the spell of Polearn had fallen, for from year's beginning to year's end he never left it. There was a solid roofed shelter, open on one side to the air, built for me in the garden, and here I lived and slept, passing scarcely one hour out of the twenty-four behind walls and windows. I was out on the bay with the fisher-folk, or wandering along the gorse-clad cliffs that climbed steeply to right and left of the deep combe where the village lay, or pottering about on the pier-head, or bird's-nesting in the bushes with boys of the village. Except on Sunday and for the few daily hours of my lessons, I might do what I pleased so long as I remained in the open air. About the lessons there was nothing formidable; my uncle conducted me through flowering bypaths among the thickets of arithmetic, and made pleasant excursions into the elements of Latin grammar, and above all, he made me daily give him an account, in clear and grammatical sentences, of what had been occupying my mind or my movements. Should I select to tell him about a walk along the cliffs, my speech must be orderly, not vague, slip-shod notes of what I had observed. In this way, too, he trained my observation, for he would bid me tell him what flowers were in bloom, and what birds hovered fishing over the sea or were building in the bushes. For that I owe him a perennial gratitude, for to observe and to express my thoughts in the clear spoken word became my life's profession.

But far more formidable than my weekdays tasks was the prescribed routine for Sunday. Some dark embers compounded of Calvinism and mysticism smouldered in my uncle's soul, and made it a day of terror. His sermon in the morning scorched us with a foretaste of the eternal ,fires reserved for unrepentant sinners, and he was hardly less terrifying at the children's service in the afternoon. Well do I remember his exposition of the doctrine of guardian angels. A child, he said, might think himself secure in such angelic care, but let him beware of committing any of those numerous offences which would cause his guardian to turn his face from him, for as sure as there were angels to protect us, there were also evil and awful presences which were ready to pounce; and on them he dwelt with peculiar gusto. Well, too, do I remember in the morning sermon his commentary on the carved panels of the altar-rails to which I have already alluded. There was the angel of the Annunciation there, and the angel of the Resurrection, but not less was there the witch of Endor, and, on the fourth panel, a scene that concerned me most of all. This fourth panel (he came down from his pulpit to trace its time-worn features) represented the lych-gate of the church-yard at Polearn itself, and indeed the resemblance when thus pointed out was remarkable. In the entry stood the figure of a robed priest holding up a cross, with which he faced a terrible creature like a gigantic slug, that reared itself up in front of him. That, so ran my uncle's interpretation, was some evil agency, such as he had spoken about to us children, of almost infinite malignity and power, which could alone be combated by firm faith and a pure heart. Below ran the legend *"Negotium perambulans in tenebris"* from the ninety-first Psalm. We should find it translated there, "the pestilence that walketh in darkness," which but feebly rendered the Latin. It was more deadly to the soul than any pestilence that can only kill the body: it was the Thing, the Creature, the Business that trafficked in the outer Darkness, a minister of God's wrath on the unrighteous. . . .

I could see, as he spoke, the looks which the congregation exchanged with each other, and knew that his words were evoking a surmise, a remembrance. Nods and whispers passed between them, they understood to what he alluded, and with the inquisitiveness of boyhood I could not rest till I had wormed the story

out of my friends among the fisher-boys, as, next morning, we
sat basking and naked in the sun after our bathe. One knew one
bit of it, one another, but it pieced together into a truly alarming
legend. In bald outline it was as follows:

A church far more ancient than that in which my uncle terrified us every Sunday had once stood not three hundred yards
away, on the shelf of level ground below the quarry from which its
stones were hewn. The owner of the land had pulled this down,
and erected for himself a house on the same site out of these
materials, keeping, in a very ecstasy of wickedness, the altar, and
on this he dined and played dice afterwards. But as he grew old
some black melancholy seized him, and he would have lights
burning there all night, for he had deadly fear of the darkness.
On one winter evening there sprang up such a gale as was never
before known, which broke in the windows of the room where he
had supped, and extinguished the lamps. Yells of terror brought
in his servants, who found him lying on the floor with the blood
streaming from his throat. As they entered some huge black
shadow seemed to move away from him, crawled across the floor
and up the wall and out of the broken window.

"There he lay a-dying," said the last of my informants, "and
him that had been a great burly man withered to a bag o' skin,
for the critter had drained all the blood from him. His last
breath was a scream, and he hollered out the same words as
passon read off the screen."

"*Negotium perambulans in tenebris,*" I suggested eagerly.

"Thereabout. Latin anyhow."

"And after that?" I asked.

"Nobody would go near the place, and the old house rotted
and fell in ruins three years ago, when along comes Mr. Dooliss
from Penzance, and built the half of it up again. But he don't
care much about such critters, nor about Latin neither. He takes
his bottle of whisky a day and gets drunk's a lord in the evening.
Eh, I'm gwine home to my dinner."

Whatever the authenticity of the legend, I had certainly heard
the truth about Mr. Dooliss from Penzance, who from that day

became an object of keen curiosity on my part, the more so because the quarry-house adjoined my uncle's garden. The Thing that walked in the dark failed to stir my imagination, and already I was so used to sleeping alone in my shelter that the night had no terrors for me. But it would be intensely exciting to wake at some timeless hour and hear Mr. Dooliss yelling, and conjecture that the Thing had got him.

But by degrees the whole story faded from my mind, overscored by the more vivid interest of the day, and, for the last two years of my out-door life in the vicarage garden, I seldom thought about Mr. Dooliss and the possible fate that might await him for his temerity in living in the place where that Thing of darkness had done business. Occasionally I saw him over the garden fence, a great yellow lump of a man, with slow and staggering gait, but never did I set eyes on him outside his gate, either in the village street or down on the beach. He interfered with none, and no one interfered with him. If he wanted to run the risk of being the prey of the legendary nocturnal monster, or quietly drink himself to death, it was his affair. My uncle, so I gathered, had made several attempts to see him when he first came to live at Polearn, but Mr. Dooliss appeared to have no use for parsons, said he was not at home, and never returned the call.

After three years of sun, wind, and rain, I had completely outgrown my early symptoms and had become a tough, strapping youngster of thirteen. I was sent to Eton and Cambridge, and in due course ate my dinners and became a barrister. In twenty years from that time I was earning a yearly income of five figures, and had already laid by in some securities a sum that brought me dividends which would, for one of my simple tastes and frugal habits, supply me with all the material comforts I needed on this side of the grave. The great prizes of my profession were already within my reach, but I had no ambition beckoning me on, nor did I want a wife and children, being, I must suppose, a natural celibate. In fact there was only one ambition which through these busy years had held the lure of blue and far-off hills to me, and that was to get back to Polearn, and live once more isolated from the world with the sea and the gorse-clad hills for play-fellows, and the secrets that lurked there for exploration. The spell of it had been woven about my heart, and I can truly say that there had hardly passed a day in all those years in which the thought of it and the desire for it had been wholly absent from my mind. Though I had been in frequent communication with my uncle there during his lifetime, and, after his death, with his widow who still lived there, I had never been back to it since I embarked on my profession, for I knew that if I went there, it would be a wrench beyond my power to tear myself away again. But I had made up my mind that when once I had provided for my own independence, I would go back there not to leave it again. And yet I did leave it again, and now nothing in the world would induce me to turn down the lane from the road that leads from Penzance to the Land's End, and see the sides of the combe rise steep above the roofs of the village and hear the gulls chiding as they fish in the bay. One of the things invisible, of the dark powers, leaped into light, and I saw it with my eyes.

The house where I had spent those three years of boyhood had been left for life to my aunt, and when I made known to her my intention of coming back to Polearn, she suggested that, till I found a suitable house or found her proposal unsuitable, I should come to live with her.

"The house is too big for a lone old woman," she wrote, "and I have often thought of quitting and taking a little cottage suffi-cient for me and my requirements. But come and share it, my dear, and if you find me troublesome, you or I can go. You may want solitude—most people in Polearn do—and will leave me. Or else I will leave you: one of the main reasons of my stopping here all these years was a feeling that I must not let the old house starve. Houses starve, you know, if they are not lived in. They die a lingering death; the spirit in them grows weaker and weaker, and at last fades out of them. Isn't this nonsense to your London notions? . . ."

Naturally I accepted with warmth this tentative arrangement, and on an evening in June found myself at the head of the lane leading down to Polearn, and once more I descended into the steep valley between the hills. Time had stood still aparently for the combe, the dilapidated signpost (or its successor) pointed a rickety finger down the lane, and a few hundred yards farther on was the white box for the exchange of letters. Point after remembered point met my eye, and what I saw was not shrunk, as is often the case with the revisited scenes of childhood, into a smaller scale. There stood the post-office, and there the church and close beside the vicarage, and beyond, the tall shrubberies which separated the house for which I was bound from the road, and beyond that again the grey roofs of the quarry-house, damp and shining with the moist evening wind from the sea. All was exactly as I remembered it, and, above all, that sense of seclusion and isolation. Somewhere above the treetops climbed the lane which joined the main road to Penzance, but all that had become immeasurably distant. The years that had passed since last I turned in at the well-known gate faded like a frosty breath, and vanished in this warm, soft air. There were law-courts somewhere in memory's dull book which, if I cared to turn the pages, would tell me that I had made a name and a great income there. But the dull book was closed now, for I was back in Polearn, and the spell was woven around me again.

And if Polearn was unchanged, so too was Aunt Hester, who met me at the door. Dainty and china-white she had always been, and the years had not aged but only refined her. As we sat and talked after dinner she spoke of all that had happened in Polearn in that score of years, and yet somehow the changes of which she spoke seemed but to confirm the immutability of it all. As the recollection of names came back to me, I asked her about the quarry-house and Mr. Dooliss, and her face gloomed a little as with the shadow of a cloud on a spring day.

"Yes, Mr. Dooliss," she said, "poor Mr. Dooliss, how well I remember him, though it must be ten years and more since he died. I never wrote to you about it, for it was all very dreadful my dear, and I did not want to darken your memories of Polearn. Your uncle always thought that something of the sort might happen if he went on in his wicked, drunken ways, and worse than that, and though nobody knew exactly what took place, it was the sort of thing that might have been anticipated."

"But what more or less happened, Aunt Hester?" I asked.

"Well, of course, I can't tell you everything, for no one knew it. But he was a very sinful man, and the scandal about him at Newlyn was shocking. And then he lived, too, in the quarry-house. . . . I wonder if by any chance you remember a sermon of your uncle's when he got out of the pulpit and explained that panel in the altar-rails, the one, I mean, with the horrible creature rearing itself up outside the lych-gate?"

"Yes, I remember it perfectly," said I.

"Ah. It made an impression on you, I suppose, and so it did on all who heard him, and that impression got stamped and branded on us all when the catastrophe occurred. Somehow Mr. Dooliss got to hear about your uncle's sermon, and in some drunken fit he broke into the church and smashed the panel to atoms. He seems to have thought that there was some magic in it, and that if he destroyed that he would get rid of the terrible fate that was threatening him. For I must tell you that before he committed that dreadful sacrilege he had been a haunted man: he hated and feared darkness, for he thought that the creature on the panel was on his track, but that as long as he kept lights burning it could not touch him. But the panel, to his disordered mind, was the root of his terror, and so, as I said, he broke into the church and attempted—you will see why I said 'attempted'—to destroy it. It certainly was found in splinters next morning, when your uncle went into church for matins, and knowing Mr. Dooliss's fear of the panel, he went across to the quarry-house afterwards and taxed him with its destruction. The man never denied it; he boasted of what he had done. There he sat, though it was early morning, drinking his whisky.

" 'I've settled your Thing for you,' he said, 'and your sermon too. A fig for such superstitions.'

"Your uncle left him without answering his blasphemy, meaning to go straight into Penzance and give information to the police about this outrage to the church, but on his way back from the quarry-house he went into the church again, in order to be able to give details about the damage, and there in the screen was the panel, untouched and uninjured. And yet he had himself seen it smashed, and Mr. Dooliss had confessed that the destruction of it was his work. But there it was, and whether the power of God had mended it or some other power, who knows?"

This was Polearn indeed, and it was the spirit of Polearn that made me accept all Aunt Hester was telling me as attested fact. It had happened like that. She went on in her quiet voice.

"Your uncle recognised that some power beyond police was at work, and he did not go to Penzance or give information about the outrage, for the evidence of it had vanished."

A sudden spate of scepticism swept over me.

"There must have been some mistake," I said. "It hadn't been broken. . . ."

She smiled.

"Yes, my dear, but you have been in London so long," she said. "Let me, anyhow, tell you the rest of my story. That night, for some reason, I could not sleep. It was very hot and airless; I dare say you will think that the sultry conditions accounted for my wakefulness. Once and again, as I went to the window to see if I could not admit more air, I could see from it the quarry-house, and I noticed the first time that I left my bed that it was blazing with lights. But the second time I saw that it was all in darkness, and as I wondered at that, I heard a terrible scream, and the moment afterwards the steps of someone coming at full speed down the road outside the gate. He yelled as he ran; 'Light, light!' he called out. 'Give me light, or it will catch me!' It was very terrible to hear that, and I went to rouse my husband, who was sleeping in the dressing-room across the passage. He wasted no time, but by now the whole village was aroused by the screams, and when he got down to the pier he found that all was over. The tide was low, and on the rocks at its foot was lying the body of Mr. Dooliss. He must have cut some artery when he fell on those sharp edges of stone, for he had bled to death, they thought, and though he was a big burly man, his corpse was but skin and bones. Yet there was no pool of blood round him, such as you would have expected. Just skin and bones as if every drop of blood in his body had been sucked out of him!"

She leaned forward.

"You and I, my dear, know what happened," she said, "or at least can guess. God has His instruments of vengeance on those who bring wickedness into places that have been holy. Dark and mysterious are His ways."

Now what I should have thought of such a story if it had been told me in London I can easily imagine. There was such an obvious explanation: the man in question had been a drunkard, what wonder if the demons of delirium pursued him? But here in Polearn it was different.

"And who is in the quarry-house now?" I asked. "Years ago the fisher-boys told me the story of the man who first built it and of his horrible end. And now again it has happened. Surely no one has ventured to inhabit it once more?"

I saw in her face, even before I asked that question, that somebody had done so.

"Yes, it is lived in again," said she, "for there is no end to blindness. . . . I don't know if you remember him. He was tenant of the vicarage many years ago."

"John Evans," said I.

"Yes. Such a nice fellow he was too. Your uncle was pleased to get so good a tenant. And now—"

She rose.

"Aunt Hester, you shouldn't leave your sentences unfinished," I said.

She shook her head.

"My dear, that sentence will finish itself," she said. "But what a time of night! I must go to bed, and you too, or they will think we have to keep lights burning here through the dark hours."

Before getting into bed I drew my curtains wide and opened all the windows to the warm tide of the sea air that flowed softly in. Looking out into the garden I could see in the moonlight the roof of the shelter, in which for three years I had lived, gleaming with dew. That, as much as anything, brought back the old days to which I had now returned, and they seemed of one piece with the present, as if no gap of more than twenty years sundered them. The two flowed into one like globules of mercury uniting into a softly shining globe of mysterious lights and reflections. Then, raising my eyes a little, I saw against the black hill-side the windows of the quarry-house still alight.

Morning, as is so often the case, brought no shattering of my illusion. As I began to regain consciousness, I fancied that I was a boy again waking up in the shelter of the garden, and though, as I grew more widely awake, I smiled at the impression, that on which it was based I found to be indeed true. It was sufficient now as then to be here, to wander again on the cliffs, and hear the popping of the ripened seed-pods on the gorse-bushes; to stray along the shore to the bathing-cove, to float and drift and swim in the warm tide, and bask on the sand, and watch the gulls fishing, to lounge on the pier-head with the fisher-folk, to see in their eyes and hear in their quiet speech the evidence of secret things not so much known to them as part of their instincts and their very being. There were powers and presences about me; the white poplars that stood by the stream that babbled down the valley knew of them, and showed a glimpse of their knowledge sometimes, like the gleam of their white under leaves; the very cobbles that paved the street were soaked in it. . . . All that I wanted was to lie there and grow soaked in it too; unconsciously, as a boy, I had done that, but now the process must be conscious. I must know what stir of forces, fruitful and mysterious, seethed along the hill-side at noon, and sparkled at night on the sea. They could be known, they could even be controlled by those who were masters of the spell, but never could they be spoken of, for they were dwellers in the innermost, grafted into the eternal life of the world. There were dark secrets as well as these clear, kindly powers, and to these no doubt belonged the *negotium perambulans in tenebris* which, though of deadly malignity, might be regarded not only as evil, but as the avenger of sacrilegious and impious deeds. . . . All this was part of the spell of Polearn, of which the seeds had long lain dormant in me. But now they were sprouting, and who knew what strange flower would unfold in their stems?

It was not long before I came across John Evans. One morning, as I lay on the beach, there came shambling across the sand a man stout and middle-aged with the face of Silenus. He paused as he drew near and regarded me from narrow eyes.

"Why, you're the little chap that used to live in the parson's garden," he said. "Don't you recognise me?"

I saw who it was when he spoke: his voice, I think, instructed me, and recognising it, I could see the features of the strong, alert, young man in this gross caricature.

"Yes, you're John Evans," I said. "You used to be very kind to me: you used to draw pictures for me."

"So I did, and I'll draw you some more. Been bathing? That's a risky performance. You never know what lives in the sea, nor what lives on the land for that matter. Not that I heed them. I stick to work and whisky. God! I've learned to paint since I saw you, and drink too for that matter. I live in the quarry-house, you know, and it's a powerful thirsty place. Come and have a look at my things if you're passing. Staying with your aunt, are you? I could do a wonderful portrait of her. Interesting face; she knows a lot. People who live at Polearn get to know a lot, though I don't take much stock in that sort of knowledge myself."

I do not know when I have been at once so repelled and interested. Behind the mere grossness of his face there lurked something which while it appalled, yet fascinated me. His thick lisping speech had the same quality. And his paintings, what would they be like? . . .

"I was just going home," I said. "I'll gladly come in, if you'll allow me."

He took me through the untended and overgrown garden into

the house which I had never yet entered. A great grey cat was sunning itself in the window, and an old woman was laying lunch in a corner of the cool hall into which the door opened. It was built of stone, and the carved mouldings let into the walls, the fragments of gargoyles and sculptured images, bore testimony of the truth of its having been built out of the demolished church. In one corner was an oblong and carved wooden table littered with a painter's apparatus and stacks of canvases leaned against the walls.

He jerked his thumb towards a head of an angel that was built into the mantelpiece and giggled.

"Quite a sanctified air," he said, "so we tone it down for the purposes of ordinary life by a different sort of art. Have a drink? No? Well, turn over some of my pictures while I put myself to rights."

He was justified in his own estimate of his skill: he could paint (and apparently he could paint anything), but never have I seen pictures so inexplicably hellish. There were exquisite studies of trees, and you knew something lurked in the flickering shadows. There was a drawing of his cat sunning itself in the window, even as I had just now seen it, and yet it was no cat but some beast of awful malignity. There was a boy stretched naked on the sands, not human, but some evil thing which had come out of the sea. Above all there were pictures of his garden overgrown and jungle-like, and you knew that in the bushes were presences ready to spring out on you. . . .

"Well, do you like my style?" he said as he came up, glass in hand. (The tumbler of spirits that he held had not been diluted.) "I try to paint the essence of what I see, not the mere husk and skin of it, but its nature, where it comes from and what gave it birth. There's much in common between a cat and a fuchsia-bush if you look at them closely enough. Everything came out of the slime of the pit, and it's all going back there. I should like to do a picture of you some day. I'd hold the mirror up to Nature, as the old lunatic said."

After this first meeting I saw him occasionally throughout the months of that wonderful summer. Often he kept to his house and to his painting for days together, and then perhaps some evening I would find him lounging on the pier, always alone, and every time we met thus the repulsion and interest grew, for every time he seemed to have gone farther along a path of secret knowledge towards some evil shrine where complete initiation awaited him. . . . And then suddenly the end came.

I had met him thus one evening on the cliffs while the October sunset still burned in the sky, but over it with amazing rapidity there spread from the west a great blackness of cloud such as I have never seen for denseness. The light was sucked from the sky, the dusk fell in ever thicker layers. He suddenly became conscious of this.

"I must get back as quick as I can," he said. "It will be dark in a few minutes, and my servant is out. The lamps will not be lit."

He stepped out with extraordinary briskness for one who shambled and could scarcely lift his feet, and soon broke out into a stumbling run. In the gathering darkness I could see that his face was moist with the dew of some unspoken terror.

"You must come with me," he panted, "for so we shall get the lights burning the sooner. I cannot do without light."

I had to exert myself to the full to keep up with him, for terror winged him, and even so I fell behind, so that when I came to the garden gate, he was already half-way up the path to the house. I saw him enter, leaving the door wide, and found him fumbling with matches. But his hand so trembled that he could not transfer the light to the wick of the lamp.

"But what's the hurry about?" I asked.

Suddenly his eyes focused themselves on the open door behind me, and he jumped from his seat beside the table which had once been the altar of God, with a gasp and a scream.

"No, no!" he cried. "Keep it off! . . ."

I turned and saw what he had seen. The Thing had entered and now was swiftly sliding across the floor towards him, like some gigantic caterpillar. A stale phosphorescent light came from it, for though the dusk had grown to blackness outside, I could see it quite distinctly in the awful light of its own presence. From it too there came an odour of corruption and decay, as from slime that has long lain below water. It seemed to have no head, but on the front of it was an orifice of puckered skin which opened and shut and slavered at the edges. It was hairless, and slug-like in shape and in texture. As it advanced its forepart reared itself from the ground, like a snake about to strike, and it fastened on him. . . .

At that sight, and with the yells of his agony in my ears, the panic which had struck me relaxed into a hopeless courage, and with palsied, impotent hands I tried to lay hold of the Thing. But I could not: though something material was there, it was impossible to grasp it; my hands sunk in it as in thick mud. It was like wrestling with a nightmare.

I think that but a few seconds elapsed before all was over. The screams of the wretched man sank to moans and mutterings as the Thing fell on him: he panted once or twice and was still. For a moment longer there came gurglings and sucking noises, and then it slid out even as it had entered. I lit the lamp which he had fumbled with, and there on the floor he lay, no more than a rind of skin in loose folds over projecting bones.

To end with, we have a dragon story which certainly has a moral, though it may be a little hard to say what the moral is.

THE FIFTY-FIRST DRAGON
Heywood Broun

OF ALL THE PUPILS AT THE NIGHT SCHOOL, GAWAINE LE COEUR-Hardy was among the least promising. He was tall and sturdy, but his instructors soon discovered that he lacked spirit. He would hide in the woods when the jousting class was called, although his companions and members of the faculty sought to appeal to his better nature by shouting to him to come out and break his neck like a man. Even when they told him that the lances were padded, the horses no more than ponies and the field unusually soft for late autumn, Gawaine refused to grow enthusiastic. The Headmaster and the Assistant Professor of Pleasaunce were discussing the case one spring afternoon and the Assistant Professor could see no remedy but expulsion.

"No," said the Headmaster, as he looked out at the purple hills which ringed the school, "I think I'll train him to slay dragons."

"He might be killed," objected the Assistant Professor.

"So he might," replied the Headmaster brightly, but he added, more soberly, "we must consider the greater good. We are responsible for the formation of this lad's character."

"Are the dragons particularly bad this year?" interrupted the Assistant Professor. This was characteristic. He always seemed restive when the head of the school began to talk ethics and the ideals of the institution.

"I've never known them worse," replied the Headmaster. "Up in the hills to the south last week they killed a number of peasants, two cows and a prize pig. And if this dry spell holds there's no telling when they may start a forest fire simply by breathing around indiscriminately."

"Would any refund on the tuition fee be necessary in case of an accident to young Coeur-Hardy?"

"No," the principal answered, judicially, "that's all covered in the contract. But as a matter of fact he won't be killed. Before I send him up in the hills I'm going to give him a magic word."

"That's a good idea," said the Professor. "Sometimes they work wonders."

From that day on Gawaine specialized in dragons. His course included both theory and practice. In the morning there were long lectures on the history, anatomy, manners and customs of dragons. Gawaine did not distinguish himself in these studies. He had a marvelously versatile gift for forgetting things. In the afternoon he showed to better advantage, for then he would go down to the South Meadow and practice with a battle-ax. In this exercise he was truly impressive, for he had enormous strength as well as speed and grace. He even developed a deceptive display of ferocity. Old alumni say that it was a thrilling sight to see Gawaine charging across the field toward the dummy paper dragon which had been set up for his practice. As he ran he would brandish his ax and shout "A murrain on thee!" or some other vivid bit of campus slang. It never took him more than one stroke to behead the dummy dragon.

Gradually his task was made more difficult. Paper gave way to papier-mâché and finally to wood, but even the toughest of these dummy dragons had no terrors for Gawaine. One sweep of the ax always did the business. There were those who said that when the practice was protracted until dusk and the dragons threw long, fantastic shadows across the meadow Gawaine did not charge so impetuously nor shout so loudly. It is possible there was malice in this charge. At any rate, the Headmaster decided by the end of June that it was time for the test. Only the night before a dragon had come close to the school grounds and had eaten some of the lettuce from the garden. The faculty decided that Gawaine was ready. They gave him a diploma and a new battle-ax, and the Headmaster summoned him to a private conference.

"Sit down," said the Headmaster. "Have a cigarette."

Gawaine hesitated.

"Oh, I know it's against the rules," said the Headmaster. "But after all, you have received your preliminary degree. You are no longer a boy. You are a man. To-morrow you will go out into the world, the great world of achievement."

Gawaine took a cigarette. The Headmaster offered him a match, but he produced one of his own and began to puff away with a dexterity which quite amazed the principal.

"Here you have learned the theories of life," continued the Headmaster, resuming the thread of his discourse, "but after all, life is not a matter of theories. Life is a matter of facts. It calls on the young and the old alike to face these facts, even though they are hard and sometimes unpleasant. Your problem, for example, is to slay dragons."

"They say that those dragons down in the south wood are five hundred feet long," ventured Gawaine, timorously.

"Stuff and nonsense!" said the Headmaster. "The curate saw one last week from the top of Arthur's Hill. The dragon was sunning himself down in the valley. The curate didn't have an opportunity to look at him very long because he felt it was his duty to hurry back to make a report to me. He said the monster, or shall I say, the big lizard?—wasn't an inch over two hundred feet. But the size has nothing at all to do with it. You'll find the big ones even easier than the little ones. They're far slower on their feet and less aggressive, I'm told. Besides, before you go I'm going to equip you in such fashion that you need have no fear of all the dragons in the world."

"I'd like an enchanted cap," said Gawaine.

"What's that?" answered the Headmaster, testily.

"A cap to make me disappear," explained Gawaine.

The Headmaster laughed indulgently. "You mustn't believe all those old wives' stories," he said. "There isn't any such thing. A cap to make you disappear, indeed! What would you do with it? You haven't even appeared yet. Why, my boy, you could walk from here to London, and nobody would so much as look at you. You're nobody. You couldn't be more invisible than that."

Gawaine seemed dangerously close to a relapse into his old

habit of whimpering. The Headmaster reassured him: "Don't worry; I'll give you something much better than an enchanted cap. I'm going to give you a magic word. All you have to do is repeat this magic charm once and no dragon can possibly harm a hair of your head. You can cut off his head at your leisure."

He took a heavy book from the shelf behind his desk and began to run through it. "Sometimes," he said, "the charm is a whole phrase or even a sentence. I might, for instance, give you 'To make the'— No, that might not do. I think a single word would be best for dragons."

"A short word," suggested Gawaine.

"It can't be too short or it wouldn't be potent. There isn't so much hurry as all that. Here's a splendid magic word: 'Rumplesnitz.' Do you think you can learn that?"

Gawaine tried and in an hour or so he seemed to have the word well in hand. Again and again he interrupted the lesson to inquire, "And if I say 'Rumplesnitz' the dragon can't possibly hurt me?" And always the Headmaster replied, "If you only say 'Rumplesnitz,' you are perfectly safe."

Toward morning Gawaine seemed resigned to his career. At daybreak the Headmaster saw him to the edge of the forest and pointed him to the direction in which he should proceed. About a mile away to the southwest a cloud of steam hovered over an open meadow in the woods and the Headmaster assured Gawaine that under the steam he would find a dragon. Gawaine went forward slowly. He wondered whether it would be best to approach the dragon on the run as he did in his practice in the South Meadow or to walk slowly toward him, shouting "Rumplesnitz" all the way.

The problem was decided for him. No sooner had he come to the fringe of the meadow than the dragon spied him and began to charge. It was a large dragon and yet it seemed decidedly aggressive in spite of the Headmaster's statement to the contrary. As the dragon charged it released huge clouds of hissing steam through its nostrils. It was almost as if a gigantic teapot had gone mad. The dragon came forward so fast and Gawaine was so frightened that he had time to say "Rumplesnitz" only once. As he said it, he swung his battle-ax and off popped the head of the dragon. Gawaine had to admit that it was even easier to kill a real dragon than a wooden one if only you said "Rumplesnitz."

Gawaine brought the ears home and a small section of the tail. His schoolmates and the faculty made much of him, but the Headmaster wisely kept him from being spoiled by insisting that he go on with his work. Every clear day Gawaine rose at dawn and went out to kill dragons. The Headmaster kept him at home when it rained, because he said the woods were damp and unhealthy at such times and that he didn't want the boy to run needless risks. Few good days passed in which Gawaine failed to get a dragon. On one particularly fortunate day he killed three, a husband and wife and a visiting relative. Gradually he developed a technique. Pupils who sometimes watched him from the hilltops a long way off said that he often allowed the dragon to come within a few feet before he said "Rumplesnitz." He came to say it with a mocking sneer. Occasionally he did stunts. Once when an excursion party from London was watching him he went into action with his right hand tied behind his back. The dragon's head came off just as easily.

As Gawaine's record of killings mounted higher the Headmaster found it impossible to keep him completely in hand. He fell into the habit of stealing out at night and engaging in long drinking bouts at the village tavern. It was after such a debauch that he rose a little before dawn one fine August morning and started out after his fiftieth dragon. His head was heavy and his mind sluggish. He was heavy in other respects as well, for he had adopted the somewhat vulgar practice of wearing his medals, ribbons and all, when he went out dragon hunting. The decorations began on his chest and ran all the way down to his abdomen. They must have weighed at least eight pounds.

Gawaine found a dragon in the same meadow where he had killed the first one. It was a fair-sized dragon, but evidently an old one. Its face was wrinkled and Gawaine thought he had never seen so hideous a countenance. Much to the lad's disgust, the monster refused to charge and Gawaine was obliged to walk toward him. He whistled as he went. The dragon regarded him hopelessly, but craftily. Of course it had heard of Gawaine. Even when the lad raised his battle-ax the dragon made no move. It knew that there was no salvation in the quickest thrust of the head, for it had been informed that this hunter was protected by an enchantment. It merely waited, hoping something would turn up. Gawaine raised the battle-ax and suddenly lowered it again. He had grown very pale and he trembled violently. The dragon suspected a trick. "What's the matter?" it asked, with false solicitude.

"I've forgotten the magic word," stammered Gawaine.

"What a pity," said the dragon. "So that was the secret. It doesn't seem quite sporting to me, all this magic stuff, you know. Not cricket, as we used to say when I was a little dragon; but after all, that's a matter of opinion."

Gawaine was so helpless with terror that the dragon's confidence rose immeasurably and it could not resist the temptation to show off a bit.

"Could I possibly be of any assistance?" it asked. "What's the first letter of the magic word?"

"It begins with an 'r,' " said Gawaine weakly.

"Let's see," mused the dragon, "that doesn't tell us much, does it? What sort of a word is this? Is it an epithet, do you think?"

Gawaine could do no more than nod.

"Why, of course," exclaimed the dragon, "reactionary Republican."

Gawaine shook his head.

"Well, then," said the dragon, "we'd better get down to business. Will you surrender?"

With the suggestion of a compromise Gawaine mustered up enough courage to speak.

"What will you do if I surrender?" he asked.

"Why, I'll eat you," said the dragon.

"And if I don't surrender?"

"I'll eat you just the same."

"Then it doesn't mean any difference, does it?" moaned Gawaine.

"It does to me," said the dragon with a smile. "I'd rather you didn't surrender. You'd taste much better if you didn't."

The dragon waited for a long time for Gawaine to ask "Why?" but the boy was too frightened to speak. At last the dragon had to give the explanation without his cue line. "You see," he said, "if you don't surrender you'll taste better because you'll die game."

This was an old and ancient trick of the dragon's. By means of some such quip he was accustomed to paralyze his victims with laughter and then to destroy them. Gawaine was sufficiently paralyzed as it was, but laughter had no part in his helplessness. With the last word of the joke the dragon drew back his head and struck. In that second there flashed into the mind of Gawaine the magic word of "Rumplesnitz," but there was no time to say it. There was time only to strike and, without a word, Gawaine met the onrush of the dragon with a full swing. He put all his back and shoulders into it. The impact was terrific and the head of the dragon flew almost a hundred yards and landed in a thicket.

Gawaine did not remain frightened very long after the death of the dragon. His mood was one of wonder. He was enormously puzzled. He cut off the ears of the monster almost in a trance. Again and again he thought to himself, "I didn't say 'Rumplesnitz'!" He was sure of that and yet there was no question that he had killed the dragon. In fact, he had never killed one so utterly. Never before had he driven a head for anything like the same distance. Twenty-five yards was perhaps his best previous record. All the way back to the knight school he kept rumbling about in his mind seeking an explanation for what had occurred. He went to the Headmaster immediately and after closing the door told him what had happened. "I didn't say 'Rumplesnitz,' " he explained with great earnestness.

The Headmaster laughed. "I'm glad you've found out," he said. "It makes you ever so much more of a hero. Don't you see that? Now you know that it was you who killed all these dragons and not that foolish little word 'Rumplesnitz.'"

Gawaine frowned. "Then it wasn't a magic word after all?" he asked.

"Of course not," said the Headmaster, "you ought to be too old for such foolishness. There isn't any such thing as a magic word."

"But you told me it was magic," protested Gawaine. "You said it was magic and now you say it isn't."

"It wasn't magic in a literal sense," answered the Headmaster, "but it was much more wonderful than that. The word gave you confidence. It took away your fears. If I hadn't told you that you might have been killed the very first time. It was your battle-ax did the trick."

Gawaine surprised the Headmaster by his attitude. He was obviously distressed by the explanation. He interrupted a long philosophic and ethical discourse by the Headmaster with, "If I hadn't of hit 'em mighty hard and fast any one of 'em might have crushed me like a, like a—" He fumbled for a word.

"Egg shell," suggested the Headmaster.

"Like a egg shell," assented Gawaine, and he said it many times. All through the evening meal people who sat near him heard him muttering, "Like a egg shell, like a egg shell."

The next day was clear, but Gawaine did not get up at dawn. Indeed, it was almost noon when the Headmaster found him cowering in bed, with the clothes pulled over his head. The principal called the Assistant Professor of Pleasaunce, and together they dragged the boy toward the forest.

"He'll be all right as soon as he gets a couple more dragons under his belt," explained the Headmaster.

The Assistant Professor of Pleasaunce agreed. "It would be a shame to stop such a fine run," he said. "Why, counting that one yesterday, he's killed fifty dragons."

They pushed the boy into a thicket above which hung a meager cloud of steam. It was obviously quite a small dragon. But Gawaine did not come back that night or the next. In fact, he never came back. Some weeks afterward brave spirits from the school explored the thicket, but they could find nothing to remind them of Gawaine except the metal parts of his medals. Even the ribbons had been devoured.

The Headmaster and the Assistant Professor of Pleasaunce agreed that it would be just as well not to tell the school how Gawaine had achieved his record and still less how he came to die. They held that it might have a bad effect on school spirit. Accordingly, Gawaine has lived in the memory of the school as its greatest hero. No visitor succeeds in leaving the building to-day without seeing a great shield which hangs on the wall of the dining hall. Fifty pairs of dragons' ears are mounted upon the shield and underneath in gilt letters is "Gawaine le Coeur-Hardy," followed by the simple inscription, "He killed fifty dragons." The record has never been equalled.